Big Medicine

Big Medicine

Louis L'Amour

LEISURE BOOKS NEW YORK CITY

A LEISURE BOOK®

January 2009

Published by special arrangement with Golden West Literary Agency.

Dorchester Publishing Co., Inc.
200 Madison Avenue
New York, NY 10016

ISBN 10: 0-8439-6068-X
ISBN 13: 978-0-8439-6068-6

The name "Leisure Books" and the stylized "L" with design are trademarks of Dorchester Publishing Co., Inc.

Printed in the United States of America.

10 9 8 7 6 5 4 3 2 1

TABLE OF CONTENTS

Introduction

by
Jon Tuska

Louis Dearborn LaMoore (1908-1988) was born in Jamestown, North Dakota. He left home at fifteen and subsequently held a variety of jobs although he worked mostly as a merchant seaman. From his earliest youth, L'Amour had a love of verse. His first published work was a poem, "The Chap Worth While," appearing when he was eighteen years old in his former hometown's newspaper, the *Jamestown Sun*. It is the only poem from his early years that he left out of *Smoke From This Altar*, which appeared in 1939 from Lusk Publishers in Oklahoma City, a book which L'Amour published himself; however, this poem is reproduced in *The Louis L'Amour Companion* (Andrews and McMeel, 1992) edited by Robert Weinberg. L'Amour wrote poems and articles for a number of small circulation arts magazines all through the early 1930s and, after hundreds of rejection slips, finally had his first story accepted, "Anything for a Pal" in *True Gang Life* (10/35). He returned in 1938 to live with his family where they settled in Choctaw, Oklahoma, determined to make writing his career. He wrote a fight story bought by Standard Magazines that year and became acquainted with editor Leo Margulies who was to play an important role later in L'Amour's life. "The Town No Guns Could Tame" in *New Western* (3/40) was his first published Western story.

During the Second World War L'Amour was drafted and ultimately served with the U.S. Army Transportation Corps in Europe. However, in the two years before he was shipped out, he managed to write a great many adventure stories for Standard Magazines. The first story he published in 1946, the year of his discharge, was a Western, "Law of the Desert Born" in *Dime Western* (4/46). A call to Leo Margulies resulted in L'Amour's agreeing to write Western stories for the various Western pulp magazines published by Standard Magazines, a third of which appeared under the byline Jim Mayo, the name of a character in L'Amour's earlier adventure fiction. The proposal for L'Amour to write new Hopalong Cassidy novels came from Margulies who wanted to launch *Hopalong Cassidy's Western Magazine* to take advantage of the popularity William Boyd's old films and new television series were enjoying with a new generation. Doubleday & Company agreed to publish the pulp novelettes in hardcover books. L'Amour was paid $500 a story, no royalties, and he was assigned the house name Tex Burns. L'Amour read Clarence E. Mulford's books about the Bar-20 and based his Hopalong Cassidy on Mulford's original creation. Only two issues of the magazine appeared before it ceased publication. Doubleday felt that the Hopalong character had to appear exactly as William Boyd did in the films and on television and thus even the first two novels had to be revamped to meet with this requirement prior to publication in book form.

L'Amour's first Western novel under his own by-line was *Westward the Tide* (World's Work, 1950). It was rejected by every American publisher to which it was submitted. World's Work paid a flat £75 without royalties for British Empire rights in perpetuity. L'Amour sold his first Western short story to a slick magazine a year later, "The Gift of Cochise" in *Collier's* (7/5/52). Robert Fellows and John Wayne purchased screen rights to this story from L'Amour for $4,000 and James Edward Grant, one of Wayne's favorite screenwriters, developed a script from it, changing L'Amour's Ches Lane to Hondo Lane. L'Amour retained the right to novelize Grant's screenplay, which differs substantially from his short story, and he was able to get an endorsement from Wayne to be used as a blurb, stating that *Hondo* was the finest Western Wayne had ever read. *Hondo* (Fawcett Gold Medal, 1953) by Louis L'Amour was released on the same day as the film, *Hondo* (Warner, 1953), with a first printing of 320,000 copies.

With *Showdown at Yellow Butte* (Ace, 1953) by Jim Mayo, L'Amour began a series of short Western novels for Don Wollheim that could be doubled with other short novels in Ace Publishing's paperback two-fers. Advances on these were $800 and usually the author never earned any royalties. *Heller With A Gun* (Fawcett Gold Medal, 1955) was the first of a series of original Westerns L'Amour had agreed to write under his own name following the success for Fawcett of *Hondo*. L'Amour wanted even this early to have his Western novels published in hardcover editions. He expanded "Guns of the Timberland" by

Jim Mayo in *West* (9/50) for *Guns of the Timberlands* (Jason Press, 1955), a hardcover Western for which he was paid an advance of $250. Another novel for Jason Press followed and then *Silver Cañon* (Avalon Books, 1956) for Thomas Bouregy & Company. These were basically lending library publishers and the books seldom earned much money above small advances paid.

The great turn in L'Amour's fortunes came about because of problems Saul David was having with his original paperback Westerns program at Bantam Books. Fred Glidden had been signed to a contract to produce two original paperback Luke Short Western novels a year for an advance of $15,000 each. It was a long-term contract but, in the first ten years of it, Fred only wrote six novels. Literary agent Marguerite Harper then pursuaded Bantam that Fred's brother, Jon, could help fulfill the contract and Jon was signed for eight Peter Dawson Western novels. When Jon died suddenly before completing even one book for Bantam, Harper managed to engage a ghost writer at the Disney studios to write these eight "Peter Dawson" novels, beginning with *The Savages* (Bantam, 1955). They proved inferior to anything Jon had ever written and what sales they had seemed to be due only to the Peter Dawson name.

Saul David wanted to know from L'Amour if *he* could deliver two Western novels a year. L'Amour said that he could, and he did. In fact, by 1962 this number was increased to three original paperback novels a year. The first L'Amour novel to appear under the Bantam contract was *Radigan* (Bantam, 1958).

A basic element to many a range war plot is the villian's means for crowding out the other ranchers in a district. He brings a giant herd that requires all the available grass and forces all the smaller ranchers out of business. It was this same strategy Bantam used in marketing L'Amour. *All* of his Western titles were continuously kept in print. Independent distributors were required to buy titles in lots of 10,000 copies if they wanted access to other Bantam titles at significantly discounted prices. In time L'Amour's paperbacks forced almost every one else off the racks in Western sections. L'Amour himself comprised the other half of this successful strategy. He dressed up in cowboy outfits, traveled about the country in a motor home visiting with independent distributors, taking them to dinner and charming them, making them personal friends. He promoted himself at every available opportunity. L'Amour insisted that he was telling the stories of the people who had made America a great nation and he appealed to patriotism as much as to commercialism in his rhetoric.

Once when we were talking and Louis had showed me his topographical maps and his library of thousands of volumes that he claimed he used for research, he asserted that, if he claimed there was a rock in a road at a certain point in a story, his readers knew that if they went to that spot they would find a rock just as he described it. I told him that might be so but I personally was troubled by the many inconsistencies in his stories. Take *Last Stand At Papago Wells* (Fawcett Gold Medal, 1957). Five characters are killed during an Indian raid. One of the surviving characters emerges from seclusion after the attact and counts *six* corpses.

"I'll have to go back and count them again," L'Amour said, and smiled. "But, you know, I don't think the people who read my books would really care."

There are many fine, and some spectacular, moments in Louis L'Amour's Western fiction. I think he was at his best in the shorter forms, especially his magazine stories, and the two best stories he ever wrote appeared in the 1950s, "The Gift of the Cochise" early in the decade and "War Party" in *The Saturday Evening Post* (6/59). The latter was expanded by L'Amour to serve as the opening chapters for *Bendigo Shafter* (Dutton, 1979). "War Party" possesses several of the characteristics in purest form which I suspect, no matter how diluted they ultimately would become, account in largest measure for the loyal following Louis L'Amour won from his readers: the young male narrator who is in the process of growing into manhood and who is evaluating other human beings and his own experiences; a resourceful frontier woman who has beauty as well as fortitude; a strong male character who is single and hence marriageable; and the powerful, romantic, strangely compelling vision of the American West which invests L'Amour's Western fiction and makes it such a delightful escape from the cares of a later time—in this author's words from this story, that "big country needing big men and women to live in it" and where there was no place for "the frightened or the mean."

Big Medicine

Old Billy Dunbar was down flat on his face in a dry wash swearing into his beard. The best gold-bearing gravel he had found in a year, and then the Apaches would have to show up!

It was like them, the mean, ornery critters. He hugged the ground for dear life and hoped they would not see him, tucked away as he was between some stones where an eddy of the water that once ran through the wash had dug a trench between the stones.

There were nine of them. Not many, but enough to take his scalp if they found him, and it would be just as bad if they saw his burros or any of the prospect holes he had been sinking.

He was sweating like a stuck hog bleeds, lying there with his beard in the sand and the old Sharps .50 ready beside him. He wouldn't have much a chance if they found him, slithery fighters like they were, but if that old Sharps threw down on them, he'd take at least one along to the happy hunting ground with him.

He could hear them now, moving along the

desert above the wash. Where in tarnation were they going? He wouldn't be safe as long as they were in the country, and this was country where not many white men came. Those few who did come were just as miserable to run into as the Apaches.

The Apache leader was a lean-muscled man with a hawk nose. All of them slim and brown without much meat on them, the way Apaches were, and wearing nothing but breechclouts and headbands.

He lay perfectly still. Old Billy was too knowing in Indian ways to start moving until he was sure they were gone. He lay right there for almost a half hour after he had last heard them, and then he came out of it, cautious as a bear reaching for a honey tree.

When he got on his feet, he hightailed it for the edge of the wash and took a look. The Apaches had vanished. He turned and went down the wash, taking his time and keeping the old Sharps handy. It was a mile to his burros and to the place where his prospect holes were. Luckily he had them back in a draw where there wasn't much chance of their being found.

Billy Dunbar pulled his old gray felt hat down a little tighter and hurried on. Jennie and Julie were waiting for him, standing head to tail so they could brush flies off each other's noses.

When he got to them, he gathered up his tools and took them back up the draw to the rocks at the end. His canteens were full, and he had plenty of grub and ammunition. He was lucky that he hadn't shot that rabbit when he saw it. The Apaches would have heard the bellow of the old

Sharps and come for him, sure. He was going to have to be careful.

If they would just kill a man, it wouldn't be so bad, but these Apaches liked to stake a man out on an anthill and let the hot sun and ants do for him, or maybe the buzzards—if they got there soon enough.

This wash looked good, too. Not only because water had run there, but because it was actually cutting into the edge of an old riverbed. If he could sink a couple of holes down to bedrock, he'd bet there'd be gold and gold aplenty.

***

When he awakened in the morning, he took a careful look around his hiding place. One thing, the way he was located, if they caught him in camp, they couldn't get at him to do much. The hollow was perhaps sixty feet across, but over half of it was covered by shelving rock from above; the cliff ran straight up from there for an easy fifty feet. There was water in a spring and enough grass to last the burros for quite some time.

After a careful scouting around, he made a fire of dead mesquite, which made almost no smoke, and fixed some coffee. When he had eaten, Dunbar gathered up his pan, pick, shovel, and rifle, and moved out. He was loaded more than he liked, but it couldn't be helped.

The place he had selected to work was the inside of the little desert stream. The stream took a bend and left a gravel bank on the inside of the elbow.

That gravel looked good. Putting his Sharps down within easy reach, Old Billy got busy.

Before sundown he had moved a lot of dirt and tried several pans, loading them up and going over to the stream. Holding the pan under the water, he began to stir the gravel, breaking up the lumps of clay and stirring until every piece was wet. Then he picked out the larger stones and pebbles and threw them to one side. He put his hands on opposite sides of the pan and began to oscillate it vigorously under water, moving it in a circular motion so the contents were shaken from side to side.

With a quick glance to make sure there were no Apaches in sight, he tipped the pan slightly, to an angle of about thirty degrees so the lighter sands, already buoyed up by the water, could slip out over the side.

He struck the pan several good blows to help settle the gold, if any, and then dipped for more water and continued the process. He worked steadily at the pan, with occasional glances around until all the refuse had washed over the side but the heavier particles. Then, with a little clean water, he washed the black sand and gold into another pan, which he took from the brush where it had been concealed the day before.

For some time he worked steadily. Then, as the light was getting bad, he gathered up his tools and, concealing the empty pan, carried the other with him back up the wash to his hideout.

He took his Sharps and crept out of the hideout and up the wall of the cañon. The desert was still and empty on every side.

"Too empty, durn it!" he grumbled. "Them Injuns'll be back. You can't fool an Apache."

***

Rolling out of his blankets at sunup, he prepared a quick breakfast, and then went over his takings of the day with a magnet. The black sand was mostly particles of magnetite, ilmenite, and black magnetic iron oxide. What he couldn't draw off, he next eliminated by using a blow box.

"Too slow, with them Apaches around," he grumbled. "A man workin' down there could mebbe do sixty, seventy pans a day in that sort of gravel, but watchin' for Injuns ain't goin' t'help much."

Yet he worked steadily, and by nightfall, despite interruptions, he had handled more than fifty pans. When the second day was over, he grinned at the gold he had. It was sufficient color to show he was on the right track. Right here, by using a rocker, he could have made it pay, but he wasn't looking for peanuts.

He had cached his tools along with the empty pan in the brush at the edge of the wash. When morning came, he rolled out and was just coming out of the hideout when he saw the Apache. He was squatted in the sand, staring at something, and, despite his efforts to keep his trail covered, Dunbar had a good idea what that something would be. He drew back into the hideout.

Lying on his middle, he watched the Indian get to his feet and start working downstream. When he got down there a little farther, he was going to see those prospect holes. There would be nothing Dunbar could do then. Nor was there anything he could do now. So far as he could see, only one Apache had found him. If he fired to kill the Indian, the others would be aware of the situation and come running.

Old Billy squinted his eyes and pondered the question. He had a hunch that Indian wasn't going to go for help. He was going to try to get Dunbar by himself, so he could take his weapons and whatever else he had of value.

The Indian went downstream farther and slipped out of sight. Billy instantly ducked out into the open and scooted down the cañon into the mesquite. He dropped flat there, and inched along in the direction the Indian had gone.

He was creeping along, getting nearer and nearer to his prospect holes, when suddenly instinct or the subconscious hearing of a sound warned him. Like a flash, he rolled over, just in time to see the Indian leap at him, knife in hand!

Billy Dunbar was no longer a youngster, but he had lived a life in the desert, and he was as hard and tough as whalebone. As the Apache leaped, he caught the knife wrist in his left hand, and stabbed at the Indian's ribs with his own knife. The Apache twisted away, and Billy gave a heave. The Indian lost balance. They rolled over, and then fell over the eight-foot bank into the wash.

Luck was with Billy. The Indian hit first, and Billy's knife arm was around him, with the point gouging at the Indian's back. When they landed, the knife went in to the hilt.

Billy rolled off, gasping for breath. Hurriedly he

glanced around. There was no one in sight. Swiftly he clawed at the bank, causing the loosened gravel to cave down, and in a few minutes of hot, sweating work the Indian was buried.

Turning, Billy lit out for his hideaway, and, when he made it, he lay there, gasping for breath, his Sharps ready. There would be no work this day. He was going to lie low and watch. The other Indians would come looking, he knew.

After dark, he slipped out and covered the Indian better, and then he used a mesquite bush to wipe out as well as possible the signs of their fighting. Then he cat-footed it back to the hollow and tied a rawhide string across the entrance with a can of loose pebbles at the end to warn him if Indians found him. Then he went to sleep.

***

At dawn he was up. He checked the Sharps, and then cleaned his .50 again. He loaded his pockets with cartridges, just in case and settled down for a day of it.

Luckily he had shade. It was hot out there, plenty hot. You could fry an egg on those rocks by 10:00 in the morning—not that he had any eggs. He hadn't even seen an egg since the last time he was in Fremont, and that had been four months ago.

He bit off a chew of tobacco and rolled it in his jaws. Then he studied the banks of the draw. An Apache could move like a ghost and look like part of the landscape. He had known them to come within fifteen feet of a man in grassy country without being seen, and not tall grass at that.

It wouldn't be so bad if his time hadn't been so short. When he had left Fremont, Sally had six months to go to pay off the loan on her ranch, or out she would go. Sally's husband had been killed by a bronco down on the Sandy. She was alone with the kids, and that loan was about to take their home away.

When the situation became serious, Old Billy thought of this wash. Once, several years before, he had washed out some color here, and it looked rich. He had left the country about two jumps ahead of the Apaches and swore he'd never come back. Nobody else was coming out of here with gold, either, so he knew it was still like he remembered. Several optimistic prospectors had tried it and were never heard of again. However, Old Billy had decided to take a chance. After all, Sally was all he had, and those two grandchildren of his deserved a better chance than they'd get if she lost the place.

The day moved along, a story told by the shadows on the sides of the wash. You could almost tell the time by those shadows. It wasn't long before Dunbar knew every bush, every clump of greasewood and mesquite along its length, and every rock.

He wiped the sweat from his brow and waited. Sally was a good girl. Pretty, too, too pretty to be a widow at twenty-two. It was almost midafternoon when his questing eye halted suddenly on the bank of the wash. He lay perfectly still, eyes studying the bank intently. Yet his eyes had moved past the spot before they detected something amiss. He scowled, trying to remember. Then it came to him.

There had been a torn place there, as though somebody had started to pull up a clump of greasewood and then abandoned it. The earth had been exposed and a handful of roots. Now it was blotted out. Straining his eyes, he could see nothing, distinguish no contours that seemed human, only that the spot was no longer visible. The spot was mottled by shadows and sunlight through the leaves of the bush.

Then there was a movement, so slight that his eye scarcely detected it, and suddenly the earth and torn roots were visible again. They had come back. Their stealth told him they knew he was somewhere nearby, and the logical place for him would be right where he was.

Now he was in for it. Luckily he had food, water, and ammunition. There should be just eight of them unless more had come. Probably they had found his prospect holes and trailed him back this way.

There was no way they could see into his hollow, no way they could shoot into it except through the narrow entrance, which was rock and brush. There was no concealed approach to it. He dug into the bank a little to get more earth in front of himself.

No one needed to warn him of the gravity of the situation. It was 150 miles to Fremont and sixty miles to the nearest white young man, Sid Barton, a cowhand turned rancher who had started running some cattle on the edge of the Apache country.

Nor could he expect help. Nobody ever came into this country, and nobody knew where he was but Sally, and she only knew in a general way. Prospectors did not reveal locations where they had found color.

Well, he wasn't one of these restless young coots who'd have to be out there tangling with the Apaches. He could wait. And he would wait in the shade while they were in the sun. Night didn't worry him much. Apaches had never cared much for night fighting, and he wouldn't have much trouble with them.

One of them showed himself suddenly—only one arm and a rifle. But he fired, the bullet striking the rock overhead. Old Billy chuckled. *Tryin' t'draw fire*, he thought, *get me located*.

Billy Dunbar waited, grinning through his beard. There was another shot, and then more stillness. He lay absolutely motionless. A hand showed, and then a foot. He rolled his quid in his jaws and spat. An Indian suddenly showed himself, and then vanished as though he had never been there. Old Billy watched the banks cynically. An Indian showed again and hesitated briefly this time, but Dunbar waited.

Suddenly, within twenty feet of the spot where Dunbar lay, an Indian slid down the bank and, with a shrill whoop, darted for the entrance to the hideaway. It was point-blank, even though a moving target. Billy let him have it.

The old Sharps bellowed like a stricken bull and leaped in his hands. The Apache screamed wildly and toppled over backward, carried off his feet by the sheer force of the heavy-caliber bullet. Yells of rage greeted the shot.

Dunbar could see the Indian's body sprawled under the sun. He picked up an edged pieced of white stone and made a straight mark on the rack wall beside him, then seven more. He drew a diagonal line through the first one. *Seven t' go*, he mused.

A hail of bullets began kicking sand and dirt up around the opening. One shot hit overhead and showered dirt down almost in his face. "Durn you," he mumbled. He took his hat off and laid it beside him, his six-shooter atop of it, ready to hand.

No more Indians showed themselves, and the day drew on. It was hot out there. In the vast brassy vault of the sky a lone buzzard wheeled.

He tried no more shots, just waiting. They were trying to tire him out. Dog-gone it. In this place he could outwait all the Apaches in the Southwest—not that he wanted to!

Keeping well below the bank, he got hold of a stone about the size of his head and rolled it into the entrance. Instantly a shot smacked the dirt below it and kicked dirt into his eyes. He wiped them and swore viciously. Then he got another stone and rolled that in place, pushing dirt up behind them. He scooped his hollow deeper and peered thoughtfully at the banks of the draw.

Jennie and Julie were eating grass, undisturbed and unworried. They had been with Old Billy too long to be disturbed by these—to them meaningless—fusses and fights. The shadow from the west bank reached farther toward the east, and Old Billy waited, watching.

He detected an almost indiscernible movement atop the bank in the same spot where he had first seen an Indian. Taking careful aim, he drew a bead on the exposed roots and waited.

He saw no movement, nothing, yet suddenly he focused his eyes more sharply and saw the roots were no longer exposed. Nestling the stock against his shoulder, his finger eased back on the trigger. The old Sharps wavered, and he waited. The rifle steadied, and he squeezed the trigger.

The gun jumped suddenly and there was a shrill yell from the Apache, who lunged to full height and rose on his tiptoes, both hands clasping his chest. The stricken Indian then plunged face forward down the bank in a shower of gravel. Billy reloaded and waited. The Apache lay still, lying in the shadow below the bank. After watching him for a few minutes, alternating between the still form and the banks of the draw, Dunbar picked up his white stone and marked another diagonal white mark, across the second straight line.

He stared at the figures with satisfaction. "Six left," he said. He was growing hungry. Jennie and Julie had both decided to lie down and call it a day.

As luck would have it, his shovel and pick were concealed in the brush at the point where the draw opened into the wider wash. He scanned the banks suddenly, and then drew back. Grasping a bush, he pulled it from the earth under the huge rocks. He then took the brush and some stones and added to his parapet. With some lumps of earth and rock he gradually built it stronger.

Always he returned to the parapet, but the Apaches were cautious and he saw nothing of them. Yet his instinct told him they were there, somewhere. And that, he knew, was the trouble. It was the fact he had been avoiding ever since he had holed up for the fight. They would always be around somewhere now. Three of their braves were missing—dead. They would never let him leave the country alive.

If he had patience, so had they, and they could afford to wait. He could not. It was not merely a matter of getting home before the six-month period was up—and less than two months remained of that—it was a matter of getting home with enough money to pay off the loan. And with the best of luck it would require weeks upon weeks of hard, uninterrupted work.

And then he saw the wolf.

It was no more than a glimpse, and a fleeting glimpse. Billy Dunbar saw the sharply pointed nose and bright eyes and then the swish of a tail. The wolf vanished somewhere at the base of the shelf of rock that shaded the pocket. It vanished in proximity to the spring.

Old Billy frowned and studied the spot. He wasn't the only one holed up here! The wolf evidently had a hole somewhere in the back of the pocket, and perhaps some young, as the time of year was right. His stillness after he had finished work on the entrance had evidently fooled the wolf into believing the white man was gone.

Obviously the wolf had been lying there, waiting for him to leave so it could come out and hunt. The cubs would be getting hungry. If there were cubs.

The idea came to him then. An idea utterly fantastic, yet one that suddenly made him chuckle. It might work! It could work! At least, it was a chance, and somehow, some way, he had to be rid of those Apaches.

He knew something of their superstitions and beliefs. It was a gamble, but as suddenly as he conceived the idea, he knew it was a chance he was going to take.

Digging his change of clothes out of the saddlebags, he got into them. Then he took his own clothing and laid it out on the ground in plain sight—the pants, then the coat, the boots, and, nearby, the hat.

Taking some sticks, he went to the entrance of the wolf den and built a small fire close by. Then he hastily went back and took a quick look around. The draw was empty, but he knew the place was watched. He went back and got out of line of the wolf den, and waited.

The smoke was slight, but it was going into the den. It wouldn't take long. The wolf came out with a rush, ran to the middle of the pocket, took a quick, snarling look around, and then went over the parapet and down the draw.

Working swiftly, he moved the fire and scattered the few sticks and coals in his other fireplace. Then he brushed the ground with a branch. It would be a few minutes before they moved, and perhaps longer.

Crawling into the wolf den, he next got some wolf hair, which he took back to his clothing. He put some of the hair in his shirt and some near his pants. A quick look down the draw showed no sign of an Indian, but that they had seen the wolf, he knew, and he could picture their surprise and puzzlement.

Hurrying to the spring, he dug from the bank near the water a large quantity of mud. This was an added touch, but one that might help. From the mud, he formed two roughly human figures. About the head of each he tied a blade of grass.

Hurrying to the parapet for a stolen look down the draw, he worked until six such figures were made. Then, using thorns and some old porcupine quills he found near a rock, he thrust one or more through each of the mud figures.

They stood in a neat row, facing the parapet. Quickly he hurried for one last look into the draw. An Indian had emerged. He stood there in plain sight, staring toward the place.

They would be cautious, Billy knew, and he chuckled to himself as he thought of what was to follow. Gathering up his rifle, the ammunition, a canteen, and a little food, he hurried to the wolf den and crawled back inside.

On his first trip he had ascertained that there were no cubs. At the end of the den there was room to sit up, topped by the stone of the shelving rock itself. To his right, a lighted match told him there was a smaller hole of some sort.

Cautiously, Billy crawled back to the entrance, and, careful to avoid the wolf tracks in the dust outside, he brushed out his own tracks, and then retreated into the depths of the cave. From where he lay he could see the parapet.

Almost a half hour passed before the first head lifted above the poorly made wall. Black straight hair, a red headband, and the sharp, hard features of their leader.

Then other heads lifted beside him, and one by one the six Apaches stepped over the wall and into the pocket. They did not rush, but looked cautiously about, and their eyes were large, frightened. They looked all around, then at the clothing, and then at the images. One of the Indians grunted and pointed.

They drew closer, and then stopped in an awed line, staring at the mud figures. They knew too well what they meant. Those figures meant a witch doctor had put a death spell on each one of them.

One of the Indians drew back and looked at the clothing. Suddenly he gave a startled cry and pointed—at the wolf hair!

They gathered around, talking excitedly, and then glancing over their shoulders fearfully.

They had trapped what they believed to be a white man, and, knowing Apaches, Old Billy would have guessed they knew his height, weight, and approximate age. Those things they could tell from the length of his stride, the way he worked, the pressure of a footprint in softer ground.

They had trapped a white man, and a wolf had escaped! Now they found his clothing lying here, and on the clothing the hair of a wolf!

All Indians knew of wolf-men, those weird creatures who changed at will from wolf to man and back again, creatures that could tear the throat from a man while he slept and could mark his children with the wolf blood.

The day had waned, and, as he lay there, Old Billy Dunbar could see that while he had worked the sun had neared the horizon. The Indians looked around uneasily. This was the den of a wolf-man, a powerful spirit who had put the death spell on each of them, who came as a man and went as a wolf.

Suddenly, out on the desert, a wolf howled!

The Apaches started as if struck, and then as a man they began to draw back. By the time they reached the parapet, they were hurrying.

***

Old Billy stayed the night in the wolf hole, lying at its mouth, waiting for dawn. He saw the wolf come back, stare about uneasily, and then go away. When light came, he crawled from the hole.

The burros were cropping grass and they looked at him. He started to pick up a pack saddle, and then dropped it. "I'll be durned if I will!" he said.

Taking the old Sharps and the extra pan, he walked down to the wash and went to work. He kept a careful eye out, but saw no Apaches. The gold was panning out even better than he had dreamed would be possible. A few more days—suddenly he looked up.

Two Indians stood in plain sight, facing him. The nearest one walked forward and placed something on a rock, and then drew away. Crouched, waiting, Old Billy watched them go. Then he went to the rock. Wrapped in a piece of tanned buckskin was a haunch of venison!

He chuckled suddenly. He was big medicine now. He was a wolf-man. The venison was a peace offering, and he would take it. He knew now he could come and pan as much gold as he liked in Apache country.

A few days later he killed a wolf, skinned it, and then buried the carcass, but from the head he made a cap to fit over the crown of his old felt hat, and, wherever he went, he wore it.

A month later, walking into Fremont behind the switching tails of Jennie and Julie, he met Sally at the gate. She was talking with young Sid Barton.

"Hi," Sid said, grinning at him. Then he looked quizzically at the wolf-skin cap. "Better not wear that around here! Somebody might take you for a wolf!"

Old Billy chuckled. "I am," he said. "You're durned right, I am. Ask them Apaches."

Trail To Pie Town

Dusty Barron turned the steel-dust stallion down the slope toward the wash. He was going to have to find water soon or the horse and he would be done for. If Emmett Fisk and Gus Mattis had shown up in the street at any other time, it would have been all right. As it was, they had appeared just as he was making a break from the saloon, and they had blocked the road to the hill country and safety. Both men had reached for their guns when they saw him, and he had wheeled his horse and hit the desert road at a dead run. With Dan Hickman dead in the saloon it was no time to argue or engage in gun pleasantries while the clan gathered.

It had been a good idea to ride to Jarilla and make peace talk, only the idea hadn't worked. Dan Hickman had called him yellow, and then gone for a gun. Dan was a mite slow, a fact that had left him dead on the saloon floor. There were nine Hickmans in Jarilla, and there were Mattis and three Fisk boys. Dusty's own tall brothers were back in the hills southwest of Jarilla, but with his road blocked he had headed the steel-dust down the trail into the basin.

The stallion had saved his bacon. No doubt about that. It was only the speed of the big desert-bred horse and its endurance that had got him away from town before the Hickmans could catch him. The big horse had given him lead enough until night had closed in, and after that it was easier.

Dusty had turned at right angles from his original route. They would never expect that, for the turn took him down the long slope into the vast, empty expanse of the alkali basin where no man of good sense would consider going.

For him it was the only route. At Jarilla they would be watching for him, expecting him to circle back to the hill country and his own people. He should have listened to Allie when she had told him it was useless to try to settle the old blood feud.

He had been riding now, with only a few breaks, for hours. Several times he had stopped to rest the stallion, wanting to conserve its splendid strength against what must lie ahead. And occasionally he had dismounted and walked ahead of the big horse.

Dusty Barron had only the vaguest idea of what he was heading into. It was thirty-eight miles across the basin, and he was heading down the basin. According to popular rumor, there was no water for over eighty miles in that direction. And he had started with his canteen only half full.

For the first hour he had taken his course from a star. Then he had sighted a peak ahead and to his left and used that for a marker. Gradually he had worked his way toward the western side of the basin.

Somewhere over the western side was Gallo Gap, a green meadow high in the peaks off a rocky and rarely used pass. There would be water there if he could make it, yet he knew of the gap only from a story told him by a prospector he had met one day in the hills near his home.

Daybreak found him a solitary black speck in a vast wilderness of white. The sun stabbed at him with lances of fire and then, rising higher, bathed the great alkali basin in white radiance and blasting furnace heat. Dusty narrowed his eyes against the glare. It was at least twelve miles to the mountains.

He still had four miles to go through the puffing alkali dust when he saw the tracks. At first he couldn't believe the evidence of his eyes. A wagon—here!

While he allowed the steel-dust to take a blow, he dismounted and examined the tracks. It had been a heavy wagon pulled by four mules or horses. In the fine dust he could not find an outlined track to tell one from the other.

The tracks had come out of the white distance to the east and had turned north exactly on the route he was following. Gallo Gap, from the prospector's story, lay considerably north of him and a bit to the west.

Had the driver of the wagon known of the gap? Or had he merely turned on impulse to seek a route through the mountains. Glancing in first one, and then the other direction, Dusty could see no reason why the driver should have chosen either direction. Jarilla lay southwest, but from here there was no indication of it and no trail.

Mounting again, he rode on, and, when he came to the edge of the low hills fronting the mountains, he detected the wagon trail running along through the scattered rocks, parched bunch grass, and greasewood. It was still heading north. Yet when he studied the terrain before him, he could see nothing but dancing heat waves and an occasional dust devil.

The problem of the wagon occupied his mind to forgetfulness of his own troubles. It had come across the alkali basin from the east. That argued it must have come from the direction of Manzano unless the wagon had turned into the trail somewhere farther north on the road to Conejos.

Nothing about it made sense. This was Apache country and no place for wagon travel. A man on a fast horse, yes, but even then it was foolhardy to travel alone. Yet the driver of the wagon had the courage of recklessness to come across the dead white expanse of the basin, a trip that, to say the least, was miserable.

Darkness was coming again, but he rode on. The wagon interested him, and with no other goal in mind now that he had escaped the Hickmans, he was curious to see who the driver was and to learn what he had in mind. Obviously the man was a stranger to this country.

It was then, in the fading light, that he saw the mule. The steel-dust snorted and shied sharply, but Dusty kneed it closer for a better look. It had been a big mule and a fine animal, but it was dead now. It bore evidence of that brutal crossing of the basin, and here, on the far side, the animal had finally dropped dead of heat and exhaustion.

Only then did he see the trunk. It was sitting between two rocks, partly concealed. He walked to it and looked it over. Cumbersome and heavy, it had evidently been dumped from the wagon to lighten the load.

He tried to open it, but could not. It was locked tight. Beside it were a couple of chairs and a bed.

"Sheddin' his load," Dusty muttered thoughtfully. "He'd better find some water for those other mules, or they'll die, too."

Then he noticed the name on the trunk: D.C. LOWE, ST. LOUIS, MO.

"You're a long way from home," Dusty remarked. He swung a leg over the saddle and rode on. He had gone almost five miles before he saw the fire.

At first, it might have been a star, but as he drew nearer, he could see it was too low down, although higher than he was. The trail had been turning gradually deeper into the hills and had begun to climb a little. He rode on, using the light for a beacon.

When he was still some distance off, he dismounted and tied the stallion to a clump of greasewood and walked forward on foot.

The three mules were hitched to the back of the wagon, all tied loosely and lying down. A girl was bending over a fire, and a small boy, probably no more than nine years old, was gathering sticks of dried mesquite for fuel. There was no one else in sight.

Marveling, he returned to his horse and started back. When he was still a little distance away, he began to sing. His throat was dry and it was a poor job, but he didn't want to frighten them. When he walked his horse into the firelight, the boy was staring up at him, wide-eyed, and the girl had an old Frontier Model Colt.

"It's all right, ma'am," he said, swinging down, "I'm just a passin' stranger an' don't mean any harm."

"Who are you?" she demanded.

"Name of Dusty Barron, ma'am. I've been followin' your trail."

"Why?" Her voice was sharp and a little frightened. She could have been no more than seventeen or eighteen.

"Mostly because I was headed thisaway an' was wonderin' what anybody was doin' down here with a wagon, or where you might be headed."

"Doesn't this lead us anywhere?" she asked.

"Ma'am," Dusty replied, "if you're lookin' for a settlement, there ain't none thisaway in less'n a hundred miles. There's a sort of town then, place they call Pie Town."

"But where did you come from?" Her eyes were wide and dark. If she was fixed up, he reflected, she would be right pretty.

"Place they call Jarilla," he said, "but I reckon this was a better way if you're travelin' alone. Jarilla's a Hickman town, an' they sure are a no-account lot."

"My father died," she told him, putting the gun in a holster hung to the wagon bed, "back there. Billy an' I buried him."

"You come across the basin alone?" He was incredulous.

"Yes. Father died in the mountains on the other side. That was three days ago."

Dusty removed his hat and began to strip the saddle and bridle from the stallion while the girl bent over her cooking. He found a hunk of bacon in his saddle pockets. "Got plenty of bacon?" he asked. "I 'most generally pack a mite along."

She looked up, brushing a strand of hair away from her face. She was flushed from the fire. "We haven't had any bacon for a week." She looked away quickly, and her chin quivered a little and then became stubborn. "Nor much of anything else, but you're welcome to join us."

He seated himself on the ground and leaned back on his saddle while she dished up the food. It wasn't much. A few dry beans and some cornbread. "You got some relatives out here somewhere?"

"No." She handed him a plate, but he was too thirsty to eat more than a few mouthfuls. "Father had a place out here. His lungs were bad and they told him the dry air would he good for him. My mother died when Billy was born, so there was nothing to keep us back in Missouri. We just headed West."

"You say your father had a place? Where is it?"

"I'm not sure. Father loaned some man some money, or, rather, he provided him with money with which to buy stock. The man was to come West and settle on a place, stock it, and then send for Dad."

Dusty ate slowly, thinking that over. "Got anything to show for it?"

"Yes, Father had an agreement that was drawn up and notarized. It's in a leather wallet. He gave the man five thousand dollars. It was all we had."

When they had eaten, the girl and boy went to sleep in the wagon box while Dusty stretched out on the ground nearby. *What a mess!* he told himself. *Those kids comin' away out here, all by themselves now, an' the chances are that money was blowed in over a faro layout long ago!*

***

In the morning, Dusty hitched up the mules for them. "You foller me," he advised, and turned the stallion up the trail to the north.

It was almost noon before he saw the thumblike butte that marked the entrance to Gallo Gap. He turned toward it, riding ahead to scout the best trail, and at times dismounting to roll rocks aside so the wagon could get through.

Surmounting the crest of a low hill, he looked suddenly into Gallo Gap. His red-rimmed eyes stared greedily at the green grass and trees. The stallion smelled water and wanted to keep going, so waving the wagon on, he rode down into the gap.

Probably there were no more than 200 acres here, but it was waist deep in rich green grass, and the towering yellow pines were tall and very old. It was like riding from desolation into a beautiful park. He found the spring by the sound of running water, crystal clear and beautiful, the water rippling over the rocks to fall into a clear pond at least an acre in extent. Nearby, space had been cleared for a cabin, and then abandoned.

Dusty turned in the saddle as his horse stood

knee deep in the water. The wagon pulled up. "This is a little bit of heaven!" he said, grinning at the girl. "Say, what's your name, anyway?"

"Ruth Grant," she said shyly.

All the weariness seemed to have fled from her face at the sight of the water and trees. She smiled gaily, and a few minutes later, as he walked toward the trees with a rifle in the crook of his elbow, he heard laughter and then her voice, singing. He stopped suddenly, watching some deer feeding a short distance off, and listening to her voice. It made a lump of loneliness rise in his throat.

That night, after they had eaten steaks from a fat buck he'd killed, their first good meal in days, he looked across the fire at her. "Ruth," he said, "I think I'll locate me a home right here. I've been lookin' for a place of my own. I reckon what we better do is for you-all to stay here with me until you get rested up. I'll build a cabin, and those mules of yours can get some meat on their bones again. Then I'll ride on down to Pie Town and locate this hombre your father had dealin's with an' see how things look."

That was the way they left it, but in the days that followed Dusty Barron had never been happier. He felled trees on the mountainside and built a cabin, and in working around he found ways of doing things he had never tried before. Ruth was full of suggestions about the house, sensible, knowing things that helped a lot. He worked the mules a little, using only one at a time and taking them turnabout.

He hunted a good deal for food. Nearby he found a salt lick and shot an occasional antelope, and several times, using a shotgun from the wagon, he killed blue grouse. In a grove of trees he found some ripe black cherries similar to those growing wild in the Guadalupe Mountains of West Texas. There was also some Mexican plum.

When the cabin was up and there was plenty of meat on hand, he got his gear in shape. Then he carefully oiled and cleaned his guns.

Ruth noticed them, and her face paled a little. "You believe there will be trouble?" she asked quickly. "I don't want you to. . ."

"Forget it," he interrupted. "I've got troubles of my own." He explained about the killing of Dan Hickman and the long-standing feud between the families.

He left at daybreak. In his pocket he carried the leather wallet containing the agreement Roger Grant had made with Dick Lowe. It was a good day's ride from Gallo Gap to Aimless Creek, where Dusty camped the first night. The following day he rode on into Pie Town. From his talks with Ruth he knew something of Lowe and enough of the probable location of the ranch, if there was one.

A cowhand with sandy hair and crossed eyes was seated on the top rail of the corral. Dusty reined in and leaned his forearm on the saddle horn and dug for the makings. After he had rolled a smoke, he passed it on to the cross-eyed rider.

"Know anything about an' hombre name of Dick Lowe?" he asked.

"Reckon so." They shared a match and, looking at each other through the smoke, decided they were men of a kind. "He's up there in the Spur Saloon now."

Dusty made no move. After a few drags on the cigarette, he glanced at the fire end. "What kind of hombre is he?"

"Salty." The cowhand puffed for a moment on his cigarette. "Salty an' mean. Plumb poison with a shootin' iron, an', when you ride for him, he pays you what he wants to when you quit. If you don't think you got a square deal, you can always tell him so, but when you do, you better reach."

"Like that, huh?"

"Like that." He smoked quietly for a few minutes. "Four hombres haven't liked what he paid 'em. He buried all four of 'em in his own personal boothill, off to the north of the ranch house."

"Sounds bad. Do all his own work or does he have help?"

"He's got help. Cat McQuill an' Bugle Nose Bender. Only nobody calls him Bugle Nose to his face."

"What about the ranch? Nice place?"

"Best around here. He come in here with money, had near five thousand dollars. He bought plenty of cattle an' stocked his range well." The cross-eyed cowhand looked at him, squinting through the smoke. "My name's Blue Riddle. I rode for him once."

"I take it you didn't argue none," Barron said, grinning.

"My maw never raised no foolish children," Riddle replied wryly. "They had me in a cross fire. Been Lowe alone, I'd maybe've took a chance, but as it was, they would have cut me down quick. So I come away, but I'm stickin' around, just waiting. I told him I aimed to have my money, an' he just laughed."

Dusty dropped his hand back and loosened his

left-hand gun. Then he swung his leg back over the saddle and thrust his toe in the stirrup. "Well," he said, "I got papers here that say I speak for a gal that owns half his layout. I'm goin' up an' lay claim to it for her."

Riddle looked up cynically. "Why not shoot yourself and save the trouble? They'll gun you down." Then he sized Barron up again. "What did you say your name was?"

Dusty grinned. "I didn't say, but its Dusty Barron."

Blue Riddle slid off the corral rail. "One of the Barrons from Castle Rock?" He grinned again. "This I gotta see!"

***

Dusty was looking for a big man, but Dick Lowe, who he spotted at once on entering the saloon, was only a bit larger than himself, and he was the only small man among the Barrons.

Lowe turned to look at him as he entered. The man's features were sharp, and his quick eyes glanced from Dusty Barron to Riddle, and then back again. Dusty walked to the bar, and Riddle loitered near the door.

The man standing beside Lowe at the bar must be Cat McQuill. The reason for the nickname was obvious, for there was something feline about the man's facial appearance.

"Lowe?" Dusty inquired.

"That's right." Lowe turned toward him slowly. "Something you want?"

"Yeah." Dusty leaned nonchalantly on the bar

and ordered a drink. "I'm representin' your partner."

Dick Lowe's face blanched, and then turned hard as stone. His eyes glinted. However, he managed a smile with his thin lips. "Partner? I have no partner."

Dusty leaned on the bar watching his drink poured. He took his time.

Lowe watched him, slowly growing more and more angry. "Well," he said sharply, "if you've got something to say, say it!"

Dusty looked around, simulating surprise. "Why, I was just givin' you time to remember, Lowe. You can't tell me you can draw up an agreement with a man, have it properly notarized, and then take five thousand dollars of his money to stock a ranch, and not remember it!"

Dusty was pointedly speaking loudly, and the fact angered Lowe. "You have such an agreement?" Lowe demanded.

"Sure I got it."

"Where's the party this supposed agreement belongs to? Why doesn't he speak for himself?"

"He's dead. He was a lunger an' died on his way West."

Lowe's relief was evident. "I'm afraid," he said, "that this is all too obvious an attempt to get some money out of me. It won't work."

"It's nothing of the kind. Grant's dead, but he left a daughter and a son. I aim to see they get what belongs to 'em, Mister Lowe. I hope we can do it right peaceable."

Lowe's face tightened, but he forced a smile. He was aware he had enemies in Pie Town and did not relish their overhearing this conversation. He was also aware that it was pretty generally known that he had come into Pie Town with $5,000 in cash and bought cattle when everyone on the range was impoverished.

"I reckon this'll be easy settled," he said. "You bring the agreement to the ranch, an', if it's all legal, I reckon we can make a deal."

"Sure," Dusty agreed. "See you tomorrow."

On the plank steps of the hotel he waited until Riddle caught up with him. "You ain't actually goin' out there, are you?" Blue demanded. "That's just askin' for trouble!"

"I'm goin' out," Dusty agreed. "I want a look at the ranch myself. If I can ride out there, I can get an idea what kind of stock he's got and what shape the ranch is in. I've got a hunch, if we make a cash settlement, Lowe isn't goin' to give us much more chance to look around if he can help it. Besides, I've talked in front o' the folks here in town, and rough as some of them may be, they ain't goin' to see no orphans get gypped. No Western crowd would stand for that unless it's some outlaws like Lowe and his two pals."

Riddle walked slowly away, shaking his head with doubt. Dusty watched him go, and then went on inside.

***

He was throwing a saddle on the steel-dust next morning when he heard a low groan. Gun in hand he walked around the corner of the corral. Beyond a pile of poles he saw Blue Riddle pulling himself off the ground. "What happened?" Dusty demanded.

"Bender an' McQuill. They gave me my walkin' papers. Said I'd been in town too long, which didn't bother Lowe none till I took up with you. They gave me till daybreak to pull my freight." He staggered erect, holding a hand to his head. "Then Bender bent a gun over my noggin."

Barron's eyes narrowed. "Play rough, don't they?" He looked at Riddle. "What are you goin to do?"

"You don't see me out there runnin' down the road, do you?" Riddle said. "I'm sittin' tight!"

"Wash your face off, then," Dusty suggested, "an' we'll eat!"

"You go ahead," Riddle replied. "I'll be along."

Dusty glanced back over his shoulder as he left and saw Blue Riddle hiking toward the Indian huts that clustered outside of Pie Town.

***

When he rode out of town an hour later, Dusty Barron was not feeling overly optimistic. Riddle had stayed behind only at Dusty's insistence, but now that Dusty was headed toward Lowe's ranch, he no longer felt so confident. Dick Lowe was not a man to give up easily, nor to yield his ranch or any part of it without a fight. The pistol-whipping of Riddle had been ample evidence of the lengths to which he was prepared to go.

The range through which Dusty rode was good. This was what he had wanted to see. How they might have bargained in town he was not sure. He doubted if anyone there would interfere if a deal was made by him. It was his own problem to see that Ruth and Billy Grant got a fair deal, and that could not be done unless he knew something, at least, of the ranch and the stock.

Dusty was quite sure now that Lowe had never expected the consumptive Roger Grant to come West and claim his piece of the ranch. Nor had he planned to give it to him if he had. He knew very well that he himself was riding into the lion's mouth, but felt he could depend on his own abilities and that Lowe would not go too far after his talk before the bystanders who had been in the saloon. By now Lowe would know that the story would be known to all his enemies in Pie Town.

Cat McQuill was loafing on the steps when Dusty rode up, and the gunman's eyes gleamed with triumph at seeing him. "Howdy," he said affably. "Come on in. The boss is waitin' for you."

Bugle Nose Bender was leaning against the fireplace and Lowe was seated at his desk. "Here he is, boss!" McQuill said as they entered.

Lowe glanced up sharply. "Where's the agreement?" he asked, holding out his hand.

Barron handed it to him, and the rancher opened it, took a quick look, and then glanced up. "This is it, Cat!"

Too late Dusty heard the slide of gun on leather and whirled to face McQuill, but the pistol barrel crashed down over the side of his head and he hit the floor. Even as he fell, he realized what a fool he had been, yet he had been so sure they would talk a little, at least, that Lowe would try to run a blazer or to buy him off cheap.

Bender lunged toward him and kicked him in the ribs. Then Lowe reached over and, jerking him to his knees, struck him three times in the face. The pistol barrel descended again and drove him down into a sea of blackness.

How long they had pounded him, he had no idea. When he opened his eyes, he struggled, fighting his way to a realization of where he was. It took him several minutes to understand that he was almost standing on his head in the road, one foot caught in the stallion's stirrup!

The steel-dust, true to his training, was standing rigidly in the road, his head turned to look at his master. "Easy boy," Dusty groaned. "Easy does it." Twisting his foot in the stirrup, he tried to free it, but to no avail.

He realized what they had planned. After beating him, they had brought him out here, wedged his foot in the stirrup, struck the horse, and, when he started to move, ridden hastily away before they could be seen. Most horses, frightened by the unfamiliar burden in the stirrup, would have raced away over the desert and dragged him to death. It had happened to more than one unwary cowhand.

They had reckoned without the steel-dust. The stallion had been reared by Dusty Barron from a tiny colt, and the two had never been long apart. The big horse had known instantly that something was radically wrong and had gone only a little way, and then stopped. His long training told him to stand, and he stood stock-still.

Dusty twisted his foot again but couldn't get loose. Nor could he pull himself up and get hold of

the stirrup and so into the saddle. He was still trying this when hoof beats sounded on the road.

He looked around wildly, fearful of Lowe's return. Then a wave of relief went over him. It was
Blue Riddle!

"Hey!" Blue exclaimed. "What the heck happened?" He swung down from his horse and
hastily extricated Dusty from his predicament.

Barron explained. "They wanted me killed, so it
would look like I was dragged to death. Lucky they
got away from here in a hurry, afraid they might be
seen."

"But they got the agreement!" Riddle protested.

"Uhn-uh." Barron grinned, and then gasped as
his bruised face twinged with pain. "That was a
copy. I put the agreement down an' traced over it.
He took a quick look and thought it was the real
thing. Now we got to get to town before he realizes
what happened."

Despite his battered and bruised body and the
throbbing of his face, Dusty crawled into the saddle and they raced up the road to Pie Town.

***

Two men were standing on the hotel porch as they
rode up. One of them glanced at Dusty Barron.
"Howdy. Young woman inside wants to see you."

Dusty rushed into the lobby and stopped in surprise. Facing him was Ruth Grant, holding Billy by
the hand, but her smile fled when she saw his face.
"Oh!" she cried. "What's happened to you?"

Briefly he explained. Then he demanded: "How'd
you get here?"

"After you left," Ruth told him, "I was worried. After Father's death and the trouble we had before you came, there was no time to think of anything, and I had to always be thinking of where we would go and what we would do. Then I remembered a comment Father made once. You see, Mister Lowe left a trunk with us to bring West or send to him later. It wasn't quite full, so Father opened it to pack some other things in it. He found something there that worried him a great deal, and he told me several times that he was afraid he might have trouble when we got out here. From all he said I had an idea what he found, so after you were gone, we searched through the trunk and found some letters and a handbill offering a five-thousand-dollar reward for Lowe. Why he kept them I can't imagine, but the sheriff says some criminals are very vain and often keep such things about themselves."

"And then you rode on here?"

She nodded. "We met two men who were trailing you, and, as they had extra horses with them so they could travel fast, we joined them."

Dusty's face tightened. "Men looking for me?"

Riddle interrupted. "Dick Lowe's ridin' into town now!"

Dusty Barron turned, loosening his guns. He started for the door.

"I'm in on this, too!" Riddle said, trailing him.

They walked out on the porch and stepped down into the street, spreading apart. Dick Lowe and his two henchmen had dismounted and were starting into the saloon when something made them glance up the street.

"Lowe!" Dusty yelled. "You tried to kill me, an' I'm comin' for you!"

Dick Lowe's hard face twisted with fury as he wheeled, stepping down into the dust.

He stopped in the street, and Cat McQuill and Bender moved out to either side.

Dusty Barron walked steadily down the street, his eyes on Dick Lowe. All three men were dangerous, but Lowe was the man he wanted, and Lowe was the man he intended to get first.

"This man's an outlaw!" he said, speaking to Bender and McQuill. "He's wanted for murder in Saint Louis! If you want out, get out now!"

"You're lying!" Bender snarled.

Dusty Barron walked on. The sun was bright in the street, and little puffs of dust arose at every step. There were five horses tied to the hitch rail behind the three men. He found himself hoping none of them would be hit by a stray shot. To his right was Blue Riddle, walking even with him, his big hands hovering over his guns.

His eyes clung to Dick Lowe, riveted there as though he alone lived in the world. He could see the man drop into a half crouch, noticed the bulge of the tobacco sack in his breast pocket, the buttons down the two sides of his shirt. Under the brim of the hat he could see the straight bar of the man's eyebrows and the hard gleam of the eyes beneath, and then suddenly the whole tableau dissolved into flaming, shattering action.

Lowe's hand flashed for his gun and Dusty's beat him by a hair's breadth, but Dusty held his fire, lifting the gun slowly. Lowe's quick shot flamed by his ear, and he winced inwardly at the proximity of death. Then the gunman fired again and the bullet tugged impatiently at his vest. He drew a long breath and squeezed off a shot, then another.

Lowe rose on tiptoes, opened his mouth widely as if to gasp for breath, seemed to hold himself there for a long moment, and then pitched over into the street.

Dusty's gun swung with his eyes and he saw Bender was down on his knees, and so he opened up on McQuill. The cat man jerked convulsively, and then began to back away, his mouth working and his gun hammering. The man's gun stopped firing, and he stared at it, pulled the trigger again, and then reached for a cartridge from his belt.

Barron stood, spraddle-legged, in the street and saw Cat's hand fumble at his belt. The fingers came out with a cartridge and moved toward the gun, and then his eyes glazed and he dropped his iron. Turning, as though the whole affair had slipped his mind, he started for the saloon. He made three steps, and then lifted his foot, seemed to feel for the saloon step, and fell like a log across the rough board porch.

Blue Riddle was on his knees, blood staining a trouser leg. Bender was sprawled out in the dust, a darkening pool forming beneath him.

Suddenly the street was filled with people. Ruth ran up to Dusty and he slid his arm around her. With a shock, he remembered. "You said two men were looking for me. Who?"

"Only us."

He turned, staring. Two big men were facing him, grinning. "Buck and Ben! How in tarnation did you two find me?"

Buck Barron grinned. "We was wonderin' what happened to you. We come to town and had a mite of a ruckus with the Hickmans. What was left of them headed for El Paso in a mighty hurry . . . both of 'em. Then an Injun kid come ridin' up on a beat-up hoss and said you-all was in a sight of trouble, so we figgered we'd come along and see how you made out."

"An Injun?" Dusty was puzzled.

"Yeah," Riddle told him, "that was my doin'. I figgered you was headed for trouble, so I sent an Injun kid off after your brothers. Heck, if I'd knowed what you was like with a six-gun, I'd never have sent for 'em!"

Ben Barron grinned and rubbed at the stubble of whiskers. "An' if we'd knowed there was on'y three, we'd never have come!" He looked from Dusty to Ruth. "Don't look like you'll be comin' home right soon with that place at Gallo Gap an' what you've got your arm around. But what'll we tell Allie?"

"Allie?" Ruth drew away from him, eyes wide. "Who's Allie? You didn't tell me you had a girl!"

Dusty winked at his brothers. "Allie? She's war chief of the Barron tribe. Allie's my ma." He turned to Riddle. "Blue, how's about you sort of keepin' an eye on that gap place for me for a week or so? I reckon I'd better take Ruth home for a spell. Allie, she sure sets a sight of store by weddin's."

Ruth's answering pressure on his arm was all the answer he needed.

McQueen of the Tumbling K

Ward McQueen reined in the strawberry roan and squinted his eyes against the sun. Salty sweat made his eyes smart, and he dabbed at them with the end of a bandanna. Kim Sartain was hazing a couple of rambunctious steers back into line. Bud Fox was walking his horse up the slope to where Ward waited, watching the drive.

Fox drew up alongside him and said: "Ward, d'you remember that old brindle ladino with the scarred hide? This here is his range, but we haven't seen hide nor hair of him."

"That's one old mossyhorn I won't forget in a hurry. He's probably hiding back in one of the cañons. Have you cleaned them out yet?"

"Uhn-huh, we surely have. Baldy an' me both worked 'em, and no sign of him. Makes a body mighty curious."

"Yeah, I suppose you've got a point. It ain't like him to be away from the action. He'd surely be down there makin' trouble." He paused, suddenly thoughtful. "Missed any other stock since I've been gone?"

Fox shrugged. "If there's any missin', it can't be more than a few head, but you can bet if that old crowbait is gone, some others went with him. He ramrods a good-sized herd all by himself."

Baldy Jackson joined them on the slope. He jerked his head to indicate a nearby cañon mouth. "Seen some mighty queer tracks over yonder," he said, "like a man afoot."

"We'll go have a look," McQueen said. "A man afoot in this country? It isn't likely."

He started the roan across the narrow valley, with Baldy and Bud following.

The cañon was narrow and high walled. Parts of it were choked with brush and fallen rock, with only the winding watercourse to offer a trail. In the spreading fan of sand where the wash emptied into the valley, Baldy drew up.

Ward looked down at the tracks Baldy indicated. "Yes, they do look odd," said Ward. "Fixed him some homemade footgear. Wonder if that's his blood or some critter?" Leading the roan, he followed the tracks up the dry streambed.

After a few minutes, he halted. "He's been hurt. Look at the tracks headed this way. Fairly long, steady stride. I'd guess he's a tall man. But see here? Goin' back, the steps are shorter an' he's staggerin'. He stopped twice in twenty yards, each time to lean against something."

"Reckon we'd better follow him?" Baldy looked at the jumble of boulders and crowded brush. "If he doesn't aim to be ketched, he could make us a powerful lot of trouble."

"We'll follow him anyway. Baldy, you go back an' help the boys. Tell Kim an' Tennessee where we're at. Bud will stay with me. Maybe we can track him down, an' he should be grateful. It looks like he's hurt bad."

They moved along cautiously for another 100 yards. Bud Fox stopped, mopping his face. "He doesn't figure on bein' followed. He's makin' a try at losin' his trail. Even tried to wipe out a spot of blood."

Ward McQueen paused and looked up the watercourse with keen, probing eyes. There was something wrong about all this. He had been riding this range for months now and believed he knew it well, yet he remembered no such man as this must be, and had seen no such tracks. Obviously the man was injured. Just as obviously he was trying, even in his weakened condition, to obliterate his trail. That meant that he expected to be followed and that those who followed were enemies.

Pausing to study the terrain, he ran over in his mind the possibilities from among those who he knew. Who might the injured man be? And who did he fear?

They moved on, working out the trail in the close, hot air of the cañon. The tracks split suddenly and disappeared on a wide ledge of stone where the cañon divided into two.

"We're stuck," Fox said. "He won't leave tracks with those makeshift shoes of his, and there's nowhere he can go up the cañons."

The right-hand branch ended in a steep, rocky slide, impossible to climb without hours of struggle, and the left branch ended against the sheer face of a cliff against whose base lay a heaped-up pile of boulders and rocky debris.

"He may have doubled back or hidden in the brush," Fox added.

Ward shrugged. "Let's go back. He doesn't want to be found, but hurt like he is, he's apt to die out here without care."

Deliberately he had spoken loudly. Turning their mounts, they rode back down the cañon to rejoin the herd.

***

Ruth Kermitt was waiting on the steps when they left the grassy bottom and rode up to the bunkhouse. With her was a slender, narrow-faced man in a black frock coat. As Ward drew up, the man's all-encompassing glance took him in, then slid away.

"Ward, this is Jim Yount. He's buying cattle and wants to look at the herd you just brought in."

"Howdy," Ward said agreeably. He glanced at Yount's horse, and then at the tied-down gun.

Two more men sat on the steps of the bunkhouse. A big man in a checkered shirt and a slim redhead with a rifle across his knees.

"We're looking to buy five hundred to a thousand head," Yount commented. "We heard you had good stock."

"Beef?"

"No, breeding stock, mostly. We're stockin' a ranch. I'm locatin' the other side of Newton's place."

Ward commented: "We have some cattle. Or rather, Miss Kermitt has. I'm just the foreman."

"Oh?" Yount looked around at Ruth with a quick, flashing smile. "Miss, is it? Or are you a widow?"

"Miss. My brother and I came here together, but he was killed."

"Hard for a young woman to run a ranch alone, isn't it?" His smile was sympathetic.

"Miss Kermitt does very well," Ward replied coolly, "and she isn't exactly alone."

"Oh?" Yount glanced at McQueen, one eyebrow lifted. "No," he said after a minute, "I don't expect you could say she was alone as long as she had cattle on the place, and cowhands."

Ruth got up quickly, not liking the look on Ward's face. "Mister Yount? Wouldn't you like some coffee? Then we can talk business."

When they had gone inside, Ward McQueen turned on his heel and walked to the bunkhouse, leading his horse. He was mad and he didn't care who knew it. The thin-faced redhead looked at him as he drew near.

"What's the matter, friend? Somebody steal your girl?"

Ward McQueen halted and turned slowly. Baldy Jackson got up quickly and moved out of line. The move put him at the corner of the bunkhouse, leaving Yount's riders at the apex of a triangle of which McQueen and himself formed the two corners.

"Miss Kermitt"—McQueen's tone was cold—"is my boss. She is also a lady. Don't get any funny notions."

The redhead chuckled. "Yeah, and our boss is a ladies' man. He knows how to handle 'em."

Deliberately he turned his back on Baldy. "Ever been foreman on a place like this, Dodson. Maybe you or me will have a new job."

Ward walked into the bunkhouse. Bud Fox was loitering beside the window. He, too, had been watching the pair.

"Don't seem the friendly type," Bud commented, pouring warm water into the tin wash basin. "Almost like they wanted trouble."

"What would be the idea of that?" Ward inquired.

Bud was splashing in the basin and made no reply, but Ward wondered. Certainly their attitude was not typical. He glanced toward the house, and his lips tightened. Jim Yount was a slick-talking sort and probably a woman would think him good-looking.

Out beyond the ranch house was a distant light, which would be Gelvin's store in Mannerhouse. Gelvin had ranched the country beyond Newton's. Suddenly McQueen made up his mind. After chow he would ride into Mannerhouse and have a little talk with Gelvin.

Supper was served in the ranch house as always and was a quiet meal but for Ruth and Jim Yount, who laughed and talked at the head of the table.

Ward, seated opposite Yount, had little to say. Baldy, Bud, and Tennessee sat in strict silence. Only Red Lund, seated beside Pete Dodson, occasionally ventured a remark. At the foot of the table, lean, wiry Kim Sartain let his eyes rove from face to face.

When supper was over, Ward moved outside into the moonlight and Kim followed. "What goes on?" Kim whispered. "I never did see anybody so quiet."

Ward explained, adding: "Yount may be a cattle

buyer, but the two riders with him are no average cowpunchers. Red Lund is a gunhand if I ever saw one, and Dodson's right off the Owlhoot Trail or I miss my guess." He hitched his belt. "I'm ridin' into town. Keep an eye on things, will you?"

"I'll do that." He lowered his tone. "That Lund now? I don't cotton to him. Nor Yount," he added.

Gelvin's store was closed but McQueen knew where to find him. Swinging down from the saddle, he tied his horse and pushed through the batwing doors. Abel was polishing glasses behind the bar, and Gelvin was at a table with Dave Cormack, Logan Keane, and a tall, lean-bodied stranger. They were playing poker.

Two other strangers lounged at the bar. They turned to look at him as he came in.

"Howdy, Ward! How's things at the Tumblin' K?"

The two men at the bar turned abruptly and looked at Ward again, quick, searching glances. He had started to speak to Gelvin, but something warned him and instead he walked to the bar.

"Pretty good," he replied. "Diggin' some stuff out of the breaks today. Tough work. All right for a brushpopper, but I like open country."

He tossed off his drink, watching the two men in the bar mirror. "They tell me there's good range beyond Newton's. I think I'll ride over and see if there's any lyin' around loose."

Gelvin glanced up. He was a short, rather handsome man with a keen, intelligent face.

"There's plenty that you can have for the taking. That country is going back to desert as fast as it can. Sand moving in, streams drying up. You can ride a hundred miles and never find a drink.

Why"—he picked up the cards and began to shuffle them—"old Coyote Benny Chait came in two or three weeks ago. He was heading out of the country. He got euchred out of his ranch by some slick card handler. He was laughin' at the man who won it, said he'd get enough of the country in a hurry."

The two men at the bar had turned and were listening to Gelvin. One of them started to speak and the other put a cautioning hand on his arm.

"Who was it won the ranch? Did he say?"

"Sure." Gelvin began to deal. "Some driftin' cardsharp by the name of . . ."

"You talk too much!" The larger of the two men at the bar stepped toward the card table. "What d'you know about the country beyond Newton's?"

Startled by the unprovoked attack, Gelvin turned in his chair. His eyes went from one to the other of the two men. Ward McQueen had picked up the bottle.

"What is this?" Gelvin asked, keeping his tone even.

These men did not seem to be drunk, yet he was experienced enough to know he was in trouble, serious trouble. "What did I say? I was just commenting on the country beyond Newton's."

"You lied!" The big man's hand was near his gun. "You lied! That country ain't goin' back! It's as good as it ever was!"

Gelvin was a stubborn man. This man was trying to provoke a fight, but Gelvin had no intention of being killed over a trifle. "I did not lie," he replied coolly. "I lived in that country for ten years. I came in with the first white men, and I've talked with the Indians who were there earlier. I know of what I speak."

"Then you're sayin' I'm a liar?" The big man's hand spread over his gun.

Ward McQueen turned in one swift movement. His right hand knocked the bottle spinning toward the second man and he kept swinging around, his right hand grabbing the big man by the belt. With a heave he swung the big man off balance and whirled him, staggering, into the smaller man who had sprung back to avoid the bottle.

The big man staggered again, fell, and then came up with a grunt of fury. Reaching his feet, his hand went to his gun, then froze. He was looking into a gun in Ward McQueen's hand.

"That was a private conversation," Ward said mildly. "In this town we don't interfere. Understand?"

"If you didn't have the drop on me, you wouldn't be talkin' so big!"

Ward dropped his six-gun into its holster. "All right, now you've got an even break."

The two men faced him, and suddenly neither liked what they saw. This was no time for bravery, they decided.

"We ain't lookin' for trouble," the smaller man said. "We just rode into town for a drink."

"Then ride out," Ward replied. "And don't butt into conversations that don't concern you."

"Hollier 'n' me . . . ," the big man started to speak, but then suddenly stopped and started for the door.

Ward stepped back toward the bar. "Thanks, Gelvin. You told me something I needed to know."

"I don't get it," Gelvin protested. "What made them mad?"

"That card shark you mentioned? His name wouldn't be Jim Yount, would it?"

"Of course! How did you know?"

The tall stranger playing cards with Gelvin glanced up and their eyes met. "You wouldn't be the Ward McQueen from down Texas way, would you?"

"That's where I'm from. Why?"

The man smiled pleasantly. "You cut a wide swath down thataway. I heard about your run-in with the Maravillas Cañon outfit."

***

McQueen was cautious when he took the trail to the Tumbling K, but he saw nothing of the two men in the saloon. Hollier—he was the smaller one. There had been a Hollier who escaped from a lynch mob down Uvalde way a few years back. He had trailed around with a man called Packer, and the larger of these two men had a P burned on his holster with a branding iron.

What was Jim Yount's game? Obviously the two men from the saloon were connected with him somehow. They had seemed anxious Yount's name not be spoken, and they seemed eager to quiet any talk about the range beyond Newton's.

The available facts were few. Yount had won a ranch in a poker game. Gelvin implied the game was crooked. The ranch he won was going back to desert. In other words, he had won nothing but trouble. What came next?

The logical thing for a man of Yount's stamp was to shrug off the whole affair and go on about his business. He was not doing that, which implied some sort of a plan. Lund and Dodson would make likely companions to Packer and Hollier. Yount was talking of buying cattle, but he was not the sort to throw good money after bad. Did they plan to rustle the cattle?

One thing was sure. It was time he got back to the ranch to alert the boys for trouble. It would be coming sooner, perhaps, because of what happened tonight. But what about Ruth? Was she taken with Yount? Or simply talking business and being polite? Did he dare express his doubts to her?

The Tumbling K foreman was riding into the ranch yard when the shot rang out. Something had struck a wicked blow on his head, and he was already falling when he heard the shot.

***

His head felt constricted, as if a tight band had been drawn around his temples. Slowly, fighting every inch of the way, he battled his way to consciousness. His lids fluttered, then closed, too weak to force themselves open. He struggled against the heaviness and finally got his eyes open. He was lying on his back in a vague half light. The air felt damp, cool.

Awareness came. He was in a cave or mine tunnel. Turning his head carefully, he looked around. He was lying on a crude pallet on a sandy floor. Some twenty feet away was a narrow shaft of light. Nearby his gun belt hung on a peg driven into the wall and his rifle leaned against the wall.

The rift of light was blotted out and someone crawled into the cave. A man came up and threw down an armful of wood. Then he lighted a lantern and glanced at McQueen.

"Come out of it, did you? Man, I thought you never would."

He was lean and old, with twinkling blue eyes and almost white hair. He was long and tall. Ward noted the footgear suddenly. This was the man they had trailed up the cañon!

"Who are you?" he demanded.

The man smiled and squatted on his heels. "Charlie Quayle's the name. Used to ride for Chait, over beyond Newton's."

"You're the one we trailed up the cañon the other day. Yesterday, I believe it was."

"I'm the man, all right, but it wasn't yesterday. You've been lyin' here all of two weeks, delirious most of the time. I was beginning to believe you'd never come out of it."

"Two weeks?" McQueen struggled to sit up, but the effort was too much. He sank back. "Two weeks? They'll figure I'm dead back at the ranch. Why did you bring me here? Who shot me?"

"Hold your horses. I've got to wash up and fix some grub." He poured water in a basin and began to wash his face and hands. As he dried his hands, he explained. "You was shot, and I ain't sure who done it. Two of them rustlin' hands of Yount's packed you to the cañon and dropped you into the wash. Then they caved sand over you and some brush. But they weren't about to do more than need be, so figurin' you were sure enough dead, they rode off. I was almighty curious to know who'd been killed, so I pulled the brush away and dug into the pile and found you was still alive. I packed you up here, and mister, it took some packin'. You're a mighty heavy man."

"Were you trailin' them when they shot me?"

"No. To tell you the truth, I was scoutin' the layout at the ranch, figurin' to steal some coffee when I heard the shot. Then I saw them carry you off, so I follered." Quayle lighted his pipe. "There's been some changes," he added. "You friend Sartain has been fired. So have Fox and that bald-headed gent. Tennessee had a run-in with Lund and Lund killed him. Picked a fight, and then beat him to the draw. Yount is real friendly with Ruth Kermitt, and he's runnin' the ranch. One or more of those tough gunmen of his is there all the time."

Ward lay back on his pallet. Kim Sartain fired! It didn't seem reasonable. Kim had been with Ruth Kermitt longer than any of them. He had been with them when Ruth and her brother came over the trail from Montana. Kim had been with her through all that trouble at Pilot Range when Ward himself had first joined them. Kim had always ridden for the brand. Now he had been fired, run off the place. And Tennessee killed!

What sort of girl was Ruth Kermitt? She had fired her oldest and most loyal hands and taken on a bunch of rustlers with a tinhorn gambler for boss. And to think he had been getting soft on her! He'd actually been thinking she was the girl for him, and the only reason he'd held off was because he had no money, nothing to offer a woman. Well, this showed what a fool he would have been.

"You've got a hard head," Quayle was saying,

"or you'd be dead by now. That bullet hit right over your eye and skidded around your skull under the skin. Laid your scalp open. You had a concussion, too. I know the signs. And you lost blood."

"I've got to get out of here," Ward said. "I've got to see Ruth Kermitt."

"You'd be better off to sit tight and get well. Right now she's right busy with that there Yount. Rides all over the range with him, holdin' hands more'n half the time. Everybody's seen 'em. And if she fired all the rest of her hands, you can be sure she doesn't want her foreman back."

He was right, of course. What good would it do even to talk to a woman who would fire such loyal hands as she'd had?

"Where d' you fit into all this?"

Quayle sliced bacon into a frying pan. "Like I told you. I rode for Chait. Yount rooked him out of his ranch, but as a matter of fact Chait was glad to get shut of it. When Yount found what he'd won, he was sore. Me, I'd saved me nigh on a year's wages an' was fixin' to set up for myself. One of those hands of Yount's, he seen the money and trailed me down, said it was ranch money. We had us a fight and they got some lead into me. I got away an' holed up in this here cañon."

***

All day McQueen rested in the cave, his mind busy with the problem. But what could he do? If Ruth Kermitt had made her choice, it was no longer any business of his. The best thing he could do was to get his horse and ride out of there, just drop the whole thing.

It was well after dark before Quayle returned, but he had news and was eager to talk.

"That Yount is takin' over the country! He went into Mannerhouse last night, huntin' Gelvin, but Gelvin had gone off with that stranger friend of his that he plays poker with all the time. Yount had words with Dave Cormack and killed him. They say this Yount is greased lightning with a gun. Then Lund an' Pete Dodson pistol-whipped Logan Keane. Yount told them he was runnin' the Tumblin' K and was going to marry Ruth Kermitt, and he was fed up with the talk about him and his men. He thinks he's got that town treed, an' maybe he has. Takes some folks a long time to get riled."

Ruth to marry Jim Yount! Ward felt a sharp pang. He realized suddenly that he was in love with Ruth. Now that he realized it, he knew he had been in love with her for a long time. And she was to marry Yount.

"Did you see anything of Kim Sartain?"

"No," Quayle replied, "but I heard the three of them rode over into the range beyond Newton's."

***

Ward McQueen was up at daybreak. He rolled out of his blankets, and, although his head ached, he felt better. No matter. It was time to be up and doing. His long period of illness had at least given him rest, and his strength was such that he recovered rapidly. He oiled his guns and reloaded them.

Quayle watched him preparing to travel but said nothing until he pulled on his boots. "Better wait until sundown if you're huntin' trouble," he said. "I got a hoss for you. Stashed him down in the brush."

"A horse? Good for you! I'm going to have a look at the ranch. This deal doesn't figure right to me."

"Nor me." Quayle knocked the ash from his pipe. "I seen that girl's face today. They rid past as I lay in the brush. She surely didn't look like a happy woman. Not like she was ridin' with a man she loved. Maybe she ain't willin'."

"I don't like to think she'd take up with a man like Yount. Well, tonight I ride."

"We ride," Quayle insisted. "I didn't like gettin' shot up any more than you-all. I'm in this fight, too."

"I can use the help, but what I'd really like you to do is hunt down Kim Sartain and the others. I can use their help. Get them back here for a show-down. Warn them it won't be pretty."

Where Quayle had found the quick-stepping buckskin Ward neither knew nor cared. He needed a horse desperately, and the buckskin was not only a horse but a very good one.

Whatever Yount's game was he had been fast and thorough. He had moved in on the Tumbling K, had Ward McQueen dry-gulched, had Ruth Kermitt fire her old hands, replaced them with his own men, and then rode into Mannerhouse and quieted all outward opposition by killing Dave Cormack and beating another man. If there was to have been opposition, it would have been Cormack and Keane who would have led it. Tennessee, too, had been killed, but Tennessee was not known in town, and that might be passed off as a simple dispute between cowhands. Yount had proved to be fast, ruthless, and quick of decision. As he acted with the real or apparent consent of Ruth Kermitt, there was nothing to he done by the townspeople in the village of Mannerhouse.

Probably, with Cormack and Keane out of the picture and Gelvin off God knew where, they were not inclined to do anything. None of them was suffering any personal loss, and nothing was to be gained by bucking a man already proven to be dangerous. Obviously the gambler was in control. He had erred in only two things. He had failed to kill Charlie Quayle and to make sure that McQueen was dead.

The buckskin had a liking for the trail and moved out fast. Ward rode toward the Tumbling K, keeping out of sight. Quayle had ridden off earlier in the day to find Kim, Baldy, and Bud Fox. The latter two were good cowhands and trustworthy, but the slim, dark-faced youngster, Kim Sartain, was one of the fastest men with a gun Ward had ever seen.

"With him," Ward told the buckskin, "I'd tackle an army."

He left the buckskin in a clump of willows near the stream, and then crossed on stepping-stones, working his way through the brush toward the Tumbling K ranch house.

He had no plan of action, or anything on which to base a plan. If he could find Ruth and talk to her, or if he could figure out what it was that Yount was trying to accomplish, it would be a beginning.

The windows were brightly lit. For a time he lay in the brush studying the situation. An error now would be fatal, if not to him, at least to their plans.

There would be someone around, he was sure.

Quayle had said one of the gunmen was always on the ranch, for the gambler was a careful man.

A cigarette glowed suddenly from the steps of the bunkhouse. Evidently the man had just turned toward him. Had he inadvertently made a sound? At least he knew that somebody was there, on guard.

Ward eased off to the left until the house was between himself and the guard. Then he crossed swiftly to the side of the house. He eased a window a little higher. It was a warm night and the window had been open at the bottom.

Jim Yount was playing solitaire at the dining room table. Red Lund was oiling a pistol. Packer was leaning his elbows on the table and smoking, watching Yount's cards.

"I always wanted a ranch," Yount was saying, "and this is it. No use gallivanting around the country when a man can live in style. I'd have had it over beyond Newton's if that damned sand bed I got from Chait had been any good. Then I saw this place. It was too good to be true."

"You worked fast," Packer said, "but you had a streak of luck when Hollier an' me got McQueen. From what I hear, he was nobody to fool around with."

Yount shrugged. "Maybe so, but all sorts of stories get started and half of them aren't true. He might be fast with a gun, but he had no brains, and it takes brains to win in this kind of game." He glanced at Lund. "Look, that Logan Keane outfit lies south of Hosstail Creek, and it joins onto this one. Nice piece of country, thousands of acres with good water, running right up to the edge of town. Keane's scared now. Once me and Ruth Kermitt are married so our title to this ranch is cinched, we'll go to work on Keane. We'll rustle his stock, run off his hands, and force him to sell. I figure the whole job shouldn't take more than a month, at the outside."

Red glanced up from his pistol. "You get the ranches, what do we get?"

Yount smiled. "You don't want a ranch, and I do, but I happen to know that Ruth has ten thousand dollars cached. You boys"—for a moment his eyes held those of Red Lund—"can split that among you. You can work out some way of dividing it even up all around."

Lund's eyes showed his understanding, and McQueen glanced at Packer, but the big horse thief showed no sign of having seen the exchange of glances. Ward could see how the split would be made; it would be done with Red Lund's six-shooter. They would get the lead; he'd take the cash. It had the added advantage to Jim Yount of leaving only one witness to his treachery.

Crouched below the window, Ward McQueen calculated his chances. Jim Yount was reputed to be a fast man with a gun. Red Lund had already proved his skill. Packer would, also, be good, even if not an artist like the others. Three to one made the odds much too long, and at the bunkhouse would be Hollier and Pete Dodson, neither a man to be trifled with.

A *clatter* of horses' hoofs on the hard-packed trail, and a horseman showed briefly in the door and was ushered into the room. It was the lean stranger who had played poker with Gelvin and Keane.

"You Jim Yount? Just riding by and wanted to tell you there's an express package at the station for Miss Kermitt. She can drop in tomorrow to pick it up if she likes."

"Express package? Why didn't you bring it out?"

"Wouldn't let me. Seems like its money or something like that. A package of *dinero* that's payment for some property in Wyoming. She's got to sign for it herself. They won't let anybody else have it."

Yount nodded. "All right. She's asleep, I think, but come morning I'll tell her."

The rider went out, and a few minutes later Ward heard his horse's hoofs on the trail.

"More money?" Packer grinned. "Not bad, boss! She can pick it up for us and we'll split it."

Red Lund was wiping off his pistol. "I don't like it," he spoke suddenly. "Looks like a move to get us off the ranch and the girl into town."

Yount shrugged. "I doubt it, but suppose that's it? Who in town has the guts or the skill to tackle us? Personally I believe it's the truth, but if it ain't, why worry? We'll send Packer in ahead to scout. If there's any strangers around, he can warn us. I think it's all right. We'll ride in tomorrow."

***

An hour later, and far back on a brush-covered hillside, Ward McQueen bedded down for the night. From where he lay, he could see anybody who arrived at or left the ranch. One thing he knew. Tomorrow was the payoff. Ruth Kermitt would not be returning to the ranch.

At daylight he was awake and watching, his buckskin saddled and ready. It had been a damp, uncomfortable night, and he stretched, trying to get the chill from his muscles. The sunshine caught reflected light from the window. Hollier emerged and began roping horses in the corral. He saddled his own, Ruth's brown mare, and Yount's big gray.

Ward McQueen tried to foresee what would happen. He was convinced, as was Red Lund, that the package was a trick. There were only nine buildings on the town's main street, scarcely more than two dozen houses scattered about. The express and stage office was next to the saloon. Gelvin's store was across the street.

Whatever happened, Ruth would be in danger. She would be with Yount, closely surrounded by the others. To fire on them was to endanger her.

And where did that young rider stand? He had been called Rip, and he had known of McQueen's gun battle in Maravillas Cañon. Ward was sure he was not the aimless drifter he was supposed to be. His face was too keen, his eyes too sharp. If he had baited a trap with money, he had used the only bait to which these men would rise. But what was he hoping to accomplish?

There were no men in Mannerhouse who could draw a gun in the same league with Yount or Lund. Gelvin would try, if he was there, but Gelvin had only courage, and no particular skill with a handgun, and courage alone was not enough.

It was an hour after daylight when Packer mounted his paint gelding and started for town. Ward watched him go, speculating on what must follow. He had resolved upon his own course of action. His was no elaborate plan. He intended to slip into town and at the right moment kill Jim Yount and, if possible, Red Lund.

The only law in Mannerhouse was old John Binns, a thoroughly good man of some seventy years who had been given the job largely in lieu of a pension. He had been a hardworking man who owned his home and a few acres of ground, and he had a wife only a few years younger.

Mannerhouse had never been on the route of trail drives, land booms, or mining discoveries, and in consequence the town had few disturbances or characters likely to cause them. The jail had been used but once, when the town first came into being, and few citizens could remember the occasion. John Binns's enforcement of the law usually was a quiet suggestion to be a little less noisy or to go home and sleep it off.

Ward McQueen, a law-abiding man, found himself faced with a situation where right, justice, and the simple rules of civilized society were being pushed aside by men who did not hesitate to kill. One prominent citizen had been murdered, another pistol-whipped. Their stated intention was to do more of the same, to say nothing of Jim Yount's plan to marry Ruth, and his implication had been that it was simply a means to seize her land. Once they had won what they wished, there was no reason to believe the violence would cease. Gangrene had infected the area, and the only solution open to Ward McQueen was to amputate.

Yet he was no fool. He knew something of the gun skills of the men he would face. Even if he was killed himself, he must eliminate them. The townspeople could take care of such as Hollier and Packer. If he succeeded, Kim Sartain could handle the rest of it, and would. That was Kim's way.

Mounting the buckskin, he started down the trail toward Mannerhouse, only a few miles away. When he had ridden but a few hundred yards, he saw from his vantage point above the ranch that three riders were also headed for town. Jim Yount, Ruth, and, a few yards behind, Red Lund.

Pete Dodson, riding a sorrel horse, was also headed for town but by another route. Jim Yount was taking no chances.

***

The dusty main street of Mannerhouse lay warm under the morning sun. On the steps of the express office Rip was sunning himself. Abel, behind his bar, watched nervously both his window and his door. He was on edge and aware, aware as a wild animal is when a strange creature nears its lair. Trouble was in the wind.

Gelvin's store was closed, unusual for this time of day. Abel glanced at Rip, and his brow furrowed. Rip was wearing two tied-down guns this morning, unusual for him.

Abel finished polishing the glass and put it down, glancing nervously at Packer. Suddenly Packer downed the drink and got to his feet. Walking to the door, he glanced up and down the street. All was quiet, yet the big man was worried. A man left the post office and walked along the boardwalk to the barbershop, and entered. The sound of the closing door was the only sound. A hen pecked at something in the mouth of the alley near Gelvin's store. As he watched, he saw Pete Dodson stop his horse behind Gelvin's. Pete was carrying a rifle. Packer glanced over at Rip, noting the guns.

Packer turned suddenly, glaring at Abel. "Give me that scattergun you got under the bar!"

"Huh?" Abel was frightened. "I ain't got . . ."

"Don't give me that! I want that gun!"

There was an instant when Abel considered covering Packer or even shooting him, but the big man frightened him and he put the shotgun on the bar. Packer picked it up and tiptoed to the window and put the gun down beside it. Careful to make no sound, he eased the window up a few inches. His position now covered Rip's side and back.

Abel cringed at what he had done. He liked Rip. The lean, easygoing, friendly young man might now be killed because of him. He'd been a coward. He should have refused, covered Packer, and called Rip inside. And he could have done that. If he wasn't such a coward. Now, because of him, a good man might be murdered, shot in the back. What was going on, anyway? This had been such a quiet little town.

Jim Yount rode up the street with Ruth beside him. Her face was pale and strained, and her eyes seemed unnaturally large.

Red Lund trailed a few yards behind. He drew up, and tied his horse across the street.

From the saloon Abel could see it all. Jim Yount and Ruth Kermitt were approaching Rip from the west. North and west was Red Lund. Due north and in the shadow of Gelvin's was Pete Dodson. In the saloon was Packer. Rip was very neatly boxed, signed, and sealed. All but delivered.

Jim Keane, Logan's much older brother, was the express agent. He saw Jim Yount come, saw Red Lund across the street.

Rip got up lazily, smiling at Ruth.

"Come for your package, Miss Kermitt?" he asked politely. "While you're here, would you mind answering some questions."

"By whose authority?" Yount demanded sharply.

Ward McQueen, crouched behind the saloon, heard the reply clearly. "The state of Texas, Yount," Rip replied. "I'm a Texas Ranger."

Jim Yount's short laugh held no humor. "This ain't Texas, and she answers no questions."

Ward McQueen opened the back door of the saloon and stepped inside.

Packer, intent on the scene before him, heard the door open. Startled and angry, he whirled around. Ward McQueen, who he had buried, was standing just inside the door. The shotgun was resting on the windowsill behind Rip. Packer went for his six-gun, but even as he reached, he knew it was hopeless. He saw the stab of flame, felt the solid blow of the bullet, and felt his knees turn to butter under him. He pitched forward on his face.

Outside all hell broke loose. Ruth Kermitt, seeing Rip's situation, spurred her horse to bump Yount's, throwing him out of position. Instantly she slid from the saddle and threw herself to the ground near the edge of the walk.

All seemed to have begun firing at once. Yount, cursing bitterly, fired at Rip. He in turn was firing at Red Lund. Ward stepped suddenly from the saloon and saw himself facing Yount, who had brought his mount under control. He fired at Yount, and a bullet from Dodson's rifle knocked splinters from the post in front of his face.

Yount's gun was coming into line and McQueen fired an instant sooner. Yount fired and they both missed. Ward's second shot hit Yount, who grabbed for the pommel. Ward walked a step forward, but something hit him and he went to his knee. Red Lund loomed from somewhere, and Ward got off another shot. Lund's face was covered with blood.

There was firing from the stage station and from Gelvin's store. There was a thunder of hoofs, and a blood-red horse came charging down the street, its rider hung low like an Indian, shooting under the horse's neck.

Yount was down, crawling on his belly in the dust. He had lost hold of his six-shooter, but his right hand held a knife and he was crawling toward Ruth. McQueen's six-shooter *clicked* on an empty chamber. How many shots were left in his other gun? He lifted it with his left hand. Something was suddenly wrong with his right. He rarely shot with his left hand, but now . . . .

Yount was closer. Ruth was staring across the street, unaware. McQueen shot past Ruth, squeezing off the shot with his left hand. He saw Yount contract sharply as the bullet struck. McQueen fired again, and the gambler rolled over on his side and the knife slipped from his fingers.

Abel ran from the saloon with a shotgun, and Gelvin from his store with a rifle. Then Ruth was running toward him, and he saw Kim Sartain coming back up the street, walking the red horse. Ward tried to rise to meet Ruth, but his knees gave way and he went over on his face, thinking how weak she must think him. He started to rise again, and blacked out.

***

When he could see again Ruth was beside him. Kim was squatting on his heels. "Come on, Ward!" he said. "You've only been hit twice and neither of 'em bad. Can't you handle lead any more?"

"What happened?"

"Clean sweep, looks like. Charlie Quayle got to us and we hightailed it to the ranch. Hollier wanted to give us trouble, but we smoked him out. I believe there were others around, but if there were, they skipped the country. Whilst they were cleanin' up, I took it on the run for town. Halfway here, I thought I heard a shot, and, when I hit the street, everybody in town was shootin', or that's what it looked like. Reg'lar Fourth of July celebration! Pete Dodson is dead, and Red Lund's dying with four bullets in him. Yount's alive, but he won't make it, either. Packer's dead."

Ward's head was aching and he felt weak and sick, but he did not want to move, even to get out of the street. He just wanted to sit, to forget all that had taken place. With fumbling fingers, from long habit, he started to reload his pistols. Oddly he found one of them contained three live shells. Somehow he must have reloaded, but he had no memory of it.

Rip came over. "My name's Coker, Ward. I couldn't figure any way to bust up Yount's operation without getting Ruth Kermitt away from him first, so I faked that package to get them into town, hoping I could get her away from them. I didn't figure they'd gang up on me like they did."

They helped Ward up and into the saloon. Gelvin brought the doctor in. "Yount just died," Gelvin said, "cussing you and everybody concerned."

He sat back in a chair while the doctor patched him up. Again he had lost blood. "I've got to find a bed," he said to Kim. "There must be a hotel in town."

"You're coming back to the ranch," Ruth said. "We need you there. They told me you left me, Ward. Jim Yount said you pulled out and Kim with you. I hadn't seen him, and Yount said he'd manage the ranch until I found someone. Then he brought his own men in and fired Kim, who I hadn't seen, and I was surrounded and scared. If you had been there, or if I'd even known you were around, I . . ."

"Don't worry about it." Ward leaned his head back. All he wanted was rest.

Baldy Jackson helped him into a buckboard, Bud Fox driving. "You know that old brindle longhorn who turned up missin'? Well, I found him. He's got about thirty head with him, holed up in the prettiest little valley you ever did see. Looks like he's there to stay."

"He's like me," Ward commented, "so used to his range he wouldn't he happy anywhere else."

"Then why think of anywhere else?" Ruth said. "I want you to stay."

Showdown on the Hogback

I

Everything was quiet in Mustang. Three whole days had passed without a killing. The townsfolk, knowing their community, were not fooled, but rather had long since resigned themselves to the inevitable and would, in fact, be relieved when the situation was back to normal with a killing every day, or more on hot days. When there had been no killing for several days, pressure mounted because no one knew who would be next. Moreover, with Clay Allison, who had killed thirty men, playing poker over at the Morrison House, and Black Jack Ketchum who richly deserved the hanging he was soon to get, sleeping off a drunk at the St. James, trouble could be expected.

The walk before the St. James was cool at this hour, and Captain Tom Kedrick, a stranger in town, sat in a well-polished chair and studied the street with interested eyes. He was a tall young man with rusty brown hair and green eyes, quiet-mannered and quick to smile. Women never failed to look twice, and, when their eyes met his, their hearts pounded, a fact of which Tom Kedrick was totally unaware. He knew women seemed to like him, but it never failed to leave him mildly astonished when they liked him very much, which they often did.

The street he watched was crowded with buckboards, freight wagons, a newly arrived stage and one about to depart. All the hitch rails were lined with saddled horses wearing a variety of brands. Kedrick was suddenly aware that a young man stood beside him, and he glanced up. The fellow was scarcely more than a boy and he had soft brown eyes and hair that needed cutting. "Cap'n Kedrick?" he inquired. "John Gunter sent me. I'm Dornie Shaw."

"Oh, yes!" Kedrick got to his feet, smiling, and thrust out his hand. "Nice to know you, Shaw. Are you working for Gunter?"

Shaw's soft brown eyes were faintly ironic. "With him," he corrected. "I work for no man."

"I see."

Kedrick did not see at all, but he was prepared to wait and find out. There was something oddly disturbing about this young man, something that had Kedrick on edge and queerly alert. "Where's Gunter now?"

"Down the street. He asked me to check an' see if you were here, an', if you were, to ask you to stick around close to the hotel. He'll be along soon."

"All right. Sit down, why don't you?"

Shaw glanced briefly at the chairs. "I'll stand. I never sit in no chair with arms on them. Apt to get in the way."

"In the way?" Kedrick glanced up, and then his eyes fell to the two guns Shaw wore, their butts hanging wide. "Oh, yes! I see." He nodded at the guns. "The town marshal doesn't object?"

Dornie Shaw looked at him, smiling slowly. "Not to me, he don't. Wouldn't do him no good if he did." He added after a minute: "Anyway, not in Mustang. Too many hardcases. I never seen a marshal could make it stick in this town."

Kedrick smiled. "Hickok? Earp? Masterson?"

"Maybe"—Dornie Shaw was openly skeptical— "but I doubt it. Allison's here. So's Ketchum. Billy the Kid's been around, and some of that crowd. A marshal in this town would have to be mighty fast, an' prove it ever' day."

"Maybe you're right." He studied Shaw surreptitiously. What was it about him that was so disturbing? Not the two guns, for he had seen many men who wore guns, had been reared among them, in fact. No, it was something else, some quality he could not define, but it was a sort of lurking menace, an odd feeling with such a calm-eyed young man.

"We've got some good men," Shaw volunteered, after a minute. "Picked up a couple today. Laredo Shad's goin' to be one of the best, I'm thinkin'. He's a tough hand, an' gun-wise as all get out. Three more come in today. Fessenden, Poinsett, an' Goff."

Obviously, from the manner in which he spoke, the names meant much to Shaw, but they meant exactly nothing to Kedrick. Fessenden seemed to strike some sort of a responsive note but he could not put a finger on it. His eyes strayed down the street, studying the crowd. "You think they'll really fight?" he asked, studying the crowd. "Are there enough of them?"

"That bunch?" Shaw's voice was dry. "They'll fight, all right. You got some tough boys in that outfit. Injun scrappers, an' such like. They won't scare worth a damn." He glanced curiously at Kedrick. "Gunter says you're a fighter."

Was that doubt in Shaw's voice? Kedrick smiled, then shrugged. "I get along. I was in the Army, if that means anything."

"Been West before?"

"Sure! I was born in California, just before the rush. When the war broke out, I was sixteen, but I went in with a bunch from Nevada. Stayed in a couple of years after the war, fighting Apaches."

Shaw nodded, as if satisfied. "Gunter thinks well of you, but he's the only one of them, an' not the most important one."

A short, thick-set man with a square-cut beard looking enough like General Grant to be his twin was pushing through the crowd toward them. He even smoked a thick, black cigar. The man walking beside him was as tall as Kedrick, who stood an easy inch above six feet. He had a sharply cut face and his eyes were cold, but they were the eyes of a man born to command, a man who could be utterly ruthless. That would be Colonel Loren Keith. That meant there was one yet, who he must meet. The man Burwick. The three were partners, and of the three only Burwick was from the area.

Gunter smiled quickly, his lips parting over clenched white teeth that gripped his cigar. He thrust out his hand. "Good to see you, Kedrick! Colonel, this is our man! If there ever was a man born to ramrod this thing through, this is the one. I told you of that drive he made for Patterson. Took those cattle through without losing a head, rustlers an' Comanches be damned."

Keith nodded, his cold eyes taking in Kedrick at a glance. "Captain . . . that was an Army title, Kedrick?"

"Army. The War Between the States."

"I see. There was a Thomas Kedrick who was a sergeant in the fighting against the Apaches."

"That was me. All of us went down some in rank after the troops were discharged."

"How much time in the war?" Keith's eyes still studied him.

"Four years, and two campaigning in the Southwest."

"Not bad. You should know what to expect in a fight." His eyes went to Kedrick's, faintly supercilious. "I have twelve years, myself. Regular Army."

Kedrick found that Keith's attitude irritated him. He had meant to say nothing about it, but suddenly he was speaking. "My American Army experience, Colonel, was only part of mine. I was with Bazaine, at the defense of Metz, in the Franco-Prussian War. I escaped, and was with MacMahon at the Battle of Sedan."

Keith's eyes sharpened and his lips thinned. Kedrick could feel the sharp dislike rising in the man. Keith was defiantly possessed of a strong superiority complex.

"Is that all?" he asked coolly.

"Why, no. Since you ask, it was not. I was with Wolseley, in the Second Ashanti War in Africa. And I was in the two-year campaign against the Tungans of northern T'ien Shan . . . with the rank of general."

"You seem to get around a good bit," Keith said dryly, "a genuine mercenary."

Kedrick smiled, undisturbed. "If you like. That's what you want here, isn't it? Men who can fight? Isn't it customary for some men to hire others to do their fighting for them?"

Colonel Keith's face flamed, then went white, but before he could speak, a big, square-faced man thrust himself through the crowd and stopped to face them. "You, is it, Gunter? Well, I've heard tell the reason why you're here, an', if you expect to take from hard-workin' men the land they've slaved for, you better come a-shootin'!"

Before anyone could speak, Dornie slid between Keith and Gunter and fronted the man. "You lookin' for trouble? You want to start your shootin' now?"

His voice was low, almost a purr, but Kedrick was startled by the shocked expression on the man's face. He drew back, holding his hands wide. "I wasn't bracin' you, Dornie. Didn't even know you was around."

"Then get out!" Shaw snarled, passion suddenly breaking through his calmness, and something else, something Kedrick spotted with a shock—the driving urge to kill!

"Get out!" Shaw repeated. "An' if you want to live, keep goin'!"

Stumblingly the man turned and ducked into the hastily assembled crowd, and Tom Kedrick, scanning their faces, found hard indifference there, or hatred. In no face did he see warmth or friendly feeling. He frowned thoughtfully, then turned away.

Gunter caught his arm, eager to take advantage of the break the interruption had made to bring peace between the two. "You see what we're up against?" he began. "Now that was Peters. He's harmless, but there's others would have drawn, and drawn fast. They won't be all like that. Let's go meet Burwick."

Kedrick fell in beside Gunter who carefully interposed himself between the two men. Once, Tom glanced back. What had become of Dornie Shaw he did not know, but he did know his second in command, which job was Shaw's, was a killer. He knew the type from of old.

Yet he was disturbed more than he cared to admit by the man who had braced them. Peters had the look of an honest man, even if not an intelligent one. Of course, there might be honest men among them, if they were men of Peters's stripe. He was always a follower, and he might follow where the wrong men led. Certainly, if this land was going to Gunter, Keith, and Burwick through a government bill, there could be nothing wrong with it. If the government sold the land to them, squatters had no rights there. Still, if there were many like Peters, the job was not going to be all he had expected.

Gunter stopped before a square stone house set back from the street. "This here's headquarters," he said. "We hole up here when in town. Come on in."

A wide verandah skirted the house, and, as they stepped upon it, they saw a girl in a gray skirt and white blouse sitting a few feet away with an open book in her lap. Gunter halted. "Colonel, you've met Miss Duane."

"Cap'n Kedrick, my niece, Consuelo Duane."

Their eyes met—and held. For a breathless moment, no voice was lifted. Tom Kedrick felt as though his muscles had gone dead, for he could not move. Her own eyes were wide, startled.

Kedrick recovered himself with a start. He bowed. "Miss Duane!"

"Captain Kedrick"—somehow she was on her feet and moving toward him—"I hope you'll like it here!"

His eyes had not left hers, and now color was coming into her cheeks. "I shall," he said gently. "Nothing can prevent me now."

"Don't be too sure of that, Captain." Keith's voice was sharp and cold. "We are late for our visit. Let's be going. Your pardon, Connie. Burwick is waiting."

Kedrick glanced back as he went through the door, and the girl was still standing there, poised, motionless.

Keith's irritation was obvious, but Gunter seemed to have noticed nothing. Dornie Shaw, who had materialized from somewhere, glanced briefly at Kedrick, but said nothing at all. Coolly he began to roll a smoke.

II

Burwick crouched behind a table. He was an incredibly fat man, and incredibly dirty. A stubble of graying beard covered his jowls and his several chins, yet the eyes that measured Kedrick from beneath the almost hairless brows were sharp, malignant, and set close alongside a nose too small for his face. His shirt was open, and the edge of the collar was greasy. Rims of black marked each fingernail.

He glanced at the others, then back at Kedrick. "Sit down!" he said. "You're late! Business won't wait!" His bulbous head swung from Kedrick to Gunter. "John, this the man who'll ramrod those skunks off that land? This him?"

"Yes, that's Kedrick," Gunter said hastily. Oddly enough, he seemed almost frightened of Burwick. Keith had said nothing since they entered the room. Quietly he seemed to have withdrawn, stepped momentarily from the picture. It was, Kedrick was to discover, a faculty he had when Burwick was near. "He'll do the job, all right."

Burwick turned his eyes on Kedrick after a

moment and nodded: "Know a good deal about you, son." His voice was almost genial. "You'll do, if you don't get too soft with them. We've no time to waste, you understand. They've had notice to move. Give 'em one more notice, then get 'em off or bury 'em! That's your business, not mine. I'll ask the questions," he added sharply, "an' I'll see nobody else does. What happens here is our business."

He dismissed Kedrick from his mind and turned his attention to Gunter. "You've ordered like I told you? Grub for fifty men for fifty days? Once this situation is cleaned up, I want to get started at once. The sooner we have work started, the sooner we'll be all set. I want no backfiring on this job."

Burwick turned sharply to Tom Kedrick. "Ten days! I give you ten days! If you need more than five, I'll be disappointed. If you've not the heart for it, turn Dornie loose. Dornie'll show 'em." He cackled suddenly. "That's right! Dornie'll show 'em!" He sobered down, glanced at the papers on his desk, then without looking up: "Kedrick, you can go. Dornie, you run along, too."

Kedrick hesitated, then arose. "How many of these men are there?" he asked suddenly. "Have any of them families?"

Gunter turned on him nervously: "I'll tell you all you need to know, Tom. See you later."

Kedrick shrugged and, picking up his hat, walked out. Dornie Shaw had already vanished. Yet when he reached the verandah, Connie Duane still sat there, only now she was not reading, merely staring over the top of her book at the dusty, sun-swept street.

He paused, hat in hand. "Have you been in Mustang long?"

She looked up, studying him for a long minute before she spoke. "Why, no. Not long. Yet long enough to learn to love and hate." She turned her eyes to the hills, then back to him. "I love this country, Captain, can you understand that? I'm a city girl, born and bred in the city, and yet when I first saw those red rock walls, those lonely mesas, the desert, the Indian ponies . . . why, Captain, I fell in love! This is my country! I could stay here forever!"

Surprised, he studied her again, more pleased than he could easily have admitted. "That's the way I feel about it. But you said to love and to hate. You love the country. Now what do you hate?"

"Some of the men who infest it, Captain. Some of the human wolves it breeds, and others, bred somewhere, who come to it to feed off the ones who came earlier and were more courageous but are less knowing, less tricky."

More and more surprised, he leaned on the rail. "I don't know if I follow you, Miss Duane. I haven't been here long, but I haven't met any of those you speak of."

She looked up at him, her eyes frank and cool. Slowly she closed her book and turned toward the door. "You haven't, Captain?" Her voice was suddenly cool. "Are you sure? At this moment, I am wondering if you are not one of them." She stepped through the door and was gone.

Tom Kedrick stood for a moment, staring after her. When he turned away, it was with a puzzled frown on his face. Now what did she mean by that?

What did she know about him that could incline her to such a view? Despite himself, he was both irritated and disturbed. Coupled with the anger of the man Peters, it offered a new element to his thinking. Yet, how could Consuelo Duane, John Gunter's niece, have the same opinions owned by Peters? No doubt they stemmed from different sources.

Troubled, he walked on down to the street of the town and stood there, looking around. He had not yet changed into Western clothes, and wore a flat-crowned, flat-brimmed black hat, which he would retain, and a tailored gray suit with black Western-style boots. Pausing on the corner, he slowly rolled a cigarette and lighted it. He made a dashing, handsome figure as he stood there in his perfectly fitted suit, his lean, bronzed face strong, intelligent, and interesting. Both men and women glanced at him, and most of them twice. His military erectness, broad shoulders, and cool self-possession were enough to mark him in any crowd. His mind had escaped his immediate problem now and was lost in the never-ending excitement of a crowded Western street. Such places held, all jammed together without rhyme or reason, all types and manner of men.

For the West was of all things a melting pot. Adventurers came to seek gold, new lands, excitement. Gamblers, women of the oldest and most active profession, thugs, gunmen, cow rustlers, horse thieves, miners, cowhands, freighters, and just drifters, all crowded the street. That bearded man in the sun-faded red wool shirt might, if prompted, start to spout Shakespeare. The slender young man talking to the girl in the buckboard might have graduated from Oxford, and the white-faced gambler might be the scion of an old Southern family.

There was no knowing in this strangest, most exciting, and colorful of countries, during its most exciting time. All classes, types, and nationalities had come West, all looking for the pot of gold at the foot of any available rainbow, and most of them were more engrossed in the looking than the finding. All men wore guns, most of them in plain sight. Few of them would hesitate to use them if need be. The man who fought with his fists was a rarity, although present.

A big man lurched from the crowd. Tom glanced at him, and their eyes met. Obviously the man had been drinking and was hunting trouble, and, as their eyes met, he stopped. Sensing trouble, other passersby stopped, too.

"So?" The big man stood, wide-legged, his sleeves rolled above thick, hairy forearms. " 'Nother one of them durn thieves. Land stealers!" He chuckled suddenly. "Well, your murderer ain't with you now to save your bacon, an' I aim to git my share of you right now. Reach!"

Kedrick's mouth was dry, but his eyes were calm. He held the cigarette in his right hand near his mouth. "Sorry, friend, I'm not packing a gun. If I were, I'd still not kill you. You're mistaken, man, about that land. My people have a rightful claim to it."

"Have they, now?" The big man came a step nearer, his hand on the butt of his gun. "The right to take from a man the land he's sweated over? To tear down his home? To run his kids out on the desert?"

Despite the fact that the man was drunk, Tom Kedrick saw beyond it a sullen and honest fury—and fear. Not fear of him, for this man was not afraid, nor would he be afraid of even Dornie Shaw. He was afraid for his family. The realization of that fact struck Kedrick and disturbed him anew. More and more he was questioning the course he had chosen.

The crowd murmured and was ugly. Obviously their sympathies were with the big man, and against Kedrick. A low murmur, then a rustling in the crowd, and suddenly, deathly silence. Kedrick saw the big man's face pale, and heard someone whisper hoarsely: "Look out, Burt. It's Dornie Shaw."

Kedrick was suddenly aware that Shaw had moved up beside him. "Let me have him, Cap'n." Shaw's voice was low. "It's time this here was stopped."

Kedrick's voice was sharp, cold. "No! Move back, Shaw! I'll fight my own battles!"

"But you ain't got a gun!" Shaw's voice was sharper in protest.

Burt showed no desire to retreat. That the appearance of Shaw was a shock was evident, but this man was not Peters. He was going to stand his ground. His eyes, wary now but puzzled, shifted from Shaw to Kedrick, and Tom took an easy step forward, putting him almost within arm's length of Burt.

"Shaw's not in this, Burt," he said quietly. "I've no quarrel with you, man, but no man calls me without getting his chance. If you want what I've got, don't let the fact that I'm not armed stop you. I wanted no quarrel, but you do, so have at it!"

Suspicion was in the big man's eyes. He had seen guns come from nowhere before, and especially from men dressed as this one did. He was not prepared to believe that Kedrick would face him unarmed. "You got a gun!" he snapped. "You got a hideout, you damned coyote!"

He jerked his gun from the holster and in that instant Tom Kedrick moved. The edge of his left hand chopped down on the rising wrist of the gun hand, and he stepped in, whipping up his right in an uppercut that packed all the power in his lean, whipcord body. The punch was fast and perfectly timed, and the crack of it on the corner of Burt's jaw was like the crack of a teamster's whip. Burt hit the walk just one split second after his gun, and hit it right on his shoulder blades.

Coolly then Kedrick stooped and picked up the gun, an old 1851 Model Navy revolver. He stood over the man, his eyes searching the crowd. Wherever he looked, there were hard, blank faces. He glanced down at Burt, and the big man was slowly sitting up, shaking his big head. He darted to lift his right hand and gave a sudden gasp of pain. He stared at it, then looked up. "You broke my wrist!" he said. "It's busted! An' me with my plowin' to do!"

"Better get up," Kedrick said quietly. "You asked for it, you know." When the man was on his feet, Kedrick calmly handed him his six-shooter. Their eyes met over the gun and Kedrick smiled. "Take it. Drop it down in your holster an' forget it. I'm not worried. You're not the man to shoot another in the back."

Calmly he turned his back and walked slowly away down the street. Before the St. James he paused. His fingers trembled ever so slightly as he took out a paper and shook tobacco into it.

"That was slick." It was Dornie Shaw's soft voice. His brown eyes probed Kedrick's face curiously. "Never seen the like. Just slapped his wrist and busted it."

With Keith, John Gunter had come up, smiling broadly. "Saw it all, son. That'll do more good than a dozen killings. Just like Tom Smith used to do. Old Bear Creek Tom who handled some of the toughest rannies that ever came over the trail with nothin' but his fists."

"What would you have done if he had jerked that gun back and fired?" Keith asked.

Kedrick shrugged, wanting to forget it. "He hadn't time," he said quietly, "but there are answers to that, too."

"Some of the boys will be up to see you tonight, Tom," Gunter advised. "I've had Dornie notify Shad, Fessenden, and some of the others. Better figure on a ride out there tomorrow. Makin' a start, anyway. Just sort of ride around with some of the boys to let 'em know we ain't foolin'."

Kedrick nodded, and after a brief discussion went inside and to his room. Certainly, he reflected, the West had not changed. Things still happened fast out here.

He pulled off his coat, waistcoat, and vest, then his boots. Stripped to the waist, he sat down on the bed and dug into his valise. For a couple of minutes he dug around and then drew out two well-oiled holsters and gun belts. In the holsters were two .44 Russian pistols, a Smith & Wesson gun, manufactured on order for the Russian Army, and one of the most accurate shooting pistols on the market up to that time. Carefully he checked the loads, then returned the guns to their holsters and put them aside. Digging around, he drew out a second pair of guns, holsters and belts. Each of these was a Walch twelve-shot Navy pistol, caliber .36, and almost identical in size and weight to the Frontier Colt or the .44 Russian. Rarely seen in the West, and disliked by some, Kedrick had used the guns on many occasions and found them always satisfactory. There were times when the added firepower was a big help. As for stopping power, the .36 in the hands of a good marksman lacked but little offered by the heavier .44 caliber.

Yet, there was a time and a place for everything, and these guns had an added tactical value. Carefully he wrapped them once more and returned them to the bottom of his valise. Then he belted on the .44 Russians and, digging out his Winchester, carefully cleaned, oiled, and loaded it. Then he sat down on the bed and was about to remove his guns again and stretch out, when there was a light tap at the door.

"Come in," said Kedrick, "and, if you're an enemy, I'll be pleased to know you."

The door opened and closed all in a breath. The man that stood with his back to it, facing Kedrick, was scarcely five feet four, yet almost as broad as he was tall, but all of it sheer power of bone and muscle and not an ounce of fat anywhere. His

broad, brown face might have been graved from stone, and the bristle of short-cropped hair above it was black as a crow's wing. The man's neck spread to broad, thick shoulders. On his right hip he packed a gun. In his hand he held a narrow-brimmed hard hat.

Kedrick leaped to his feet. "Dai!" The name was an explosion of sound. "Dai Reid! And what are you doing in this country?"

"Ah? So it's that you ask, is it? Well, it's trouble there is, bye, much of trouble! An' you that's by way of bringin' it!"

"Me?" Kedrick waved to a chair. "Tell me what you mean."

The Welshman searched his face, then seated himself, his huge palms resting on his knees. His legs were thick-muscled and bowed. "It's the man Burwick you're with? An' you've the job taken to run us off the land? There is changed you are, Tom, an' for the worse."

"You're one of them? You're on the land Burwick, Keith, and Gunter claim?"

"I am that. And a sight of work I've done on it, too. An' now the rascals would be puttin' me off. Well, they'll have a fight to move me, an' you, too, if you're to stay one of them."

Kedrick studied the Welshman thoughtfully. All his doubts had come to a head now, for this man he knew. His own father had been Welsh, his mother Irish, and Dai Reid had been friend to them both. Dai had come from the old country with his father, had worked beside him when he courted his mother, and, although much younger than Gwilym Kedrick, he had come West with him, too.

"Dai," he said slowly, "I'll admit that today I've been having doubts of all this. You see, I knew John Gunter after the war, and I took a herd of cattle over the trail for a friend of his. There was trouble that year, the Indians holding every herd and demanding large numbers of cattle for themselves, the rustlers trying to steal whole herds, and others demanding money for passage across land they claimed. I took my herd through without paying anything but a few fat beefs for the Indians, who richly deserved them. But not what they demanded . . . they got what I wanted to give. Gunter remembered me from that and knew something of my war record, so when he approached me in New Orleans, his proposition sounded good. And this is what he told me.

"His firm . . . Burwick, Keith, and Gunter . . . had filed application for the survey and purchase of all or parts of nearly three hundred sections of land. They made oath that this land was swampland or overflowed and came under the General Land Office ruling that it was land too wet for irrigation at seeding time, though later requiring irrigation, and therefore subject to sale as swamp. He went on to say that they had arranged to buy the land, but that a bunch of squatters were on it who refused to leave. He wanted to hire me to lead a force to see the land was cleared, and he said that as most of them were rustlers, outlaws, or renegades of one sort or another, there would be fighting and force would be necessary."

Dai nodded. "Right he was as to the fighting, but renegades, no. Well,"—he smiled grimly past his pipe—"I'd not be saying that now, but there's mighty few. There are bad apples in all barrels, one or two, but most of us be good people, with homes built and crops in. An' did he tell you that their oath was given that the land was unoccupied? Well, given it was! And let me tell you. Ninety-four sections have homes on them, some mighty poor, but homes. Shrewd they were with the planning. Six months the notices must be posted, but they posted them in fine print and where few men could read, and three months are by before anything is noticed, and by accident only. So now they come to force us off, to be sure the land is unoccupied and ready. As for swamp, 'tis desert now, and always desert. Crops can only be grown where the water is, an' little enough of that." Dai shook his head and knocked out his short-stemmed pipe. "Money we've none to fight them, no lawyers among us, although one who's as likely to help, a newspaper man, he is. But what good without money to send him to Washington?" The Welshman's face was gloomy. "They'll beat us, that we know. They've money to fight us with, and tough men, but some of them will die on the ground and pay for it with their red blood, and those among us there are who plan to see 'tis not only the hired gunners who die, but the high an' mighty. You, too, lad, if among them you stay."

Kedrick was thoughtful. "Dai, this story is different from the one I've had. I'll have to think about it, and tomorrow we ride out to look the land over and show ourselves."

Reid looked up sharply. "Don't you be one of them, bye! We've plans made to see no man gets off alive if we can help it."

"Look, man." Kedrick leaned forward. "You've got to change that. I mean, for now. Tomorrow it's mainly a show of force, a threat. There will be no shooting, I promise you. We'll ride out, look around, then ride back. If there's shooting, your men will start it. Now you go back to them and stop it. Let them hold off, and let me look around."

Dai Reid got slowly to his feet. "Ah, lad, 'tis good to see you again, but under happier circumstances I wish it were! I'd like to have you to the house for supper and a game, as in the old days. You'd like the wife I have."

"You? Married?" Kedrick was incredulous. "I'd never believe it!"

Dai grinned sheepishly. "Married it is, all right, and happy, Tom." His face darkened. "Happy if I can keep my ground. But one promise I make. If your bloody riders take my ground, my body will be there where they ride past, and it will be not alone, but with dead men around."

Long after the Welshman had gone, Tom Kedrick sat silently and studied the street beyond the window. Was this what Consuelo Duane had meant? Whose side was she on? First, he must ride over the land, see it for himself, and then he must have another talk with Gunter. Uneasily he looked again at the faces of the men in his mind. The cold, wolflike face of Keith, the fat, slobby face of Burwick, underlined with harsh, domineering power, and the face of Gunter, friendly, affable, but was it not a little—sly?

From outside came the noise of a tinny piano and a strident female voice, singing. Chips rattled, and there was the constant rustle of movement and of booted feet. Somewhere a spur jingled, and Tom Kedrick got to his feet and slipped into a shirt. When he was dressed again, with his guns belted on, he left his room and walked down the hall to the lobby.

From a room beside his, a man stepped and stared after him. It was Dornie Shaw.

III

Only the dweller in the deserts can know such mornings, such silences, drowsy with warmth and the song of the cicadas; nowhere but in the desert shall the far miles stand out so clearly, the mesas, towers, and cliffs so boldly outlined. Nowhere will the cloud shadows island themselves as on the desert, offering their brief respite from the sun.

Six riders, their saddles creaking, six hard men, each lost in the twisted arroyos of his own thoughts, were emerging upon the broad desert. They were men who had used their guns to kill and would use them so again. Some of them were already doomed by the relentless and ruthless tide of events, and to the others their time, too, would come. Each of them was alone, as men who live by the gun are always alone, each man a potential enemy, each shadow a danger. They rode jealously, their gestures marked by restraint, their eyes by watchfulness.

A horse blew through his nostrils, a hoof clicked on a stone, someone shifted in his saddle and sighed. These were the only sounds. Tom Kedrick rode an Appaloosa gelding, fifteen hands even, with iron-gray forequarters and starkly white hindquarters splashed with tear-shaped spots of solid black—a clean-limbed horse, strong and fast, with quick, intelligent eyes and interested ears.

When they had bunched to start their ride, Laredo Shad had stopped to stare at the horse, walking around it admiringly. "You're lucky, friend. That's a horse! Where'd you find him?"

"Navajo remuda. He's a Nez Percé war horse, a long ways off his reservation."

Kedrick had noticed the men as they gathered and how they all sized him up carefully, noting his Western garb, and especially the low-hung, tied-down guns. They had seen him yesterday, in the store clothes he had worn from New Orleans, but now they could size him up better, judge him with their own kind.

He was tall and straight, and of his yesterday's clothing only the black, flat-crowned hat remained, the hat, and the high-heeled rider's boots. He wore a gray wool shirt now and a black silk kerchief around his neck. His jeans were black, and the two guns rode easily in position, ready for the swing of his hand.

Kedrick had seen them bunch, and, while they all were there, he had said simply: "All right, let's go!"

They had mounted up. Kedrick had noted slender, wiry Dornie Shaw, the great bulk of Si Fessenden, lean, bitter Poinsett, the square, blond Lee Goff, sour-faced Clauson, the oldest of the lot, and the lean Texan, Laredo Shad. Moving out, he had glanced at them. Whatever else they might be, they were fighting men. Several times Shaw had glanced at his guns.

"You ain't wearin' Colts?"

"No, Forty-Four Russians. They are a good gun, one of the most accurate ever built." He had indicated the trail ahead with a nod. "You've been out this way before?"

"Yeah, we got quite a ride. We'll noon at a spring I know just over the North Fork. There's some deep cañons to cross, then a big peak. The Indians an' Spanish called it The Orphan. All wild country. Right behind there we'll begin strikin' a few of 'em." He grinned a little, showing his white, even teeth. "They are scattered all over hell's half acre."

"Dornie," Goff had asked suddenly, "you figure on ridin' over to the *malpais* this trip?"

Clauson had chuckled. "Sure, he will! He should've give up long ago, but he's sure hard to whip! That girl has set her sights higher'n any west-country gunslinger."

"She's shapely, at that!" Goff was openly admiring. "Right shapely, but playin' no fav'rites."

"Maybe they're playin' each other for what they can git," Poinsett had said wryly. "Maybe that's where he gets all the news he's tellin' Keith. He sure seems to know a sight o' what's goin' around."

Dornie Shaw had turned in his saddle, and his thin features had sharpened. "Shut up!" he had said coldly.

The older man had tightened and his eyes had blazed back with genuine hate, yet he had held his peace. It was educational to see how quickly he quieted down; for Poinsett, a hard, vicious man with no love for anybody or anything obviously wanted no part of what Shaw could give him.

As the day drew on, Kedrick studied the men, and noticed they all avoided giving offense to Shaw, even the burly Fessenden who had killed twenty men and was the only one of the group Kedrick had ever seen before. He wondered if Fessenden remembered him and decided he would know before the day was out.

Around the noon camp there was less friendly banter than in a cow camp. These men were surly and touchy. Only Shaw seemed to relax much, and everything came easily for him. Clauson seemed to take over the cooking job by tacit consent, and the reason was soon obvious. He was really an excellent cook.

As he ate, Tom Kedrick studied his situation with care. He had taken this job in New Orleans, and at the time had needed money badly. Gunter had put up the cash to get him out here, and, if he did back out, he would have to find a way to repay him. Yet the more he looked over this group, the more he believed that he was into something that he wanted out of, but fast.

He had fought as a soldier of fortune in several wars. War had been his profession, and he had been a skilled fighting man almost from the beginning. His father, a one-time soldier, had a love for tactics, and Tom had grown up with an interest in things military. His education had mostly come from his father and from a newspaperman who lived with them for a winter and helped to teach the boy what he could.

Kedrick had grown up with his interest in tactics, and had entered the Army and fought through the War Between the States. The subsequent fighting had given him a practical background to accompany his study and theory, but with all his fighting and the killing it had entailed, he had not become callous. To run a bunch of renegades off the land seemed simple enough and it promised action and excitement. It was a job he could do. Now he was no longer sure it was a job he wanted to do, for his talk with Dai Reid as well as the attitude of so many people in Mustang had convinced him that all was not as simple as it had first appeared. Now, before taking a final step, he wanted to survey the situation and see just who he would be fighting, and where. At the same time he knew the men who rode with him were going to ask few questions. They would do their killing, collect their money, and ride on.

Of them all, only Shad might think as he did, and Kedrick made a mental note to talk with the Texan before the day was over, find out where he stood and what he knew. He was inclined to agree with Shaw's original judgment, that Shad was one of the best of the lot with a gun. The man's easy way was not only natural to him, he was simply confident with that hard confidence that comes only from having measured his ability and knowing what he could do when the chips were down.

After he finished his coffee, he got to his feet and strolled over to the spring, had a drink, then arose and walked to his horse, tightening the cinch he had loosened when they stopped. The air was clear, and despite their lowered voices he could catch most of what was said.

The first question he missed, but Fessenden's reply he heard. "Don't you fret about him. He's a scrapper from way back, Dornie. I found that out. This here ain't our first meetin'."

Even at this distance and with his horse between him and the circle of men, Kedrick could sense their attention.

"Tried to finagle him out of that Patterson herd, up in Injun Territory. He didn't finagle worth a damn."

"What happened?" Goff demanded. "Any shootin'?"

"Some. I was ridin' partners with Chuck Gibbons, the Llano gunman, an' Chuck was always on the prod, sort of. One, two times I figured I might have to shoot it out with him my own self, but wasn't exactly honin' for trouble. We had too good a thing there to bust it up quarrelin'. But Chuck, he was plumb salty, an', when Kedrick faced him an' wouldn't back down or deliver the cattle, Chuck called him."

Fessenden sipped his coffee, while they waited impatiently. When they could stand the suspense no longer, Goff demanded: "Well, what happened?"

The big man shrugged. "Kedrick's here, ain't he?"

"I mean . . . what was the story?"

"Gibbons never cleared leather. None of us even seen Kedrick draw, but you could have put a half dollar over the two holes in Chuck's left shirt pocket."

Nobody spoke after that, and Tom Kedrick took his time over the cinch, then with his horse between them he walked away farther and circled, scouting the terrain thoughtfully.

He was too experienced a man to fail to appreciate how important is knowledge of terrain. All this country from Mustang to the territorial line would become a battleground in the near future, and a man's life might depend on what he knew, so he wanted an opportunity to study the country or ask questions. He had handled tough groups before, and he was not disturbed over the problem they presented, although in this case he knew the situation was much more serious. In a group they would be easier to handle than separately, for these men were individualists all, and without any group loyalty. They had faith in only two things in the last analysis: six-gun skill and money. By these they lived and by these they would die. That Fessenden had talked was pleasing, for it would settle the doubts of some of them, at least. Knowing him for a gun hand, they would more willingly accept orders from him, not because of fear, but rather because they knew him for one of their own, and not some stranger brought in for command.

***

When they moved out, taking their time, the heat had increased. Not a thing stirred on the wide, shallow face of the desert but a far and lonely buzzard that floated, high and alone, over a far-off mesa. Tom Kedrick's eyes roamed the country ceaselessly, and yet from time to time his thoughts kept reverting to the girl on the verandah. Connie Duane was a beautiful girl—Gunter's niece, but apparently not approving all he did. Why was she here? What was her connection with Keith? Kedrick sensed the animosity of Keith and welcomed it. A quiet man, he was slow to anger, but tough, and, when pushed, a deep-seated anger arose within him in a black tide that made him a driving fury. Knowing this rage that lay dormant within him, he rode carefully, talked carefully, and held his temper and his hand.

Dornie Shaw drew up suddenly. "This here is Cañon Largo"—he said, waving his hand down the rift before them—"that peak ahead an' on your right is The Orphan. Injuns won't let no white man up there, but they say there's a spring with a good flow of water on top. Yonder begins the country in the Burwick, Keith, and Gunter buy. They don't have the land solid to the Arizona border, but they've got a big chunk of it. The center of the squatters is a town called Yellow Butte. There's maybe ten, twelve buildin's there, among 'em a store, a stable, corrals, a saloon, an' a bank."

Kedrick nodded thoughtfully. The country before him was high desert and could under no circumstances be called swamp. In the area where he stood there was little growth, a few patches of curly mesquite grass or black grama, with prickly pear, soapweed, creosote bush, and catclaw scattered through it. In some of the washes he saw the deeper green of piñon or juniper.

They pushed on, entered the cañon, and emerged from it, heading due west. He rode warily, and once, far off on his left, he glimpsed a horseman. Later, seeing the same rider, nearer than before, he deduced they were under observation and hoped there would be no attack.

Dornie Shaw said: "The country where most of the squatters are is right smack dab in the middle o' the range the company is after. The hombre most likely to head 'em is Bob McLennon. He's got him two right-hand men name of Pete Slagle an' Pit Laine. Now, you asked me the other day if they would fight. Them three are shinnery oak. Slagle's an oldish feller, but McLennon's in his forties an' was once a cow-town marshal. Laine, well, he's a tough one to figure, but he packs two guns an' cuts him a wide swath over there. I hear tell he had him some gun trouble up Durango way an' he didn't need no help to handle it."

From behind him Kedrick heard a low voice mutter: " 'Most as hard to figure as his sister!"

Shaw's mouth tightened, but he gave no other evidence that he had heard, but the comment added a little to Kedrick's information. Obviously Dornie Shaw had a friend in the enemy's camp, and the information with which he had been supplying Keith must come from that source. Was the girl betraying her own brother and her friends? It could be, but could Shaw come and go among them without danger? Or did he worry himself about it? There had been no mention of Dai Reid, yet the powerful little Welshman was sure to be a figure wherever he stood, and he was definitely a man to be reckoned with.

Suddenly a rider appeared from an arroyo not thirty yards off and walked her horse toward them. Dornie Shaw swore softly and drew up. As one man, they all stopped.

The girl was small, well-made, her skin as brown as that of an Indian, her hair coal black. She had large, beautiful eyes and small hands. Her eyes flashed from Dornie to the others, then clung to Tom Kedrick, measuring him for a long minute. "Who's your friend, Dornie?" she said. "Introduce me."

Shaw's eyes were dark and hard as he turned slightly. "Cap'n Kedrick, I want you to meet Sue Laine."

"Captain?" She studied him anew. "Were you in the Army?"

"Yes," he said quietly. Her pinto was not the horse of the rider who had been observing them; therefore, there was another rider out there somewhere. Who was he?

"You're ridin' quite a ways from home, Sue," Shaw interrupted. "You think that's wise?"

"I can take care of myself, Dornie!" Her reply was cool, and Kedrick saw blood rise under Shaw's skin. "However, I came to warn you, or Captain Kedrick, if he is in charge. It won't be safe to ride any farther. McLennon called a meeting this morning and they voted to open fire on any party of surveyors or strange riders they see. From now on, this country is closed. A rider is going to Mustang tonight with the news."

"There she is," Goff said dryly. "They are sure enough askin' for it! What if we ride on, anyway?"

She glanced at him. "Then there will be fighting," she said quietly.

"Well," Poinsett said impatiently, "what are we talkin' for? We come here to fight, didn't we? Let's ride on an' see how much battle they got in them."

Tom Kedrick studied the girl thoughtfully. She was pretty, all right, very pretty. She lacked the quiet beauty of Connie Duane, but she did have beauty. "Do they have scouts out?" he asked.

She glanced at him. "Not yet, but they will have." She smiled. "If they had, I'd never have dared ride to warn you."

"Whose side are you on, Miss Laine?" Kedrick asked.

Dornie Shaw's head came around sharply and his eyes blazed. Before he could speak, Sue Laine answered for herself: "That decision I make for myself. My brother does not make it for me, nor any one of them. They are fools! To fight over this desert!" Contemptuously she waved a hand at it. "There's no more than a bare living on it, anyway! If they lose, maybe we can leave this country." She swung her horse abruptly. "Well, you've had your warning. Now I'll go back."

"I'll be ridin' your way," Shaw interposed.

Her eyes swung back to him. "Don't bother!" Then she turned her attention deliberately to Kedrick and measured him again with her cool eyes, a hint of a smile in them now. "If anybody comes, let Captain Kedrick come. They don't know him!"

Somebody in the group chuckled, and Dornie Shaw swung his horse, his face white as death. His teeth were bared, his right hand poised. "Who laughed?" he said, his voice almost trembling.

"Miss Laine," Kedrick said quietly, "I think Dornie Shaw could make the trip better than I. He knows the country."

Shaw's eyes glittered. "I asked . . . *who laughed?*"

Kedrick turned his head. "Forget it, Shaw." His voice was crisp. "There'll be no fighting with other men in the outfit while I'm in command!"

For an instant, Dornie Shaw held his pose, then his eyes, suddenly opaque as a rattler's, swung toward Kedrick. "You're tellin' *me?*" Incredulity was mixed with sarcasm.

Tom Kedrick knew danger when he saw it, but he only nodded. "You, or anybody, Dornie. We have a job to do. You've hired me for that job as much as any man here. If we begin to fight among ourselves, we'll get nothing done, and right now we can't afford to lose a good man. I scarcely think," he added, "that either Keith or Burwick would like the idea of a killing among their own men."

Shaw's eyes held Kedrick's and for an instant there was no sound. A cicada hummed in the brush, and Sue Laine's horse stamped at a fly. Tom Kedrick knew in that instant that Dornie Shaw hated him, and he had an idea that this was the first time Shaw had ever been thwarted in any purpose he held.

Then Shaw's right hand slowly lowered. "You got me on that one, Cap'n." His voice was empty, dry. "I reckon this is too soon to start shootin' . . . an' old man Burwick is right touchy."

Sue Laine glanced again at Kedrick, genuine surprise and not a little respect in her eyes. "I'll be going. Watch yourselves!"

Before her horse could more than start, Kedrick asked: "Miss Laine, which of your outfit rides a long-legged grulla?"

She turned on him, her face pale as death. "A . . . a grulla?"

"Yes," he said, "such a rider has been watching us

most of the morning, and such a rider is not over a half mile away now. Also," he added, "he has a field glass!"

Fessenden turned with an oath, and Poinsett glared around. Only Shaw spoke. His voice was strained and queer. "A grulla? Here?"

He refused to say more, but Kedrick studied him, puzzled by the remark. It was almost as if Shaw knew the grulla horse, but had not expected it to be seen here. The same might be true of Sue Laine, obviously upset by his comment. Long after they rode on, turning back toward the spring on the North Fork, Kedrick puzzled over it. This was an entirely new element that might mean anything or nothing.

There was little talking on the way back. Poinsett was obviously irritated that they had not ridden on in, yet he seemed content enough to settle down into another camp.

IV

Dornie Shaw was silent, saying nothing at all. Only when Tom Kedrick arose after supper and began to saddle his horse did he look up. Kedrick glanced at him. "Shaw, I'm ridin' to Yellow Butte. I'm going to look that setup over at firsthand. I don't want trouble, an' I'm not huntin' any, but I want to know what we're tacklin'."

Shaw was standing, staring after him, when he rode off. He rode swiftly, pushing due west at a good pace to take advantage of the remaining light. He had more than one reason for the ride. He wanted to study the town and the terrain, but also he wanted to see what the people were like. Were they family men? Or were they outlaws? He had seen little thus far that tended to prove the outlaw theory.

The town of Yellow Butte lay huddled at the base of the long, oval-shaped mesa from which it took its name. There, on a bit of flat land, the stone and frame buildings of the town had gathered together. Most of them backed against the higher land behind them, and faced toward the arroyo. Only three buildings and the corrals were on the arroyo side, but one thing was obvious. The town had never been planned for defense.

A rifleman or two on top of Yellow Butte could cover any movement in the village, and the town was exposed to fire from both the high ground behind the town, and the bed of the arroyo where there was shelter under its banks. The butte itself was scarcely one hundred and fifty feet higher than the town and looked right down the wide street before the buildings.

Obviously, however, some move had been made toward defense, or was in the process of being made, for there were some piles of earth, plainly from recent digging, near several of the buildings. He studied them, puzzled over their origin and cause. Finally he gave up and scouted the area.

He glanced at the butte thoughtfully. Had they thought of putting their own riflemen up there? It would seem the obvious thing, yet more than one competent commander had forgotten the obvious at some time during his career, and it might also be true of these men. The top of the butte not only commanded the town, but most of the country around, and was the highest point within several miles.

That could come later. Now Kedrick turned his Appaloosa down the hill toward the town, riding in the open, his right hand hanging free at his side. Yet, if he was seen, nothing was done to disturb him. How would it have been if there were more than one rider?

He swung down before the Butte Saloon, and tied his horse at the rail. The animal was weary, he knew, and in no shape for a long ride, but he had made his own plans and they did not require such a ride. The street was empty, so he stepped up on the walk and pushed through the swinging doors into the bright lights of the interior. A man sitting alone at a table saw him, scowled, and started to speak, then went on with his solitaire. Tom Kedrick crossed to the bar. "Rye," he said quietly.

The bartender nodded and, without looking up, poured the drink. It was not until Kedrick dropped his coin on the bar that he did raise his glance. Instantly his face stiffened: "Who're you?" he demanded. "I never saw you before!"

Kedrick was aware that men had closed in on both sides of him, both of them strangers. One was a sharp-looking, oldish man, the other an obviously belligerent redhead. "Pour a drink for my friends, too," he said, and then he turned slowly, so they would not mistake his intentions, until his back was to the bar. Carefully he surveyed the room. There were a dozen men here, and all eyes were on him. "I'm buying," he said quietly. "Will you gentlemen join me?"

Nobody moved, and he shrugged. He turned back to the bar. His drink was gone.

Slowly he lifted his eyes to the bartender. "I bought a drink," he said quietly.

The man stared back at him, his eyes hard. "Never noticed it," he said.

"I bought a drink, paid my money, and I want my drink."

All was still. The men on either side of him leaned on the bar, ignoring him.

"I'm a patient man," he persisted, "I bought a drink, an' I want it . . . now."

"Mister"—the bartender thrust his wide face across the bar—"we don't serve drinks to your kind here. Now get out before we throw you out!"

Kedrick's forearms were resting on the edge of the bar, and what happened was done so swiftly that neither man beside him had a chance to move. Tom Kedrick's right hand shot out and grabbed the bartender by the shirt collar under his chin, then he turned swiftly back to the bar, and heaved! The bartender came over the bar as if greased and hit the floor with a crash. Instantly Kedrick spun away from the two men beside him and stood facing the room, gun in hand.

Men had started to their feet, and several had moved toward him. Now they froze where they were. The .44 Russian had appeared as if materialized from thin air.

"Gentlemen," Kedrick said quietly, "I did not come here hunting trouble. I have been hired for a job as all of you, at some time or another, have been hired for a job. I came to see if you were the manner of men you have been represented as being. Evidently your bartender is hard of hearing, or lacking in true hospitality. I ordered a drink. You"— Kedrick gestured at the man playing solitaire— "look like a man of judgment. You pour my drink and pour it on the end of the bar nearest me. Then"—his eyes held the room—"pour each of these gentlemen a drink." With his left hand he extracted a gold eagle from his pocket and slapped it on the bar. "That pays."

He took another step back, then coolly he holstered his gun. Eyes studied him, but nobody moved. The redhead did not like it. He had an urge to show how tough he was and Kedrick could see it building. "You!" Kedrick asked quickly. "Are you married? Children?"

The redhead stared at him, then said, his voice surly: "Yeah, I'm married, and I got two kids. What's it to you?"

"I told you," Kedrick replied evenly. "I came to see what manner of men you are."

The man who was pouring the drinks looked up. "I'll answer your questions. I'm Pete Slagle."

"I've heard of you."

A slight smile came to Slagle's mouth. "Yeah," he said, "an' I've heard of you."

Nobody moved or spoke while Slagle calmly poured the drinks, then he straightened and glanced around the room. "Men," he said, "I reckon there's no use goin' off half-cocked an' getting' somebody killed. Let's give this man a chance to speak his piece. We sure don't have to buy what he wants to sell us if we don't like his argument."

"Thanks, Slagle." Kedrick studied the room. Two of the faces seemed hard, unrelenting. Another was genuinely interested, but at the door in the rear a man loitered who had shifty eyes and a sour face. He could have been, in disposition at least, a twin brother to the former outlaw, Clauson.

"The land around here," Kedrick said quietly, "is about to be purchased from the government by the firm who has employed me. The firm of Burwick, Keith, and Gunter. In New Orleans, where I was hired, I was told that there were squatters on the land, a bunch of outlaws, renegades, and wasters, that they would resist being put off, and would aim to keep the badlands for themselves. My job was to clean them out, to clear the land for the company. I have come here for that purpose."

There was a low murmur from the back of the room. Kedrick took time to toss off his drink, and then calmly begin to roll a smoke. To his right, the door opened and two men came in. One of these was as tall as himself with coal-black hair turning gray at the temples. His eyes were gray and cold, his face firmly cut. He glanced sharply around the room, then at Kedrick.

"Cap'n Tom Kedrick, Bob," Slagle said quietly, "speakin' his piece. He's just explained that we've been represented as a bunch of renegades."

"That sounds like Burwick," McLennon said. "Get on with it, Kedrick."

"I've little to say but this. Naturally, like any good fighting man, I wanted to look over the terrain. Moreover, since arriving in Mustang, certain rumors and hints have reached me that the picture is not one-sided. I have come out here to look you over, to see exactly what sort of people you are, and if you are the outlaws and wasters you have been represented to be. Also, I would like to have a statement from you."

Red's face was ugly. "We got nothin' to say to you, Kedrick," he said harshly, "nothin' at all! Just you come down here with your killers an' see how many get away alive!"

"Wait a minute, Red!" Slagle interrupted. "Let Tom have his say."

"Aw, why bother?" Red said roughly. "The man is scared or he'd never have come huntin' information!"

Kedrick's eyes held Red's thoughtfully, and he

said slowly: "No, Red, I'm not scared. If I decide the company is right and you are to be run off, that is exactly what I'll do. If the men I have are not enough, I'll get more. I'm used to war, Red. I've been at it all my life, and I know how to win. I'm not here because I'm scared. I have come simply because I make a pass at being a just man. If you have a just claim to your places here, and are not as represented, I'll step out of this.

"Naturally," he added, "I can't speak for the others, but I will advise them as to my conclusions."

"Fair enough," McLennon agreed. "All right, I'll state our case. This land is government land like all of it. The Navajos an' Utes claim some of it, an' some of us have dickered with them for land. We've moved in an' settled on this land. Four or five of us have been here upwards of ten years, most of us have been here more than three. We've barns built, springs cleaned out, some fences. We've stocked some land, lived through a few bad summers and worse winters. Some of us have wives, an' some of us children. We're makin' homes here. The company is tryin' to gyp us. The law says we were to have six months' notice. That is, it was to be posted six months before the sale by the government to the company. This land, as we understand it, is supposed to be unoccupied. Well, it isn't. We live on it. Moreover, that notice was posted five months ago, stuck in out-of-the-way places, in print so fine a man can scarcely read it without a magnifyin' glass. A month ago one of the boys read it, but it took him a few days to sort out the meanin' out of the legal phrasin', and then he hightailed it to me. We ain't got the money to send a man to the government. So all we can do is fight. That's what we figure on. If the company runs us off, which I don't figure you or nobody can do, they'll buy ever' inch of it with their blood, believe me."

A murmur of appreciation went through the room, and Kedrick scanned their faces thoughtfully. Dornie Shaw had judged these men correctly. They would fight. Moreover, with men like McLennon and Slagle to lead them, they would be hard to handle. Legally the company seemed to be in the best position; the squatters were bucking a stacked deck. From here it would take a man all of two weeks, and possibly three, even to get to Washington, let alone cut through all the government red tape to get to the men who could block the sale—if it could be blocked.

"This here's a speculation on their part," McLennon stated. "There's rumor this here land is goin' into an Injun reservation, an', if it does, that means they'll stick the government a nice price for the land."

"Or you will," Kedrick replied. "Looks like there's two sides to this question, McLennon. The company has an argument. If the federal government does make this a reservation, you'll have to move, anyway."

"We'll face that when it comes," Slagle said. "Right now we're buckin' the company. Our folks aren't speculators. We aren't gunmen, either."

Another man had entered the room, and Kedrick spotted him instantly. It was Burt, the big man he had whipped in the street fight. The man stopped by the wall, and surveyed the room.

"None of you?" Kedrick asked gently. "I have heard some stories about Pit Laine."

"Laine's a good man!" Red burst out heatedly. "He'll do to ride any river with!"

Neither McLennon nor Slagle spoke, and the latter shifted his feet uneasily. Evidently there was a difference of opinion here. He made a note to check on Laine, to find out more about him.

"Well," Kedrick said finally, "I reckon I'll study it a little. In the meantime, let's keep the peace. I'll keep my men off, if you will do likewise."

"We aren't huntin' trouble," McLennon said. "As long as there's no shootin' at us, an' as long as the company men stay off our land, there'll be no trouble from us."

"Fact is," Slagle said, "we sent Roberts ridin' in with a message to Burwick to that effect. We ain't huntin' for no trouble."

Kedrick turned toward the door, but the bartender's voice stopped him. "You forgot your change," he said dryly.

Kedrick glanced at him, grinned, then picked it up. "Be seein' you," he said, and stepped to the door. At that instant, the door burst open and a man staggered into the room, his arm about another man, who he dropped to the floor. "Roberts!" the man said. "He's been murdered!"

All eyes stared at the man on the floor. That he had been shot many times was obvious. He had also been ridden over, for his body was torn and beaten by the hoofs of running horses. Tom Kedrick felt his stomach turn over. Sick with pity and shock, he lifted his eyes. He looked up into a circle of accusation: McLennon, shocked and unbelieving, Slagle, horrified. Red pointed a finger that trembled with anger. "While he stands an' talks to us, his outfit murders Bob!"

"Git him!" somebody yelled. "Git him! I got a rope!"

Kedrick was standing at the door, and he knew there was no reasoning with these men. Later, they might think, and reason that he might have known nothing about the killing of Roberts. Now, they would not listen. As the man yelled, he hurled himself through the swinging doors and, jerking loose his reins, hit the saddle of the Appaloosa. The startled horse swung and lined out, not down the street, but between the buildings.

Behind him men shouted and cursed. A shot rang out, and he heard a bullet clip past his head as he swung between buildings. Then he knew his escape had driven him into a *cul-de-sac*, for he was now facing, not more than two hundred yards away, the rim around the flat where the town lay. Whether there was a break in that wall he could not guess, but he had an idea both the route upstream and that downstream of the arroyo would be covered by guards, so he swung his horse and charged into the darkness toward Yellow Butte itself.

As he had come into town, he had seemed to see a V-shaped opening near its base. Whether there was a cut through the rim there he did not know. It might only be a box cañon, and a worse trap than the one into which he had run on his first break.

He slowed his pace, knowing that silence was the first necessity now, for, if they heard him, he could easily be bottled up. The flat was small, and aside from crossing the arroyo there were but two routes of escape, and both would be watched, as he had first surmised. The butte towered high above him now, and his horse walked softly in the abysmal darkness of its foot. His safety was a matter of minutes, for they must know they had him.

The Appaloosa was tired, he knew, for he had been going all day, and the day had been warm and he was a big man. He was in no shape for a hard run against fresh horses, so the only possible escape lay in some shrewd move that would have them guessing and give him time. Yet he must be gone before daylight or he was through. By day they would comb this area and surely discover him.

Now the cañon mouth yawned before him. The walls were not high but were deep enough to allow no escape on horseback, at least. The shouts of pursuit had stopped, but he knew they were hard at work to find him. By now they would know from the guards on the stream that he was still on the flat, and had not escaped. Those guards might be creatures of his own imagination, but knowing the men with whom he dealt, he was shrewd enough to realize that, if they had not guarded the openings before his arrival, they certainly would have sent guards out at once.

The cañon was narrow and he rode on, moving with extreme caution, yet when he had gone but a short distance, he saw the end of the cañon rising above him, black and somber. His throat tightened and his mouth went dry. The Appaloosa stopped and Tom Kedrick sat silently, feeling the labored breathing of the horse and knowing this was an end. He was trapped. Fairly trapped!

Behind him, a light flared briefly, then went out, but there was a shout. That had been a struck match, somebody looking for tracks. And they had found them. In a few minutes more, for they would move cautiously, they would be here. There would be no reasoning with them now. They had him. He was trapped.

V

Captain Tom Kedrick sat very still, listening. He heard some gravel stir; a stone rattled down the cañon. Every move would count now, and he must take no unnecessary chance. He was cornered, and, while he did not want to kill any of these men, he had no intention of being killed.

Carefully he dismounted. As his boot touched the sand, he tested it to make sure no sound would result when his weight settled. Haste now was his greatest danger. There might be nothing he could do, but he was a man of many experiences, and in the past there had always been a way out. Usually there was, if a man took his time and kept his head.

Standing still beside the Appaloosa, he studied the situation. His eyes had grown accustomed to the darkness under the bulk of Yellow Butte. He stared around, seeing the faint gray of sand underfoot, the black bulk of boulders, and the more ragged bulk of underbrush. Leading his horse, he followed a narrow strip of gray that showed an opening between boulders. Scarcely wide enough to admit his horse, the opening led back for some twenty feet, then widened. These were low boulders, rising scarcely above his waist, with the brush somewhat higher. The horse seemed to sense the danger, for it, too, walked quietly and almost without sound.

Literally he was feeling his way in the dark, but that trail of sand must come from somewhere, for water had run here, and that water might spill off the cliff edge, or might come through some opening. Walking steadily, he found himself going deeper into a tangle of boulders, weaving his way along that thin gray trail, into he knew not what.

Twice he paused and, with his hat, worked back along the path brushing out the tracks. He could not see how good a job he was doing, but the opening was narrow enough to give him a good chance of success. When he had pushed back into the tangle for all of ten minutes, he was brought up sharply by the cliff itself. He had found his way up the slope, through the talus, brush, and scattered boulders, to the very face of the rock. Above him, and apparently out of reach, was a notch in the cliff, and this was probably the source of the sandy trail he had followed. Worried now, he ground-hitched the Appaloosa and moved along the cliff, feeling his way along the face, searching each crack.

To his left, he found nothing. Several times he paused to listen, but no sound came from down the cañon. If this were a box cañon, with no exit, they would probably know it and make no attempt to close in until daylight. In the darkness a man could put up quite a fight in here. Yet, because of their eagerness to avenge the dead man, they might push on. Speaking softly to the horse, he worked his way along the face to the right, but here the pile of talus fell off sharply and he dipped into a hollow. It was cool and the air felt damp. There might even be a spring there, but he heard no water running.

Despite the coolness he was sweating, and he paused, mopping his face and listening. As he stood there, he felt a faint breath of wind against his cheek! He stiffened with surprise, then with a sudden surge of hope he turned and eagerly explored the rocky face, but could find no source for that breeze. He started on, moving more cautiously, then the talus began to steepen under his feet, so he worked his way up the cliff alone. He carried with him his rifle.

At the top he could turn and glance back down the cañon and the faint grayness in the distance that indicated the way he had come. Here the cañon turned a bit, ending in a sort of blind alley on an angle from the true direction of the cañon. There, breaking the edge of the cliff above him, was a notch, and a steep slide led to the top! It must have been some vague stirring of wind from up there on the rim that had touched his cheek, but the slide was steeper than a stairway, and might start sliding underfoot. Certainly the rattle would give away his attempt, and it would be the matter of a few minutes only for them to circle around. As far as that went, they could even now be patrolling the rim above him.

Turning, his foot went from under him and only a frenzied grasp at some brush kept him from falling into whatever hole he had stumbled upon. Scrambling back to good footing, he dropped a pebble and heard it strike some fifteen or twenty feet down. Working his way along the edge, he reached the foot of the slide, or nearly there, and knew what he had come upon. Water, flooding down that slide during heavy rains, had struck a soft stratum of sand or mud at this point and, striking it with force, had gouged out a deep hole that probably ran back into the cañon itself. There was always a chance that deep within this crack there might be some hiding place, some concealment. Turning abruptly, he returned for his horse.

The slide continued steeply to the bottom of the crevasse scooped from the earth, and, when they reached bottom, he glanced up. He was walking, leading the horse, but the opening of the hole in which he stood was at least fifteen feet above him, and not more than seven or eight feet in width. He moved on into it, and after only a short distance it was almost covered on top by a thick growth of brush growing on the surface or from the sides near the top.

It was cool and still down here, and he pushed on until he found a spot where the rush of water had made a turn, and had gouged deeply under the bank, making a sort of cave beneath the overhang. Into this he led his horse, and here he stopped. A little water stood at the deepest part of the turn, and he allowed the Appaloosa to drink. When the horse had finished, the shallow pool was gone.

Kedrick tried the water in his canteen, then stripped the saddle from the horse, and rubbed him down with a handful of coarse grass. Then he tied the horse and, spreading his blanket, rolled up in it. He was philosophical. He had done what he could. If they found him now, there was nothing to do but shoot it out where he was.

Surprisingly he slept, and, when he awakened, it was the startled breathing of the Appaloosa that warned him. Instantly he was on his feet, speaking in a whisper to the horse and resting his hand on its shoulder. Day had come, and somewhere above them, yet some distance, there were voices!

The cave in which he stood was sandstone, no more than fifteen feet in depth, and probably eight feet high at the opening. Kedrick moved to the mouth, studied the crevasse down which he had come, and it was as he had supposed, a deep-cut watercourse from the notch in the cliff. Evidently during heavy rains this roared full of water, almost to the brim.

At the place where he now stood, the brush on either side almost met over the top, and at one point a fallen slab bridged the crack. Glancing back the way he had come, Kedrick saw that much of it was also covered by brush, and there was a chance that he would not be found. A very, very slim chance, but a chance. He could ask for no more.

He wanted to smoke, but dared not, for the smell of it might warn them of his presence. Several times he heard voices, some of them quite near. He glanced toward the back of the cave and saw the gelding drinking again. Evidently the water had seeped through during the night, even though not much. His canteen was over half full, and as yet water was not a problem.

His rifle across his knees, he waited, from time to time staring down the crevasse in the direction he had been going. Where did this water flow? It must flow into the arroyo below, near town, and in that case they would certainly know of it. The men and women of the town might not know of it, but the children would without doubt. Trust them to find every cave, every niche in the rock within miles!

Yet as the morning wore on, although he heard occasionally the sound of voices, nobody approached his place of concealment, nor did they seem aware of it. Once, he ventured out into the crevasse itself, and pulled a few handfuls of grass growing on a slight mound of earth. This he fed to the horse, that ate gratefully. He dug some jerky from his own pack and chewed on it, wishing for a cup of coffee.

Later, he ventured farther down the crevasse which seemed to dip steeply from where he was, and, hearing no voices, he pushed on, coming to a point where the crevasse turned sharply again, the force of the water having hollowed out a huge cave like a bowl standing on edge, and then the water turned and shot down an even steeper declivity into the black maw of a cavern!

Having come this far, he took a chance on leaving his horse alone and walked on down toward the cave. The entrance was high and wide and the cave extended deep into the mountain with several shelves or ledges that seemed to show no signs of water. There was a pool in the bottom, and apparently the water filled a large basin, but lost itself through some cracks in the bottom of the larger hollow. Although he penetrated no great distance, he could find no evidence of another outlet, nor could he feel any motion of air. Yet, as he looked around him, he realized that with some food a man might well hide in this place for weeks, and, unless they went to the foot of the slide and found the opening into the crevasse, this place might never be discovered. The run-off from the cliff, then, did not go to the arroyo, but ended here, in this deep cavern.

The day wore on slowly, and twice he walked back down to the cavern to smoke, but left his horse where it was, for he had an idea he could escape later. Yet when dusk came, and he worked his way back up the crevasse slide, he crawled out on the edge where he could look toward the entrance and saw two men, squatting there beside a fire, with rifles under their hands. They believed him concealed inside, and hoped to starve him out.

By this time Dornie Shaw must have returned to Mustang with news of his disappearance and, probably, of their murder of the messenger. For he was sure that it had been his own group who had committed the crime. It was scarcely likely that Gunter or Keith would countenance such a thing near town where it would not fail to be seen and reported upon by unfriendly witnesses.

Returning, he studied the slide to the rim. It was barely possible that a horse might scramble up there. It would be no trick for an active man, and the Appaloosa was probably a mountain horse. It was worth a gamble—if there was no one on top to greet him. Pulling an armful of grass from near the brush and boulders, he returned to the horse, and watched it gratefully munch the rich green grass.

***

Connie Duane was disturbed. She had seen the messenger come to her uncle and the others, and had heard their reply. Then, at almost noon the following day, Dornie Shaw and the others had come in, and they had returned without Tom Kedrick. Why that should disturb her she could not have said, but the fact remained that it did. Since he had stepped up on the verandah, she had thought of little else, remembering the set of his chin, the way he carried his shoulders, and the startled expression when he saw her. There was something about him that was different, not only from the men around her uncle, but from any man she had known before. Now, when despite herself she had looked forward to his return, he was missing.

John Gunter came out on the verandah, nervously biting the end from a cigar. "What happened?" she asked. "Is something wrong? Where's Captain Kedrick?"

"Wish I knew!" His voice was sharp with anxiety. "He took a ride to look over those squatters an' never came back. I don't trust Shaw, no matter how much Keith does. He's too bloodthirsty. We could get into a lot of trouble here, Connie. That's why I wanted Kedrick. He has judgment, brains."

"Perhaps he decided he wanted no part of it, Uncle. Maybe he decided your squatters were not outlaws or renegades."

Gunter glanced at her sharply. "Who has been talking to you?" he demanded.

"No one. It hasn't been necessary. I have walked around town, and I've seen some of these outlaws, as you call them, have wives and children, that they buy supplies, and look like nice people. I don't like it, Uncle John, and I don't like to think that my money may be financing a part of it."

"Now, now! Don't bother your head over it. You may be sure that Loren and I will do everything we can for your best interests."

"Then drop the whole thing!" she pleaded. "There's no need for it. I've money enough, and I don't want money that comes from depriving others of their homes. They all have a right to live, a chance."

"Of course!" Gunter was impatient. "We've gone over all this before! But I tell you most of these people are trash, and no matter about that, they all will be put off that land, anyway. The government is going to buy out whoever has control. That will mean us, and that means we'll get a nice, juicy profit."

"From the government? Your own government, Uncle?" Connie studied him coolly. "I fail to understand the sort of man who will attempt to defraud his own government. There are people like that, I suppose, but somehow I never thought I'd find one in my own family."

"Don't be silly, child. You know nothing of business . . . you aren't practical."

"I suppose not. Only I seem to remember that a lot of worthwhile things don't seem practical at the moment. No, I believe I'll withdraw my investment in this deal and buy a small ranch somewhere nearby. I will have no part in it."

"You can't do that!" Gunter exploded impatiently. "Your money is already in, and there's no way of getting it out until this business is closed. Now, why don't you trust me like a good girl? You always have before!"

"Yes, I have, Uncle John, but I never believed you could be dishonest." She studied him frankly. "You aren't very happy about this yourself. You know," she persisted, "those people aren't going to move without a fight. You believed they could be frightened. Well, they can't. I've seen Bob McLennon, and he's not the kind of a man who can be frightened. Even by that choice bunch of murderers Loren has gathered together."

"They aren't that. Not murderers," Gunter protested uneasily, but refused to meet her eyes. "Reckless, yes. And temperamental. Not murderers."

"Not even Dornie Shaw? The nice-looking, boyish one who has killed a dozen men and is so coldblooded and fiendish at times that others are afraid of him? No, Uncle, there is no way you can sidestep this. If you continue, you are going to countenance murder and the killing of innocent people. Loren doesn't care. He has always been coldblooded. You've wondered why I wouldn't marry him. That's why. He has the disposition of a tiger. He would kill anything or anyone that stood in his way. Even you, Uncle John."

He started and looked at her uneasily. "Why did you say that?"

"Because it's true. I know our tall and handsome man. He will allow nothing to come between him and what he desires. You've chosen some choice companions." She got to her feet. "If you hear anything of Captain Kedrick, let me know, will you?"

Gunter stood still for a long time after she left. He swore bitterly. Connie was like her mother. She always had the faculty for putting her finger on the truth, and certainly she was right about this. It was beginning to look ugly, but away down deep in his heart he was upset less over Keith than over Burwick. That strange, fat, and dirty man was a thing of evil, of corruption. There was some evil thing within him, something cold and vicious as a striking snake. Connie Duane was not the only person who was disturbed over the strange disappearance of Tom Kedrick.

***

Bob McLennon, unofficial commander of the forces for defense, sat in his rambling ranch house on the edge of Yellow Butte. Pete Slagle, Burt Williams, Dai Reid, and Pit Laine were all gathered there. With them was Sue Laine, keeping in the background. Her dark, lively eyes were stirring from one to the other, her ears were alert for every word.

"Blazes, man!" McLennon said irritably. "Where could he have gone? I'd have sworn he went into that box cañon. There was no other place for him to go, unless he took wings and flew! He had to go in there!"

"You looked yourself," Slagle said dryly. "Did

you see him? He just ain't there, that's all! He got
plumb away!"

"He probably did that," Dai Reid commented.
"A quick man, that Tom Kedrick. Hand or mind,
he's quick." He drew out his pipe and stoked it
slowly. "You shouldn't have jumped him," he continued. "I know the lad, an' he's honest. If he said
that was what he come for, it was the truth he told.
I'd take any oath he'd no knowledge of the killin'!"

"I'd like to believe that," McLennon agreed.
"The man impressed me. We could use an honest
man on the other side, one who would temper the
wind a bit, or get this thing stopped."

"It won't be that Shaw who stops. He's a mur-
derin' little devil," Slagle said. "He'll kill like a
weasel in a chicken pen until there's naught left to
kill."

"Kedrick fought me fair," Williams said. "I'll
give him that."

"He's a fair man," Dai persisted. "Since a lad
I've known him. I'd not be wrong. I'd give fifty
acres of my holdin' for the chance to talk to him."

***

Daylight brought the first attack. It came swiftly, a
tight bunch of riders that exploded from the mouth
of the arroyo hit the dusty street of Yellow Butte on
a dead run, pistols firing, and then the deep, heavy
concussion of dynamite. As suddenly as they had
come, they were gone. Two men sprawled in the
street.

Peters, the man Shaw had faced down in the
street of Mustang, was one of them. He had taken

three .44 slugs through the chest and died before he hit the ground. He had made one final effort to win back his self-respect. He had seen Dornie Shaw in the van of the charging riders and rushed into the street to get him. He failed to get off a single shot. The second man down was shot through the thigh and arm. He was a Swede who had just put in his second crop.

The riders had planned their attack well and had worked near enough to the guards at the mouth of the arroyo, and at a time when no attack was expected. The one guard awake was knocked down by a charging horse, but miraculously suffered only bruises. Two bundles of dynamite had been thrown. One had exploded against the door of the general store, smashing it off its hinges and tearing up the porch. The sound exploded harmlessly between the buildings.

The first rattle of rifle fire brought Tom Kedrick to an observation point. He had saddled his horse, hoping for a break, and instantly he saw it. The two guards had rushed in to the scene of action, and he led his horse out of the crevasse, rode at a canter to the cañon's mouth, and, seeing dust over the town, he swung right and, skirting close to the butte, slipped out into the open, a free man once more.

VI

Kedrick did not return to Mustang. He had come this far for a purpose, and he meant to achieve it. Turning west and north, he rode upstream away from Yellow Butte and Mustang. He wanted actually to see some of the homes of which so much had been said. By the way these people lived he could tell the sort they were. It was still and warm in the morning, and after the preliminary escape he slowed his horse to a walk and studied the terrain.

Certainly nothing could be further from swampland, and in that at least the company had misrepresented. Obviously they had misrepresented in maintaining that the land was vacant, but, if the squatters were a shiftless lot, Kedrick knew he would continue his job. Already he was heartily sick of the whole mess, yet he owed Gunter money, and how to pay it back was a bigger problem. And then, although the idea lurked almost unthought in the back of his consciousness, there was Connie Duane.

In his fast moving and active life he had met

many women, and a few had interested him, but none so much as this tall girl with the quiet, interested eyes. His desire to get back to Mustang had nothing to do with the company, but only with her. At the same time, Dornie Shaw had acted without his orders, had slain the messenger, and attacked the town. Of course, they might think him dead.

Turning due north, he rode though the sagebrush and catclaw toward two towering blue mountains that stood alone this side of the rim that bordered the country to the north. On his left, he saw broken land, and what was evidently a deep arroyo. He swung the Appaloosa over and headed it toward the cañon. Suddenly he reined in.

On the ground before him were the tracks of a trotting horse, and he recognized them. They were the same tracks left by the strange rider on the grulla mustang that had scouted their approach to Yellow Butte. The tracks were fresh.

Riding more slowly, he came to the edge of the cañon and looked down at a long, green meadow, fenced and watered by a small stream. At the far side, tucked in a corner, was a stone cottage, at once more attractive and better built than any other he had seen in this section. Ahead of him a trail turned down, so without delay he rode down it and walked his horse across the meadow by a narrow lane, toward the house.

It was a pleasant place of sandstone blocks and a thatched roof. Shade trees sheltered the yard, and there were a half dozen hens pecking about. In the corral there were several horses. His heart jumped as he saw the grulla, saddled and waiting.

He drew up in the courtyard and swung down,

trailing his reins. The door opened and a girl came out with a pan of water. She started as she saw him, and he recognized her instantly. It was Sue Laine, the girl of the trail, the girl in whom Dornie was reported to be interested.

"You!" she gasped as she stared at him. "They told me you were dead!"

He shrugged. "Not dead, just hungry. Could you feed a man?"

She studied him a minute, then nodded. "Come in. Better tie your horse, though. He'll head for that meadow if you don't. And"—her voice was dry—"you may need him. This isn't exactly friendly country."

He tied his horse near the grulla and followed her inside. "Isn't it?" he said. "Somehow I gathered you weren't exactly an enemy to the company."

"Don't say that!" she flared. "Don't ever say that!" Her voice lowered. "Not around here, anyway. If my brother ever heard . . ."

So Pit Laine and his sister did not see alike? That was an interesting point. He bathed his hands and face in the basin she left him, then combed his hair. Ruefully he rubbed his chin. "Your brother got a razor? I hate to go unshaven."

She brought a razor without comment, and he shaved, then dried his face and hands and walked into the house. It was amazingly neat, and on a side table there were several books. Flowered curtains hung at the windows, and several copper dishes were burnished to brightness. He sat down and she brought him food, beef, eggs, and homemade bread with honey.

"Everybody's looking for you," she said. "Where have you been?"

He accepted the statement and ignored the question. "After that messenger was killed, I had to get out of Yellow Butte. I did. What's been happening?"

"Keith served a final ultimatum. We either move, or they run us out. McLennon refused."

"He did right."

She turned on him, her eyes questioning. "You think that? I thought you were their man?"

He looked up from his food, and shook his head. "I don't know where I stand, but I don't go for murder, nor for running people out of their homes."

"They can't stay, anyway. If this land becomes a reservation, they will all be moved off. We will, too. They are foolish to fight."

"At least, the government will buy their land and pay for their investment. In any event, the company has misrepresented things."

"Does it matter?" She sat down opposite him. "They will win. They have money, influence, and power. The settlers here have nothing." She looked around bitterly. "Perhaps you think I am going against my own people, but that's not true. These aren't my people. Pit and I don't belong here and we never have, although Pit won't see it. Do you think I want to slave my life away on this desert?" She leaned toward him. "Look, Captain Kedrick, you're one of them, not just working for them, not just a hired gunman like Dornie Shaw. You can lead the men you have to, and I wouldn't be surprised but what you could even handle Keith. You could be a big man in this country, or any country.

Why be foolish and start thinking like you are? These farmers and ranchers can do nothing for you. They can't even help themselves. The company will win, and, if you are one of them, you will have a share in the winning. Don't get foolish, Captain, stay with them, do what you have to do."

"There are things more important than money. There's self-respect."

She stared at him, her eyes widening. "You don't really believe that? Try buying supplies with it, sometime. You won't get any place. But that isn't the point. You'll do what you want, but I want a man who will take me out of this desert." She got up quickly and came around the table. "You could do it, Captain. You could become rich, right here."

He smiled at her. "Ambitious, aren't you?"

"Why not? Being a rancher's wife doesn't appeal to me. I want to get away from here, go some place, be something, and enjoy life." She hesitated, studying him. "You could edge Gunter out of it, and Keith . . . maybe even Burwick. But the first two would be easy, and I know how."

"You do?" He looked up at her. She stood very close to him, and she was smiling down at him. She was, he had to admit, a lovely girl, and an exciting one. Too exciting for comfort right now, and that was a fact she understood completely. "How?"

She shook her head. "Oh, no! That I'd tell you only if you threw in with me, joined me. But this much I'll tell you . . . John Gunter is small potatoes. They needed money, and he had that girl's money, so they roped him in. Keith is dangerous because he is ambitious and unscrupulous, but the man to reckon with is Burwick. He will be top man when this thing is over, and you can bank on it, he has a way figured, all the time!"

"You seem to know a great deal."

"I do. Men like me, and men talk. They don't have any idea how much I lead them to say, or how much I remember."

"Why tell me all this?"

"Because you're the man who can do what has to be done. You could whip that bunch into line. All of them would listen to you, even Dornie Shaw . . . and he's suspicious of you."

"Of me? Why?"

"He saw Dai Reid come from your room. He was watching you."

So that was it! He had suspected that Shaw had something on his mind. But why had Shaw been watching? What was the little gunman thinking of? And had he reported that conference to Keith?

Kedrick finished his meal and lighted a cigarette. Ever since their first meeting in the desert, this girl had puzzled him. He was inclined to doubt if any girl, reared as she must have been, could be so sincerely disdaining of all loyalty and so plainly self-seeking. And this girl was scarcely more than a child, slim, brown, and lovely, with her quick, measuring eyes and her soft lips. Now, she seemed to have selected him for the man who was to take her away from the desert. But how many others had the same idea? And then, he had no idea of leaving the desert.

"Your brother around?" he asked.

Her glance was a quick flash of alarm. "You don't want to see him, or talk to him. You'd better get out of here."

"On the contrary, Sue, I'd like to talk to Pit. I've heard about him and I'd like to know him."

"You'd better go," she warned. "He'll be back soon, and some of that Yellow Butte crowd may be with him."

"You mean he's not here? Then whose horse is that out there? That grulla?"

Her face was strange as she shook her head. "You'll think I'm a liar, but I don't know. I never saw the rider."

His eyes searched hers. He could see nothing but sincerity there, sincerity and a little fear. "You mean that horse showed up there, tied like that? And you never saw the rider?"

"That's right. I looked out this morning, shortly after Pit left, and he was tied right there. This isn't the first time! He has been here twice before, when Pit was gone, and some others have seen him, most of them women when their husbands are away. Missus Burt Williams said he was tied to her corral for three or four hours one day."

"But surely someone has seen the rider come and mount up?"

"Never. He'll be out there like he is now . . . wait! . . . he's gone!"

Kedrick came to his feet with a start and stared out the door. Sue was right. The mouse-colored horse was gone. His own Appaloosa stood where he had been left, but the grulla had disappeared.

Walking out into the yard, he looked around very carefully, but there was nothing in sight on the plain or the hills. The horse—and he was positive he had seen it only a few minutes before—was gone! He looked at her and saw the strained expression on her face, then he walked out to the Appaloosa. Pinned to his saddle was a note. He took it down and glanced at it, then passed it to Sue who had come up beside him.

Stay away

Kedrick shrugged. "Your brother do this?"

"Oh, no! I told him about the horse and he knew no more about it than I. Besides, he didn't print that. He couldn't. Pit never learned either to read or write."

***

Long after he left the Malpais Arroyo behind, he was puzzling over the strange horse. Somebody was seriously trying either to puzzle or frighten the squatters, yet it was an action unlike the company. Moreover, it must be somebody who had a lot of time to spend.

Kedrick rode north toward Blue Hill, then swung out, crossing the old Mormon Trail and skirting the rim. This was good grazing land. There was an abundance of rough foliage here and a good herd of cattle could fatten on this range without trouble. Moreover, the herding problem was solved in part by the rim that provided a natural drift fence beyond which the cattle could not go. When he reached Salt Creek, he turned down the creek toward the river, but swung east again, and, passing near Chimney Rock, he rode southeast until he struck the Hogback Trail. Once over that ridge he headed due east for Mustang.

Yet, as always, his eyes were alive and alert. He loved this land, harsh though it might be at times. He loved the dim purples and blues, the far-flung mists and mornings and nights, the gray-green of the sagebrush, and the rust-red of the sandstone. It was a good country, and there was room for all if it were left open for settlement.

His own mind was not yet resolved. The problem of his debt to Gunter weighed heavily upon him, and there were other considerations. He wanted no trouble, and to withdraw now might mean plenty of it, particularly if he remained in the country, which he had every reason to do. He would try to talk the company into withdrawing, but knew that would fail.

Just where, in all this, did Connie Duane actually stand? Was she involved more deeply than he believed? Or was it only what had been implied, that her uncle had invested her money in the land speculation? If such was the case, it might be difficult or impossible to get out at this stage—even if they would allow it. Burwick puzzled him. Obviously the controlling power, he gave no evidence of where that power came from, aside from some native shrewdness. Yet there might be much more to the man and evidently was, for that Keith and Gunter deferred to him was obvious. Purposely Kedrick had said nothing of his hideaway near Yellow Butte when talking to Sue. That young lady already knew more than was good for her, and that spot might again become useful. It was something to know.

Mustang was asleep when he rode into the town and headed for the stable. He put his horse up and rubbed it down thoroughly, gave it a good bait of corn, and forked down some hay. Then he made his way quickly to the St. James. As he neared the hotel, a tall, lean figure arose from the chair where he himself had been sitting a few days before. The build and the broad hat, the very hang of the guns left no mistake. It was Laredo Shad.

"Cap'n?" The voice was low. "You all right?"

"Yes, and you?"

Shad chuckled. "Don't worry none about Shad! I stay healthy." He motioned to a chair. "You better sit down. I've been hopin' you'd show up."

"What's the talk? Did they think I was dead, or skipped the country?"

"Some o' both, I reckon. Keith was fit to be tied. He wants to see you as soon as you show . . . no matter when."

"He'll wait. I'm tired."

Shad nodded, then lighted his cigarette, which had gone out. "You know, I ain't right sure about this business."

Kedrick nodded. "I know what you mean. I'm not the man to run folks out of their homes."

"You quittin'?"

"Not yet. I'll talk to 'em first."

"Won't do no good. They are mighty bloodthirsty. It was Poinsett shot that messenger. Dornie put him up to it. Poinsett killed him, an' then four, five of those rannies shot up the body. I don't think Fessenden shot any, an' maybe Goff didn't. You can lay your last peso I didn't shoot none. It was mighty raw, Cap'n, mighty raw."

"They'll pay for it. Were you on the Yellow Butte raid?"

"Uhn-huh, but I didn't shoot nobody. I'm no Bible packer, Cap'n, but I do figure a fightin' man shouldn't tackle folks who cain't fight back, an' I ain't the man to be firin' on no women or kids."

"What are they talkin' up now? Any plans you know of?"

Shad hesitated, then shrugged. "Reckon you'd better talk that out with them, Cap'n. I may know somethin', but I ain't tellin', not yet."

The Texan sat silently for a few minutes while both men smoked, and then he waved an impatient hand. "Cap'n, I hired on as a gun hand, an' such I am, but I didn't figure on this sort of thing. Some of those hombres on the other side o' this shindig look a damned sight more human than some on our own side. I'm getting' shut o' the whole she-bang."

"Uhn-huh"—surprisingly Kedrick found resolution coming to him—"I know how you feel, but my own way will be different. I think, if I can't talk Gunter an' the rest of them out of it, I'll change sides."

Shad nodded. "I've thought of it. I sure have."

Kedrick turned suddenly and found Dornie Shaw standing not twenty feet behind them. Slowly he got to his feet, and Laredo Shad did likewise. Shaw's eyes avoided Kedrick. "If you figure on leavin' us, Shad, you better figure on killin' me first."

"If I have to," Laredo said quietly, "then I reckon you can die as simple as any other man. Want to try it now?"

"That's enough, Shad!" Kedrick's voice was sharp. "I've said there would be no more fighting. Not in this outfit."

Dornie Shaw turned his head slowly and smiled at Kedrick. "Still like to give orders, do you? Maybe that'll be changed."

"Maybe." Tom Kedrick shrugged. "That will be time enough for me to stop giving orders. I'm turning in."

"Keith wants to see you."

"He can wait. I've had a rough time. There's nothing he wants won't wait."

"Shall I tell him that?"

"If you like."

Shaw smiled again. "You must carry a lot o' weight where you come from, Kedrick, but don't forget it ain't here. Keith is a bad man to buck. So's Burwick."

Kedrick shrugged again. "I've bucked worse. But at the moment I'm bucking nobody. I need sleep, and, by the Lord Harry, sleep is what I'll get. Whatever Keith has on his mind can wait until daylight. I'll be up then."

Shaw started to go, then hesitated, unable to restrain his curiosity. "What happened to you? We figured you were dead or taken prisoner when you didn't come back."

For the first time Kedrick began to wonder. Had Shaw wanted the messenger killed for that very reason? Had he deliberately moved that way hoping the enraged settlers would kill Kedrick? It was most likely. "It doesn't matter," he said, passing off the remark casually. "I found a way to keep out of sight."

Shaw turned away, and, when he had gone only a few steps, Tom Kedrick spoke up suddenly: "By the way, Dornie. Know anybody who rides a grulla mustang?"

Shaw stopped abruptly, but he did not turn. His whole body seemed to stiffen. Then he started on. "No," he said gruffly, "I sure don't."

Laredo Shad stared after him. "You know, pardner, you'll either kill that hombre someday or you'll be killed."

"Uhn-huh," Kedrick said quietly, "I've the same feeling."

VII

Keith was pacing the floor in the office at the gray stone building when Kedrick walked in. He stopped and turned swiftly. "Shaw tells me you came in after midnight. Why didn't you come to me according to my orders?"

"Frankly I was tired. Furthermore"—Kedrick returned Keith's look—"I'd nothing to report that wouldn't keep."

"You were hired to do a job, and you haven't done it." Keith stood with his hands on his hips. "Where've you been?"

Briefly and clearly Kedrick explained, omitting only the visit to Laines' and the story of the hideout. He continued: "Having looked the situation over, I'd say you had small chance of driving those people off. Also, you and Gunter misrepresented things to me and the government. That land is occupied not by renegades and outlaws, but by good, solid people. You can't get away with running them off."

Keith smiled contemptuously. "Getting scared? You were supposed to be a fighting man. As for what we can do or can't do, let me tell you this, Kedrick. We've started to run those people off, and we'll do it. With or without you! Hiring you was Gunter's idea, anyway."

"That's right, it was." Gunter walked into the room followed by Burwick, and he glanced swiftly from Kedrick to Keith. "If you're complainin' about his going to look over that country, you can stop. I sent him."

"Did you tell him to come back scared to death? Saying we can't swing it?"

Burwick had been silent, but now he moved to the big chair behind the desk and dropped into it. He sighed heavily and wiped the back of his hand across his mouth, then glanced at Kedrick keenly. "What did you find out?"

"That they are determined to fight. I talked to Bob McLennon and to Slagle. There's no quit in those men. They'll fight at the drop of a hat, and to the last ditch. Right now, at this minute, they are ready for anything. Your raid killed one man, wounded another. The dynamite blasted a door loose and blew a hole in the porch."

Burwick turned swiftly and glared at Keith. "You told me three men dead and a building destroyed! Hereafter, you be sure reports to me are accurate." He swung back to Kedrick. "Go on, what happened to you? You got away?"

"I'm here."

Their eyes met and held for a long time, Burwick's stone-cold and hard, examining, probing.

"What do you think of the deal?" he asked finally.

"The fight," Kedrick replied carefully, "will raise

a stink clear to Washington. Remember the Lincoln County War? We'll have us another general down here, and you know how much profit you'll make out of that place then!"

Burwick nodded his huge head. "Sensible, that's sensible. Have to think our way around that. At least"—he glared again at Keith and Gunter— "this man can bring in some sensible ideas and make a coherent report. You two could learn from him." He looked up at Kedrick. "Anything else?"

"A couple of things. There's a mysterious rider out on those plains. Rides a mouse-colored horse, and he's got those folks more jittery than all your threats."

"Hah?" Burwick was uninterested. He shuffled papers on his desk. "What's this I hear about you quittin'?"

"I won't be a party to murder. These people aren't outlaws, but good, substantial folks. I'd say buy them out or leave them alone."

"You aren't running this affair," Keith replied coldly. "We will decide what is to be done."

"Nobody quits," Burwick said quietly, his eyes on Kedrick's, "unless I say so!"

Tom Kedrick smiled suddenly. "Then you'd better say so, because I've quit as of now!"

"Tom!" Gunter protested. "Let's talk this over!"

"What of the money you owe the firm?" Keith demanded unpleasantly. "You can repay that, I suppose?"

"There's no need."

They all turned at the voice. Connie Duane stood in the door. "You have money of mine in this project. When Uncle John got it from me, he told me it was a real estate speculation. His other activities have been honest and practical, so I did not investigate. Now I have. I shall withdraw my money, and you can pay me less the sum advanced to Captain Kedrick. He may repay me when circumstances permit it."

All in the room were still. Gunter's face was pale, and Keith looked startled, then angry. He started to protest, but he was too slow. Burwick turned on Gunter. "You!" he snorted angrily. "You told me that was your money! You fool! What do you mean, bringing a woman into a deal like this? Well, you brought her in. Now you manage her or I shall!"

"Nobody," Connie replied, "is managing me or my affairs from now on. I'll handle them myself!" She turned to Kedrick. "I'm glad, Captain, that you've made this decision. I am sure you'll not be sorry for it."

Kedrick turned to follow her from the room, but Burwick's voice stopped him. "Captain!"

He turned. Keith's eyes were ugly and Gunter's face was haunted by doubt and fear. "Captain Kedrick," Burwick said, "I believe we are all being too hasty. I like your caution in this matter. Your suggestion that cleaning out those people might make trouble and cause talk in Washington is probable. I had considered that but, not knowing McLennon, had considered the chance negligible. Slagle, I know. McLennon I do not know. Your suggestion eliminates a frontal attack. We must try some other means. Also," he added, "I believe that your presence has some claim on that of Miss Duane. Consequently, as we can brook no failure now,

I have a proposition for you. How would you like to come into the firm? As a silent partner?"

Keith's face flushed angrily, but Gunter looked up, his eyes suddenly hopeful. Burwick continued. "We could give you a fifteen percent interest, which, believe me, will be adequate. I believe you could keep Miss Duane in line, and with you at the helm we might straighten this whole thing out . . . without bloodshed."

Kedrick hesitated. The money was a temptation, for he had no desire to be indebted to Connie, yet the money alone would mean nothing. It was that last phrase that gripped his attention and made him incautious. "Without bloodshed," he repeated. "On those terms, I accept. However, let's discuss this matter a bit further."

Keith spun on his heel. "Burwick, this doesn't make sense! You know the only way we'll get these people off is by driving them off! We agreed on that before. Also, this man is not reliable. I happen to know that he has friends on the other side, and has actually been in communication with them."

"So much the better." Burwick pursed his fat lips and mopped perspiration from his face. "He'll have a contact he can use then to make a deal." He chuckled. "Suppose you two run along and let me talk to Captain Kedrick?"

***

Hours later, Tom Kedrick paused on the street and studied it with care. Burwick had been more than reasonable, and, little as he was able to trust him, yet he thought it possible that Burwick was sincere in his agreement to buy off a few of them, and to try to convince others. Certainly, if the government moved in, they would have to move, anyway. With McLennon and Slagle out of the picture the chances were there would be no fight, for the others lacked leadership. No fighting meant no deaths, and the settlers would come out of it with a little money at least.

He paced the street irritably, avoiding company. Burwick stank of deceit, but the man was practical and he should realize that a sudden mess of killings preceding the sale of the land would create a furor that might cause them to lose out all around. At least, trouble had been avoided for the time, and even Connie was hopeful that something might be done. Tomorrow he was returning again to try to make some deal with McLennon and Slagle. A neutral messenger was leaving tonight.

"They won't come to town," Burwick had agreed, "so why not pick some intermediate point? Meet them, say, at Largo Cañon or Chimney Rock? Have your talk there, and I'll come with you. Just you and me, McLennon and Slagle. We can talk there and maybe make peace. Ain't it worth a try?"

It was only that chance for peace that had persuaded him and helped him to persuade Connie. She had listened in silence as he explained the situation, then she had turned to him frankly. "Captain, you don't trust them, and neither do I. Uncle John has never been this way before, and I believe somehow he has fallen under the domination of those other men. However, I think that, if Burwick is willing to talk, we should at least agree. I'll stand by you in this, and we'll hope something can come of it that will prevent trouble."

Kedrick was less hopeful than he had let it appear, and now he was studying the situation from every angle. As things stood, it was a stalemate. He was confident that with McLennon and Slagle to lead them, the settlers could manage a stiff defense of their town and their homes. Certainly they could prevent the survey being completed and prevent any use being made of the lands. Yet there were fiery elements on both sides, and Keith did not like the turn things had taken. Colonel Loren Keith had from the very beginning planned on striking fast and wiping out the opposition. It would be merely another unsolved mystery of the West. Kedrick resolved to keep an eye on the man and be prepared for anything.

He returned to the St. James and to bed, yet he awakened early and was surprised to see Keith, mounted and riding out of town at daybreak. With a bound he was out of bed and dressing. Whatever Keith had in mind he meant to know. Swiftly he descended the stairs and went to the livery stable. Mounted, he headed out of town, found Keith's tracks with ease, and followed them. Keith turned off the trail and headed west and slightly north, but after a few miles Kedrick lost the trail and took a wide swing to try and cut it again, but Keith had vanished somewhere in the vicinity of Largo Cañon.

Returning to the hotel, he found a message from Bob McLennon. He and Slagle would meet with Burwick and Kedrick at Chimney Rock at three in the afternoon on Wednesday. It was now Monday, and a whole day lay between. Yet during the remainder of Monday he saw nothing of Dornie

Shaw, although Laredo Shad appeared a couple of times, then vanished into one of the saloons.

At midnight the door of his room opened slowly and Tom Kedrick sat up, gun in hand. It was Laredo Shad.

"Somethin's up," he said, dropping on the bed, "an' she looks mighty peculiar. Couple of hours ago Poinsett an' Goff showed up an' said they had quit. No fightin' here, so they were pullin' out for Durango. About a half our later, they mounted up an took out."

"What's peculiar about that?" Kedrick inquired, building a smoke. "That's in line with Burwick's talk with me."

"Yeah," Shad replied dryly, "but both of them came in here with a good deal of gear. They lost their pack horses somewheres and went out only with what they could carry on the one horse, an' damned little o' that."

"What about Fessenden?"

"Ain't seen him."

"Any of the others gone?"

"Clauson is. At least, he ain't around in sight. I ain't seen him since morning."

That left Shaw, who had been around little himself, and Fessenden if he was still in town. Despite himself, Kedrick was disturbed, but if Burwick was getting rid of his warriors, it was a good sign, and probably, Kedrick felt, he was getting too suspicious. Nothing, Shad said, had been said to him about quitting. "In fact," he said dryly, "the Mixus boys pulled in this morning, an' they went right to Burwick."

"Who are they?"

"Killers. Dry-gulchers, mostly. Bean an' Abe Mixus. They were in that Sandoval affair. Couple of men died awful opportune in that affair, an', come to think of it, Burwick was around. Fact is, that was where I met him."

"Were you in that?"

"Uhn-uh. I was in town, though, an' had me a run-in with Roy Gangle. Roy was a mighty tough ranny who'd been ramroddin' a big spread down thataway, an', when he got into the war, he went bad, plumb bad. We'd had trouble over a steer, an' he braced me. He was a mite slow."

It made no sense—gunmen leaving, but others arriving. Of course, the Mixus boys could have been spoken to before the change of plans. That must be it. He suggested as much to Laredo, and the Texan nodded dubiously. "Maybe. I don't trust that hombre none. Your man Gunter is in over his head. Keith, well, he's all around bad when it comes to that, but neither of them can hold a candle to that Burwick."

***

Study the situation as he could, Tom Kedrick could see no answer to it, and the fact remained that they were to meet Slagle and McLennon for a peace conference. Out of that anything might come, and he had no real cause to distrust Burwick. Morning was bright and clear with the sun promising a hot day. Yet it was still cool when Kedrick appeared on the street and crossed to the little restaurant where he ate in silence. He was on his second cup of coffee when Connie came in.

Her face brightened with a smile as she saw him, and she came over to his table. "You know, you're the one bright spot in this place. I'm so tired of that old stone house and seeing that dirty old man around that I can scarcely stand it. I'll be glad when this is all over."

He studied her. "What will you do then?"

"You know, I've not really thought of that. What I want to do is to get a ranch somewhere, a place with trees, grass, and some running water. It doesn't have to be a big place."

"Cattle?"

"A few, but horses are what I want. Horses like that one of yours, I think."

"Good idea. It takes less land for horses, and there's always a market for good stock." He studied the beauty of her mouth, the quietness and humor of her eyes. "Somehow I'm glad to think you're staying. It wouldn't be the same without you. Not now."

She looked at him quickly, her eyes dancing with laughter, but with the hint of a question in their depths. "Why, Tom! That sounds almost like gallantry. Like you were trying to make love to me, like all the cowboys."

"No, Connie," he said quietly, "when I make love to you, there won't be any doubt about it. You'll know, and I won't be fooling. Over west of here, west and south, there's a great rim that stretches for miles across the country, and a splendid pine forest atop it. There's trees, water, game, and some of the finest mountain meadows a man ever saw. I know a place over there where I camped once, a good spring, some tall trees, graceful in the wind, and a long sweep of land clear to the rim's edge, and beyond it miles upon miles of rolling, sweeping range and forest."

"It sounds fascinating, like what I've been wanting ever since I came West."

He pushed back his chair. "Maybe when this is over, you'd ride over that way with me? I'd like to show it to you."

She looked up at him. "All right, Tom. We'll look at it together."

He paused, hat in hand, staring out the door. "Together," he mused. Then he glanced down at her. "You know, Connie, that's the most beautiful word in the language . . . together."

He walked away then, pausing to pay his check and hers, before stepping outside into the warmth of the street. A buckboard had stopped and a man was getting out of it, a man who moved warily and looked half frightened. He glanced around swiftly, then ducked through the door into the store.

VIII

Two men crossed the street suddenly. One of them was a man Kedrick had never seen before; the other was the sly-looking loafer he had seen hanging around the back door in the saloon at Yellow Butte. The loafer, a sour-faced man called Singer, was talking. They stopped, and he indicated the buckboard to the man with him. "That's him, Abe," Singer was saying, "he's one of that crowd from across the way. He's brother-in-law to McLennon."

"This is a good place to start," Abe replied shortly, low-voiced. "Let's go!"

Tom Kedrick turned on his heel and followed them. As they stepped into the door, he stepped after and caught it before it slammed shut. Neither man seemed to be aware of his presence, for they were intent on the man at the counter.

"Hello, Sloan," Singer said softly. "Meet Abe Mixus."

The name must have meant something to Sloan, for he turned, his face gray. He held a baby's bottle that he was in the act of buying in his right hand.

His eyes, quick and terror stricken, went from one to the other. He was frightened, and puzzled, and he seemed to be fighting for self-control. "You in this squabble, Singer? I figured you to be outside of it."

Singer chuckled. "That's what I aim for folks to think."

Mixus, a lean, stooped man with yellow eyeballs and a thin-cheeked face, drew a paper from his pocket. "That's a quit-claim deed, Sloan," he said. "You can sign it an' save yourself trouble."

Sloan's face was gray. His eyes went to the deed and seemed to hold there, then, slowly, they lifted. "I can't do that. My wife's having a child in the next couple of days. I worked too hard on that place to give it up. I reckon I can't sign."

"I say you better." Mixus' voice was cold, level. The storekeeper had vanished, and the room was empty save for the three, and for Tom Kedrick, standing in the shadows near some hanging jeans and slickers. "I say you better sign because you don't own that prop'ty anyhow. Want to call me a liar?"

Sloan's face was gray and yet resolution seemed to have overcome his immediate fear. He was a brave man, and Kedrick knew that whatever he said now, he would die. He spoke first.

"No, Abe," he said softly, "I'll call you a liar."

Mixus stiffened as if struck. He was a killer, and dangerous, but he was a smart, sure-thing killer, and he had believed himself alone but for Singer. Now somebody was behind him. He stood stock-still, then started to turn. Singer had fallen back against the wall, his eyes staring to locate Kedrick.

"It's Kedrick," he said. "The boss gunman."

Mixus scowled. "What's the matter?" he said irritably. "What yuh buttin' in for?"

"There's to be no more killing, Abe." Kedrick held his ground. "We're havin' a peace conference tomorrow. This killing is over."

"Got my orders," Mixus persisted. "You talk to Burwick."

There was a movement from Sloan, and he whirled on him. "You stand still!" he barked.

"You can go, Sloan," Kedrick said. "Get in your outfit an' tell McLennon that my word is good. You'd better stop thinking about him, Abe. You're in trouble, and I'm the trouble."

Mixus was confused. He knew Kedrick was ramrodding the gunmen for the company, and he was puzzled. Had he been about to do the wrong thing? But, no, he hadn't. "You fool!" His confusion burst into fury. "Keith tol' me to git him!"

"Shut up!" Singer yelled. "Damn it! You . . . !"

Abe Mixus was a cold-blooded killer and no heavyweight mentally. Orders and counterorders had come to him and, worked up to such a killing pitch, he had been suddenly stopped in the middle of it and switched off into this back trail where he floundered hopelessly. Now Singer seemed to be turning on him, and he swung toward him, his teeth bared, his face vicious.

"Don't you tell me, you white-livered coyote!" he snarled.

One hand hung over a gun, and Singer, frightened, grabbed for his own gun. Instantly Mixus whipped out his .44 and flame stabbed at Singer. The renegade turned on his heel. His knees slowly buckled and he slid to the floor, his head against a sack of flour, blood welling from his mouth.

Mixus stared down at him, and then, slowly, he blinked, then blinked again. Awareness seemed to return to him, and his jittery nerves calmed. He stared down at Singer almost unbelieving. "Why, I . . . I . . . kilt Singer," he said.

"That's right." Kedrick was watching him, knowing now upon what a slender thread of irritation this man's muscles were poised. "What will Keith say to that?"

Cunning came over Abe's horse-like face. "Keith? What give you the idee he had anythin' to do with this?" he demanded.

Slowly, attracted by the shooting and made confident by its end, people were gathering in front of the door. The storekeeper had come into the room and stood watching, his face drawn and frightened.

Tom Kedrick took a slow step back as Abe's eyes turned toward the front of the store. Putting the slickers between them, he moved on cat feet to the opening between the counters and slid through into the living quarters and out into the alley behind the store.

Crossing the street below the crowd, he wound up in front of the St. James, pausing there. Laredo Shad materialized beside him. "What happened?" he asked swiftly.

Kedrick explained. "I don't get it," he said. "Keith may be moving on his own, but Burwick was to hold off until we had our talk . . . and I know Keith didn't like that. He spoke right up about it."

"Ain't Singer supposed to be a settler?" Shad asked. "Won't this serve to get 'em all riled up? Who knew that Singer was with Keith an' the company?"

"You've got a point there," Kedrick said thoughtfully. "This may be the very thing that will blow the lid off. Both of them were mighty jumpy. It looked like they had Sloan marked because he was McLennon's relative. I sprung a surprise on them, an' Mixus just couldn't get himself located."

The crowd separated, then gathered in knots along the street to discuss the new event. Shad loitered there beside him, and was standing there when Loren Keith came up. He glanced sharply at Shad, then at Kedrick. "What's happened over there?"

He kept his eyes on Kedrick as he spoke, and Kedrick shrugged. "Shooting, I guess. Not unusual for Mustang from what I hear."

"Mixus was in there," Shad commented. "Wonder if he had a hand in it?"

Keith turned and looked at Laredo, suspicion in his eyes. "Who was shot?" he inquired, his eyes going from one to the other.

"Singer, they tell me," Shad said casually. "I reckon Mixus killed him."

"Mixus? Kill Singer?" Keith shook his head. "That's preposterous!"

"Don't know why," Laredo drawled. "Mixus come heah to fight, didn't he? An' ain't Singer one o' them settlers?"

Colonel Keith hesitated, his sharp, hard features a picture of doubt and uncertainty. Watching him, Kedrick was amused and pleased. The storekeeper had not seen him, and it was doubtful if anyone had but Mixus, the dead man, and the now missing Sloan.

What Abe Mixus would offer as an explanation for shooting Singer, Tom couldn't conceive, but a traitor had died, and the enemy was confounded. Little as it might mean in the long run, it was for the moment a good thing. The only fly in the ointment was the fact that Singer had been a squatter, and that few if any knew of his tie-up with Keith and the company.

Watching the crowds in the street, Tom Kedrick began to perceive a new element shaping itself. Public opinion was a force Burwick had not reckoned with, and the faces of the men talking in the streets were hard and bitter. These were mostly poor men who had made their own way or were engaged in making their way, and they resented the action of the company. Few had known Singer well, and those few had little use for the man, but the issue, from their viewpoint, was not a matter of personalities, but a matter of a bunch of hardworking men against the company, an organization largely of outsiders, seeking to profit from the work of local people. Furthermore, whatever Singer was, he was not a gunman and he was a local man. Abe Mixus was a known killer, a gunman whose gun was for hire.

Tom Kedrick nodded toward the street. "Well, Colonel," he said, "you'd better start thinking about that unless you want to stretch hemp. That bunch is sore."

Keith stared at them nervously, then nodded and hurried away toward headquarters. Shad watched him go, and turned toward Kedrick. "You know, we're sort of tied in with the company, an' I don't want to hang for 'em. Let's light a shuck out of here an' stick in the hills for a few days?"

"Can't. I've got to make that meeting with Burwick. But you might get out of town, anyway. Scout around and see what you can find of Goff and them . . . if they really left the country or not. Meet me at Chimney Rock about five tomorrow evening . . . make it later . . . about sundown."

Leaving Shad, Kedrick hurried to his room in the St. James and bundled his gear together. He carried it down to the livery stable and saddled the Appaloosa. When that was done, he headed for headquarters, staying off the main street. Yet it was Connie Duane he wanted to see, and not Burwick or Keith.

There was no sign of any of them. Gunter was not around, and Burwick and Keith seemed to have vanished. Idling in the office, Tom heard a slight movement upstairs. He called out. Feet hurried along the floor above him, and then Connie was at the stair head. "Yes?" Recognizing him, she hurried down. "Is something wrong?"

Swiftly he explained, not holding anything back. "Nothing may come of it, although it wouldn't take much to start it, and they all know that the company gunmen are mostly out of town. Burwick, Keith, and your uncle must have lit out."

"Uncle John hasn't been around all day. I saw him at breakfast, and then he disappeared."

"I'll look around. Do you have a gun?" He shook his head then. "Don't much think you'll need it, most of them like you around here, and you've been pretty outspoken. But stay close to your room. The lid's going to blow off."

He turned away, but she called to him: "Tom?" He turned when he reached the door. He seemed to see pleading in her eyes. "Be careful, Tom"

Their eyes held for a long moment, and then he nodded. "I will if I . . . can."

He went out and paused on the steps. Burwick and Keith might get out of the way, but whatever else Gunter might be, he was scarcely the man to leave his niece behind at a time of danger. Puzzled that he should be thus inconsistent, Kedrick paused and looked around him. The back street was bare and empty. The white, powdery dust lay thickly and had sifted into the foliage of the trees and shrubs.

Kedrick hitched his guns into place and walked slowly around the house. The stable lay behind it, but it was usually filled with horses. Now it seemed empty. He strode back, his spurs jingling a little and tiny puffs of dust rising from his boots as he walked. Once, nearly to the stable, he paused by a water trough and listened for noise from the town. It was quiet, altogether too quiet. He hesitated, worrying about Connie again, but then went on and into the wide door that gave entrance to the shadowed coolness of the stable.

The stalls were empty, all save one. He walked back, then paused. The chestnut was Gunter's horse, and his saddle lay nearby. Could he be somewhere around town? Kedrick considered that, then dismissed it. He removed his hat and wiped the band with his kerchief, then replaced it. His face was unusually thoughtful, and he walked to the far end of the stable, examining every stall as he walked back.

Nothing.

Puzzled, he stepped out into the bright glare of the sun, and heard no sound anywhere. He squinted his eyes around, then saw the ramshackle old building that had done duty for a stable before the present large one was built. He stared at it, and then turned in that direction. He had taken scarcely a step when he heard a rattle of hoofs, and swung swiftly around, half crouched, his hands wide.

Then he straightened. Sue Laine slid from her horse and ran to him. "Oh, I've found you, Tom!" she cried, catching him by the arms. "Tom, don't go to that meeting tomorrow. There's going to be trouble!"

"You mean, McLennon's framed something?"

"McLennon?" For an instant she was startled. "Oh, no! Not Mac!" Her expression changed. "Come home with me, Tom. Please do! Let them have this out and get it over with! Come home with me!"

"Why all this sudden worry about me?" He was sincerely puzzled. "We've met only once, and we seem to have different ideas about things."

"Don't stand there and argue! Tom, I mustn't be seen talking to you . . . not by either side. Come with me and get away from here until this is all over. I've seen Dornie, and he hates you, Tom. He hates you."

"He does, does he?" He patted her arm. "Run along home now. I've things to do here."

"Oh?" Her eyes hardened a little. "Is it that

woman? That Duane girl? I've heard all about her, how beautiful she is, how . . . how she . . . what kind of girl is she?"

"She's a lovely person," he said gravely. "You'd like her, Sue."

Sue stiffened. "Would I? I wonder how much you know about women, Tom? Or do you know anything about them? I could never like Connie Duane!" She shook his arm. "Come, if you're coming. I just heard this last night, and I can't . . . I won't see this happen."

"What? What's going to happen?"

She stamped her foot with impatience. "Oh, you fool, you! They plan to kill you, Tom! Now, come on!"

"Not now," he said quietly. "I've got to get this fight settled first, then maybe I'll ride your way. Now run along. I've got to look around."

Impatiently she turned and walked to her horse. In the saddle she glanced back at him. "If you change your mind . . ."

"Not now," he repeated.

"Then be careful. Be careful, Tom."

He watched her go, then happened to glance toward the house. Connie Duane stood in the window, looking down at him, but as he looked up, she turned sharply away. He started for the house, then hesitated. There was nothing he could say now, nothing that would have any effect or do any good at all.

He started toward the front of the house again, then stopped. On an impulse he turned and walked swiftly back to the little old building and caught the latch. The door was weathered and gray.

It creaked on rusty hinges and opened rheumatically. Inside, there was the musty odor of decay. Kedrick stood there for a minute watching the sunlight filter through the cobwebbed window and fall in a faint square upon the ancient straw that littered the earthen floor, and then he stepped forward, peering around the corner of the nearest stall.

John Gunter lay sprawled upon his face, his head pillowed upon one forearm, the back of his shirt covered with a dark, wide stain. Kedrick knelt beside him.

Connie's uncle had been stabbed in the back. Three powerful blows, from the look of the wounds, had been struck downward—evidently while he sat at a desk or table. He had been dead for several hours.

IX

Alton Burwick, for all his weight, sat his saddle easily and rode well. His horse was a blood bay, tall and long-limbed. He walked it alongside Tom Kedrick's Appaloosa, and from time to time he spurred it to a trot, then eased down. On this morning Burwick wore an ancient gray felt hat, torn at the flat crown, and a soiled handkerchief that concealed the greasy shirt collar. His shirt bulged over his belt, and he wore one gun, too high on his hip for easy use. His whiskers seemed neither to have grown nor been clipped. They were still a rough stubble of dirty, mixed gray. Yet he seemed unusually genial this morning.

"Great country, Kedrick! Country for a man to live in! If this deal goes through, you should get yourself a ranch. I aim to."

"Not a bad idea." Kedrick rode with his right hand dangling. "I was talking about that yesterday, with Connie Duane."

The smile vanished from Burwick's face. "You talked to her yesterday? What time?"

"Afternoon." Kedrick let his voice become casual,

yet he was alert to the change in Burwick's voice. Had Burwick murdered Gunter? Or had it been one of the squatters? With things as they were, it would be difficult or impossible to prove. "We had a long talk. She's a fine girl."

Burwick said nothing, but his lips tightened. The red cañon walls lifted high above them, for along here they were nearly five hundred feet above the bottom of Salt Creek. There was but little farther to go, he knew, and he was puzzled by Burwick's increased watchfulness. The man might suspect treachery, but he had said nothing to imply anything of the kind.

Tom's mind reverted to Sue's warning of the previous day—they intended to kill him—but who were "they"? She had not been specific in her warning except to say that he should not keep this rendezvous today. Kedrick turned the idea over in his mind, wondering if she were deliberately trying to prevent a settlement, or if she knew something and was genuinely worried.

Pit Laine, her gun-slinging brother, was one element in the situation he could not estimate. Laine had not been mentioned in any of the discussions and he seemed always just beyond reach, just out of sight, yet definitely in the background as was the mysterious rider of the mouse-colored horse. That whole story seemed fantastic, but Kedrick did not think Sue was inclined to fall for tall stories.

The cañon of Salt Creek widened out and several branch cañons opened into it. They left the creek bed and rode closer together to the towering cliffs, now all of seven hundred feet above the trail. They were heading south, and Burwick, mopping his

sweating face from time to time with a dirty handkerchief, was no longer talking. Kedrick pushed
back his hat and rolled a smoke. He had never seen
Burwick so jittery before, and he was puzzled. Deliberately he had said nothing to any of the company about Gunter, although he had arranged with
some of the townspeople to have the body moved.
Tom was afraid it might precipitate the very trouble he was trying to end, and bring the fight into
open battle. Moreover, he was not at all sure of why
Gunter had been killed, or who had done it. That it
could be retaliation for Singer's death was an answer to be considered, but it might have been done
by either Keith or Burwick.

He drew up suddenly, for a horse had left recent
tracks coming in alone from the northwest. Burwick followed his eyes, studying the tracks. "I've
seen those tracks before," Tom Kedrick said. "Now
whose horse is that?"

"We better step it up," Burwick said impatiently.
"They'll be there before us."

They pushed on into the bright, still morning.
The sky overhead was a vast blue dome scattered
with fleecy puffballs of clouds, like bolts of cotton
on the surface of a lake of pure blue. The red cliffs
towered high on their left, and the valley on their
right swept away in a vast, gently rolling panorama.
Glancing off over this sagebrush-dotted valley,
Tom knew that lost in the blue haze, some seven or
eight miles away, was Malpais Arroyo and Sue
Laine. Was she there this morning? Or was she riding somewhere? She was strangely attractive, that
slim, dark-haired, dark-eyed girl with her lovely
skin, soft despite the desert sun and desert wind.

She had come to him, riding all that distance to bring him a warning of danger. Why? Was it simply that she feared for him? Was she in love with him? He dismissed that idea instantly, but continued to wonder. She was, despite her beauty, a hard, calculating girl, hating the country around, and wanting only to be free of it.

Heat waves danced out over the bottomland, and shadows gathered under the red wall. A dust devil lifted and danced weirdly across the desert, then lost itself among the thick antelope brush and the catclaw. Tom Kedrick mopped his brow and swung his horse farther east, the tall spire of Chimney Rock lifting in the distance, its heavier shouldered companion looming beside and beyond it.

"Look!" Burwick's voice held a note of triumph. "There they come!"

To the south, and still three or four miles off, they could see two riders heading toward Chimney Rock. At this distance they could not be distinguished, but their destination was obvious.

"Now that's fine!" Burwick beamed. "They'll be here right on time! Say . . ."—he glanced at his heavy gold watch—"tell you what. You'll be there a shade before them, so what say you wait for them while I have me a look at a ledge up in the cañon?"

In the shadow of the rock, Kedrick swung down. There was a small pool of water there. He let the Appaloosa drink and ground-hitched him deeper in the shade, near some grass. Then he walked back and, dropping to the ground, lit a smoke. He could see the two riders nearing now. One was on a fast-stepping chestnut, the other a dappled gray.

They rode up and swung down. The first man was Pete Slagle, the second a stranger who Kedrick had not seen before. "Where's McLennon?" he asked.

"He'll be along. He hadn't come in from the ranch, so I came on with Steelman here. He's a good man, an' anything he says goes with all of us. Bob'll be along later, though, if you have to have his word."

"Burwick came. He's over lookin' at a ledge he saw in the cañon over there."

The three men bunched and Steelman studied Kedrick. "Dai Reid tells me you're a good man, trustworthy, he says."

"I aim to be." He drew a last drag on his cigarette and lifted his head to snap it out into the sand. For an instant, he stood poised, his face blank, then realization hit him. "Look out!" he yelled. "Hit the dirt!"

His voice was drowned in a roar of guns and something smashed him in the body even as he fell, then something else slugged him atop the head and a vast wave of blackness folded over him, pushing him down, down, down, deeper and deeper into a swirling darkness that closed in tightly around his body, around his throat. And then there was nothing, nothing at all.

***

Alton Burwick smiled and threw down his cigar. Calmly he swung into the saddle and rode toward the four men who were riding from behind a low parapet of rocks near Chimney Rock. As he rode up, they were standing, rifles in hand, staring toward the cluster of bloody figures sprawled on the ground in the shade. "Got 'em!" Shaw said. His eyes were hard. "That cleans it up, an' good!"

Fessenden, Clauson, and Poinsett stared at the bodies, saying nothing. Lee Goff walked toward them from his vantage point where he had awaited anyone who might have had a chance to escape. He stooped over the three.

Slagle was literally riddled with bullets, his body smashed and bloody. Off to one side lay Steelman, half the top of his head blown off. Captain Kedrick lay sprawled deeper in the shadow, his head bloody, and a dark stain on his body.

"Want I should finish 'em off for sure?" Poinsett asked.

"Finish what off?" Clauson sneered. "Look at 'em . . . shot to doll rags."

"What about Kedrick?" Fessenden asked. "He dead for sure?"

"Deader'n Columbus," Goff said.

"Hey!" Shaw interrupted. "This ain't McLennon! This here's that Joe Steelman!"

They gathered around. "Sure is!" Burwick swore viciously. "Now we're in trouble! If we don't get McLennon, we're . . . ." His voice trailed away as he looked up at Dornie Shaw. The soft brown eyes were bright and boyish.

"Why, boss," he said softly, dropping his cigarette and rubbing it out with his toe, "I reckon that's where I come in. Leave McLennon to me. I'll hunt him down before sun sets tomorrow."

"Want company?" Poinsett asked.

"Don't need it," Shaw said, "but come along. I

hear this Bob McLennon used to be a frontier marshal. I never liked marshals no way."

They drifted to their horses, then moved slowly away. Dornie Shaw, Poinsett, and Goff toward the west and Bob McLennon. Alton Burwick, his eyes thoughtful, rode toward the east and Mustang and the others rode with him. Only Fessenden turned nervously and looked back. "We should have made sure they were dead."

"Ride back if you want," Clauson said. "They are dead all right. That Kedrick! I had no use for him. I aimed my shot right for his smart skull."

***

Afternoon drew on. The sun lowered, and after the sun came coolness. Somewhere a coyote lifted his howl of anguish to the wide, white moon and the desert lay still and quiet beneath the sky.

In the deeper shadow of towering Chimney Rock and its bulkier neighbor there was no movement. A coyote moved nearer, scented the blood, but with it there was the dreaded man smell. He whined anxiously and drew back, then trotted slowly off, turning only once to look back. The Appaloosa, still ground-hitched, walked along the grass toward the pool, then stopped, nostrils wide at the smell of blood.

Well down behind some rocks and brush, the shooting had only made it lift its head, then return to cropping the thick, green grass that grew in the tiny, subirrigated area around Chimney Rock. Nothing more moved. The coolness of the night stiffened the bodies of the men who lay sprawled there.

Ten miles north Laredo Shad, late for his meeting with Kedrick, limped along the trail, leading a badly lamed horse. Two hours before, the trail along an arroyo bank had given way, and the horse had fallen. The leg was not broken, but was badly injured. Shad swore bitterly and walked on, debating as he had for the past two hours on the advisability of camping for the night. But remembering that Kedrick would be expecting him, he pushed on.

An hour later, still plodding and on blistered feet, he heard horse's hoofs and drew up, slipping his rifle into his hands. Then the rider materialized from the night, and he drew up, also. For a long minute no word was said, then Shad spoke. "Name yourself, pardner."

The other rider also held a gun. "Bob McLennon," he said. "Who are you?"

"Laredo Shad. My horse lamed himself. I'm headed for Chimney Rock. S'posed to meet Kedrick there." He stared at the rider. "Thought you was to be at the meetin'? What happened?"

"I didn't make it. Steelman an' Slagle went. I'm ridin' up here because they never come in."

"What?" Shad's exclamation was sharp. "McLennon, I was right afeared o' that. My bet is there's been dirty work. Nevah trusted that there Burwick, not no way."

McLennon studied the Texan, liking the man, but hesitant. "What's your brand read, Laredo? You a company man?"

Shad shook his head. "Well, now, it's like this. I come in here, drawin' warrior pay to do some gun slingin', but I'm a right uppity sort of a gent about some things. This here didn't size up right to me, nor to Kedrick, so we been figurin' on gettin' shut of the company. Kedrick only stayed on, hopin' he could make peace. I stayed along with him."

"Get up behind me," McLennon said. "My horse will carry double an' it ain't far."

X

His eyes were open a long time before realization came, and he was lying in a clean, orderly place with which he was totally unfamiliar. For a long time he lay there, searching his memory for clues to tie all this together. He was Captain Tom Kedrick—he had gone west from New Orleans—he had taken on a job—then he remembered. There had been a meeting at Chimney Rock and Steelman had come in place of McLennon, and then he had thrown his cigarette away and had seen those men behind the rocks, seen the sunlight flashing on their rifle barrels actually. He had yelled, and then dropped, but not fast enough. He had been hit in the head, and he had been hit in the body at least once.

How long ago was that? He turned his head and found himself in a square, stone room. One side of the room was native rock, and part of another side. The rest had been built up from loose stones gathered and shaped to fit. Besides the wide bed on which he lay, there was a table and a chair. He turned slightly, and the bed creaked. The door opened, and he looked up into the eyes of Connie Duane!

"Connie?" He was surprised. "Where is this place? What's happened?"

"You've been unconscious for days," she told him, coming to the bedside. "You have had a bad concussion and you lost a lot of blood before Laredo and Bob McLennon found you."

"What about the others?"

"Both of them are dead, and by all rights you should have been."

"But where are we? What is this place?"

"It's a cliff dwelling, a lonely one, and very ancient. It is high up in the side of the mountain called Thieving Rock. McLennon knew where it was, and he knew that, if word got out that you were alive, they would be out to complete the job at once, so they brought you here, McLennon did, with Shad."

"Are they still here?"

"Shad is. He hunts and goes to Yellow Butte for supplies, but he has to be very careful because it begins to look like they are beginning to get suspicious."

"McLennon?"

"He's dead, Tom. Dornie Shaw killed him. He went to Mustang to find a doctor for you, and encountered Dornie on the street. Bob was very fast, you know, but Dornie is incredible! He killed Bob before he could get a shot off."

"How did you get here?"

"Bob McLennon and Shad had talked about it, and also that Uncle John had been killed, so they came to me, and I came out here right away. I knew a little about nursing, but not much. Laredo has been wonderful, Tom, he's a true friend."

Kedrick nodded. "Who did the shooting? I thought it was Poinsett."

"He was one of them. I heard them talking about it but was not sure until later. Poinsett was there, Goff, Fessenden, Clauson, and Shaw."

"Anything else happened?"

"Too much. They burned Yellow Butte's saloon and livery stable, and they have driven almost half the people off the land. Their surveyors are on the land now, checking the survey they made previously. A handful of the squatters have drawn back into the mountains somewhere, under Pit Laine and that friend of yours, Dai Reid. They are trying to make a stand there."

"What about Sue?"

She looked at him quickly. "You liked her, didn't you? Well, Sue has taken up with Keith. They are together all the time. He's a big man now. They've brought in some more gunmen, and the Mixus boys are still here. Right now Alton Burwick and Loren Keith have this country right under their thumbs. In fact, they even called an election."

"An election?"

"Yes, and they counted the ballots themselves. Keith was elected mayor, and Fessenden is sheriff. Burwick stayed out of it, of course, and Dornie Shaw wouldn't take the sheriff's job."

"Looks like they've got everything their own way, doesn't it?" he mused. "So they don't know I'm alive."

"No. Shad went back there and dug three graves. He buried the other two, and then filled in the third grave and put a marker over it with your name on it."

"Good!" Kedrick was satisfied. He looked up at the girl. "And how do you get out here and back without them becoming curious?"

She flushed slightly. "I haven't been back, Tom. I stayed here with you. There was no chance of going back and forth. I just left everything and came away."

"How long before I can be up?"

"Not long, if you rest. And you've talked enough now."

Kedrick turned over the whole situation in his mind. There could be no more than a few days before the sale of the land would come off, and, if there was one thing that mattered, it was that the company not be permitted to profit from their crookedness. As he lay there resting, a plan began to form in his mind, and the details supplied themselves one by one as he considered it.

His guns hung on a nail driven into the wall close to his hand. His duffel, which he had brought away from the St. James, lay in the corner. It was almost dark before he completed his planning, and, when Laredo came in, he was ready for him.

"Cimarron?" Shad shook his head. "Bloomfield would be nearer. How's that?"

"Good!" Kedrick agreed. "Make it fast."

"That ain't worryin' me," Laredo said, rolling his tobacco in his jaws. "They've been mighty suspicious lately. Suppose they trail this place down while I'm gone?"

"We'll have to chance that. Here's the message. Hurry it up!"

***

The sun was bright in the room when Connie came through the door with his breakfast. She turned, and her face went white. "Oh, you're up!"

He grinned shakily. "That's right. I've laid abed long enough. How long has it been?"

"Almost two weeks," she told him, "but you mustn't stand up. Sit down and rest."

There was a place by a window where he had a good view of the trail below. At his request Connie brought the Winchester to him, and her own rifle. He cleaned them both, oiled them carefully, and placed them beside his window. Then he checked his guns and returned them to their holsters, digging the two Walch Navy pistols from his duffel and checking them, also.

Thoughtfully he considered. It was late to do anything now, but it was a wonder he had not thought of Ransome before. No more able legislator existed in Washington than Frederic Ransome, and the two had been brother officers in the War Between the States as well as friends in France during the Franco-Prussian War when Ransome had been there as an observer. If anybody could block the sale to the company, he could, even on such short notice. His telegram would be followed by a letter supplying all the details, and with that to go on Ransome might get something done. He was a popular and able young senator with good connections and an affable manner. Moreover, he was an excellent strategist. It would make all the difference in this situation.

The cliff-dwelling was built well back from the

face of the cliff, and evidently constructed with an eye toward concealment as well as defense. They had called this, Connie told him, Thieving Rock long before the white man appeared, and the Indians who lived here had been notorious thieves. There was a spring, so water was not a worry, and there were supplies enough for immediate purposes.

Two days dragged slowly by, and on the morning of the third Kedrick was resuming his station by the window when he saw a rider coming into the narrow cañon below. The man was moving slowly and studying the ground as he came, although from time to time he paused and searched the area with careful eyes. Kedrick pushed himself up from his chair and, taking the Winchester, worked his way along the wall to the next room.

"Connie," he called softly. There was no reply, and after a minute he called a second time. Still no answer.

Worried now, he remembered she had said something about going down below to gather some squaw cabbage to add greens to their diet.

Back at the window, he studied the terrain carefully, and then his heart gave a leap, for Connie Duane was gathering squaw cabbage from a niche in the cañon wall, not fifty yards from the unknown rider!

Lifting his rifle, Kedrick checked the range. It was all of four hundred yards and a downhill shot. Carefully he sighted on the rider, then relaxed. He was nearer the girl now, and a miss might ricochet and kill Connie, for the cañon wall would throw any bullet he fired back into the cañon itself and it might even ricochet several times in the close confines.

Yet, somehow, she had to be warned. If the rider saw her tracks, he would find both the girl and the hideout. Suddenly the ears of his horse came up sharply, and the rider stiffened warily and looked all around. Carefully Kedrick drew a bead on the man again. He hated to kill an unwarned man, but if necessary he would not hesitate.

Connie was standing straight now and appeared to be listening. Tense in every fiber, Tom Kedrick watched and waited. The two were now within fifty feet of each other, although each was concealed by a corner of rock and some desert growth including a tall cottonwood and some cedars.

Still listening, both stood rigidly, and Kedrick touched his lips with the tip of his tongue. His eyes blurred with the strain, and he brushed his hand across them.

The rider was swinging to the ground now, and he had drawn a gun. Warily he stepped out from his ground-hitched horse. Shifting his eyes to Connie, Tom saw the girl wave, and, lifting his hand, he waved back, then lifted the rifle. She waved a vigorous negation with her arm, and he relaxed, waiting.

Now the man was studying tracks in the sandy bottom of the wash, and, as he knelt, his eyes riveted upon the ground, a new element entered the picture. A flicker of movement caught the tail of Kedrick's eye, and, turning his head, he saw Laredo Shad riding into the scene. He glanced swiftly at the window and waved his hand. Then he moved forward and swung to the ground.

From his vantage point Kedrick could hear

nothing, but he saw Laredo approach, making heavy going of it in the thick sand, and then, not a dozen yards from the man, he stopped. He must have spoken, for the strange rider stiffened as if shot, then slowly got to his feet. As he turned, Tom saw his face fully in the sunlight. It was Clauson!

What happened then was too fast for the eye to follow. Somebody must have spoken, but who did not matter. Clauson's gun was drawn, and he started to swing it up. Laredo Shad in a gunman's crouch flashed his right-hand gun. It sprang clear, froze for a long instant, and then just as Clauson fired, Shad fired—but a split second sooner!

Clauson staggered a step back, and Shad fired again. The outlaw went down slowly, and Laredo walked forward and stripped his gun belts from him, then from his horse he took his saddlebags, rifle, and ammunition. Gathering up the dead man, and, working with Connie's help, they tied him to the saddle, and then turned the horse loose with a slap on the hip.

Connie Duane's face was white when she came into the room. "You saw that?"

He nodded. "We didn't dare to let him go. If we had, we would all have been dead before noon tomorrow. Now"—he said with grim satisfaction—"they have something to think about!"

Shad grinned at him when he came in. "I didn't see that gun he had drawed," he said ruefully. "Had it layin' along his leg as he was crouched there. Might've got me."

He dropped the saddlebags. "Mite of grub," he said, "an' some shells. I reckon we can use 'em even though we have some. The message got off, an' so did the letter. Feller over to the telegraph office was askin' a powerful lot of questions. Seems like they've been hearin' about this scrap."

"Good! The more the better. We can stand it, but the company can't. Hear anything?"

"Uhn-huh. Somebody from outside the state is startin' a row about Gunter's death. I hear they have you marked for that. That is, the company is sayin' you did it."

Kedrick nodded. "They would try that. Well, in a couple of days I'll be out of here and then we'll see what can be done."

"You take some time," Shad said dubiously. "That passel o' thieves ain't goin' to find us. Although," he said suddenly, "I saw the tracks of that grulla day afore yestiddy, an' not far off."

The grulla again!

***

Two more days drifted by, and Tom Kedrick ventured down the trail and the ladders to the cañon below with Laredo and visited their horses concealed in a tiny glade not far away. The Appaloosa nickered and trotted toward him, and Kedrick grinned and scratched his chest. "How's it, boy? Ready to go places?"

"He's askin' for it," Shad said. He lighted a smoke and squinted his eyes at Kedrick. "What do you aim to do when you do move?"

"Ride around a little. I aim to see Pit Laine, an' then I'm goin' to start hunting up every mother's son that was in that dry-gulching. Especially," he added, "Dornie Shaw."

"He's bad," Laredo said quietly. "I nevah seen it, but you ask Connie. Shaw's chain lightnin'. She seen him kill Bob."

"So one of us dies," Kedrick said quietly. "I'd go willing enough to take him with me, an' a few others."

"That's it. He's a killer, but the old bull o' that woods is Alton Burwick, believe me, he is. Keith is just right-hand man for him, an' the fall guy if they need one. Burwick's the pizen-mean one."

***

With Connie they made their start three days later, and rode back trails beyond the rim to the hideout Laine had established. It was Dai Reid himself who stopped them, and his eyes lighted up when he saw Kedrick.

"Ah, Tom!" His broad face beamed. "Like my own son, you are. We'd heard you were kilt dead."

Pit Laine was standing by the fire, and around him on the ground were a dozen men, most of whom Kedrick recognized. They sat up slowly as the three walked into the open space, and Pit turned. It was the first time Kedrick had seen him, and he was surprised. He was scarcely taller than his sister, but wide in the shoulders and slim in the hips. When he turned, he faced them squarely, and his eyes were sharp and bitter. This was a killing man, Kedrick decided, as dangerous in his own way as that pocket-size devil, Dornie Shaw.

"I'm Kedrick," he said, "and this is Connie Duane. I believe you know Shad."

"We know all of you." Laine watched them, his eyes alert and curious.

Quietly and concisely, Kedrick explained, and ended by saying: "So there it is. I've asked this friend of mine to start an investigation into the whole mess, and to block the sale until the truth is clear. Once the sale is blocked and that investigation started, they won't be with us long. They could get away with this only if they could keep it covered up, and they had a fair chance of doing that."

"So we wait and let them run off?" Laine demanded.

"No." Tom Kedrick shook his head decidedly. "We ride into Mustang . . . all of us. They have the mayor and the sheriff, but public opinion is largely on our side. Furthermore," he said quietly, "we ride in the minute they get the news the sale is blocked. Once that news is around town, they will have no friends. The band wagon riders will get off, and fast."

"There'll be shootin'," one told-timer opined.

"Some," Kedrick admitted, "but, if I have my way, there'll be more of hanging. There's killers in that town, the bunch that dry-gulched Steelman and Slagle. The man who killed Bob McLennon is the man I want."

Pit Laine turned. "I want him."

"Sorry, Laine. He killed Bob, an' Bob was only in town to get a doc for me. You may," he added, "get your chance, anyway."

"I'd like a shot at him my ownself," Laredo said quietly, "but somethin' else bothers me. Who's this grulla rider? Is he one of you?"

"Gets around plenty," the old-timer said, "but nobody ever sees him. I reckon he knows this here country better'n any of us. He must've been aroun' here for a long time."

"What's he want?" Shad wondered. "That don't figure."

Kedrick shrugged. "I'd like to know." He turned to Dai. "It's good to see you. I was afraid you'd had trouble."

"Trouble?" Dai smiled his wide smile. "It's trouble, you say? All my life there's been trouble, and where man is, there will be trouble to the end of time, if not of one kind, then another. But I take my trouble as it comes, bye." He drew deeply on his short-stemmed pipe and glanced at the scar around Kedrick's skull. "Looks like you'd a bit of it yourself. If you'd a less hard skull, you'd now be dead."

"I'd not have given a plugged peso for him when I saw him," Laredo said dryly. "The three of them lyin' there, bloody an' shot up. We thought for sure they was all dead. This one, he'd a hole through him, low down an' mean, an' that head of his looked like it had been smashed until we moved him. He was lucky as well as thick-skulled."

***

Morning found Laredo and Kedrick once more in the saddle. Connie Duane had stayed behind with some of the squatters' women. Together the two men were pushing on toward Mustang, but taking their time, for they had no desire to be seen or approached by any of the company riders.

"There's nothing much we can do," Kedrick agreed, "but I want to know the lay of the land in town. It's mighty important to be able to figure just what will happen when the news hits the place. Right now, everything is right for them. Alton Burwick and Loren Keith are better off than they ever were. Just size it up. They came in here with the land partly held by squatters, with a good claim on the land. That land they managed to get surveyed and they put in their claim to the best of it, posted the notices, and waited them out. If somebody hadn't seen one of those notices and read it, the whole sale might have gone through and nobody the wiser. Somebody did see it, and trouble started. They had two mighty able men to contend with, Slagle and McLennon. Well, both of them are dead now. And Steelman, another possible leader, is dead, too. So far as they are aware, nobody knows anything about the deaths of those men or who caused them. I was the one man they had learned they couldn't depend on, and they think I'm dead. John Gunter brought money into the deal, and he's dead and out of the picture completely. A few days more and the sale goes through, the land becomes theirs, and there isn't any organized opposition now. Pit Laine and his group will be named as outlaws, and hunted as such, and, believe me, once the land sale goes through, Keith will be hunting them with a posse of killers."

"Yeah," Laredo drawled, "they sure got it sewed up, looks like. But you're forgettin' one thing. You're forgettin' the girl, Connie Duane."

"What about her?"

"Look," Shad said, speaking around his cigarette,

"she sloped out of town, right after McLennon was killed. They thought she had been talking to you before, and she told 'em off in the office, said she was gettin' her money out of it. All right, so suppose she asks for it, and they can't pay? Suppose," he added, "she begins to talk and tells what she knows, and they must figure it's plenty. She was Gunter's niece, and for all they knew he told her more than he did tell her."

"You mean they'll try to get hold of her?"

"What do you think? They'll try to get hold of her, or kill her."

Tom Kedrick's eyes narrowed. "She'll be safe with Laine," he said, but an element of doubt was in his voice. "That's a good crowd."

Shad shrugged. "Maybe. Don't forget that Singer was one of them, but he didn't hesitate to try to kill Sloan, or to point him out for Abe Mixus. He was bought off by the company, so maybe there are others."

***

At that very moment, in the office of the gray stone building, such a man sat opposite Alton Burwick, while Keith sat in a chair against the wall. The man's name was Hirst. His face was sallow, but determined. "I ain't lyin'!" he said flatly. "I rode all night to git here, slippin' out o' camp on the quiet. She rode in with that gunman, Laredo Shad, and this Kedrick hombre."

"Kedrick! Alive?" Keith sat forward, his face tense.

"Alive as you or me! Had him most of the hair

clipped on one side of his head, an' a bad scar there. He sort of favored his side, too. Oh, he'd been shot all right, but he's ridin' now, believe me!"

The renegade had saved the worse until last. He smiled grimly at Burwick. "I can use some money, Mister Burwick," he said, "an' there's more I could tell you."

Burwick stared at him, his eyes glassy hard, then reached into a drawer and threw two gold eagles on the desk. "All right! What can you tell me?"

"Kedrick sent a message to some hombre in Washington name of Ransome. He's to block the sale of the land until there's a complete investigation."

"What?"

Keith came to his feet, his face ashen. This was beyond his calculations. When the idea had first been brought to his attention, it had seemed a very simple, easy way to turn a fast profit. He had excellent connections in Washington through his military career, and with Burwick managing things on the other end and Gunter with the money, it seemed impossible to beat it. He was sure to net a handsome profit, clear his business with Gunter and Burwick, then return East and live quietly on the profits. That it was a crooked deal did not disturb him, but that his friends in the East might learn of it!

"Ransome!" His voice was shocked. "Of all people!"

Frederic Ransome had served with him in the war, and their mutual relationship had been something less than friendly. There had been that episode by the bridge. He flushed at the thought of it, but

Ransome knew, and Ransome would use it as a basis for judgment. Kedrick had no way of knowing just how fortunate his choice of Ransome had been.

"That does it!" He got to his feet. "Ransome will bust this wide open, and love it!"

He was frightened, and Burwick could see it. He sat there, his gross body filling the chair, wearing the same soiled shirt. His eyes followed Keith with irritation and contempt. Was Keith going bad on him now?

"Get back there," Burwick said to Hirst, "and keep me informed of the movements. Watch everything closely now, and don't miss a trick. You will be paid."

When Hirst had gone, Burwick turned to Keith and smiled with his fat lips. "So does it matter if they slow it up a little? Let them have their investigation. It will come too late."

"Too late?" Keith was incredulous. "With such witnesses against us as Kedrick, Shad, Connie, and the rest of them?"

"When the time comes," Burwick said quietly, "there will be no witnesses! Believe me, there won't be!"

XI

Keith turned on Burwick, puzzled by the sound of his voice. "What do you mean?" he asked.

Burwick chuckled and rolled his fat lips on his cigar. There was malice and some contempt in the look he gave Keith. How much better, he thought, had Kedrick not been so namby-pamby. He was twice the man Keith was, for all the latter's commanding presence.

"Why," he said, "if there's no witnesses, there'll be no case. What can these people in town tell them? What they suspect? Suspicions won't stand in a court of law, nor with that committee. By the time they get here, this country will be peaceful and quiet, believe me."

"What do you want to do?" Keith demanded.

"Do? What is there to do? Get rid of Kedrick, Laredo Shad, and that girl. Then you'll take a posse and clean out that rat's nest back of the rim. Then who will they talk to? Gunter might have weakened, but he's dead. With the rest of them out of it . . ."

"Not Connie?" Keith protested. "Not her! For heaven's sake, man!"

Burwick snorted and his lips twisted in an angry sneer as he heaved his bulk from the chair. "Yes, Connie!" he said. "Are you a complete fool, Keith? Or have you gone soft? That girl knows more than all of them. Suppose Gunter talked to her, and he most likely did? She'll know everything, everything, I tell you!"

He paced back across the room, measuring Keith. The fool! He was irritated and angry. The sort of men they made these days, a weak and sniveling crowd. Keith had played out his time. If he finished this job alive . . . well, Dornie didn't like Keith. Burwick chuckled suddenly. Dornie! Now there was a man! The way he had killed that Bob McLennon!

"Now get this. Get the boys together. Get Fessenden, Goff, Clauson, Poinsett, and the Mixus boys and send them out with Dornie. I want those three killed, you hear me? I want them dead before the week is out, and no bodies, understand?"

Keith touched his dry lips, his eyes haunted. He had bargained for nothing like this. It had all seemed such an easy profit, and only a few poverty-stricken squatters to prevent them from acquiring wealth in a matter of a few months. Everything had started off just as Burwick had suggested, everything had gone so well. Gunter had provided the money, and he had fronted for them in Washington. Uneasily now Keith realized that, if trouble was made over this, it would be he upon whom the blame would rest. Burwick somehow had been in the background in the East as much as he, Keith, had been kept in the background here. Yet it would be his guilt if anything went wrong. And with Ransome investigating everything had gone wrong.

He sighed deeply. Of course, Burwick was right. There was only one thing to do now. At least, Dornie and the others would not hesitate. Suddenly he remembered something.

"You mentioned Clauson. He's out of it, Burwick. Clauson came in last night tied to his horse. He had been dead for hours."

"What?" Burwick stopped his pacing and walked up to Keith. "You just remembered?" He held his face inches away from Keith's and glared. "Is anybody backtracking that horse? You blithering idiot! Clauson was dynamite with a gun, so if he's dead, shot, it has to be by one of three men, and you know it!"

Burwick's face was dark with passion and he wheeled and walked the length of the room, swearing in a low, violent voice that shocked Keith with its deep, underlying passion. When he turned again, Burwick's eyes were ugly with fury. "Can't you realize," he demanded hoarsely, "those men are dangerous? That every second they are alive we are in danger? You have seen Dornie in action. Well, believe me, I'd sooner have him after me than Kedrick. I know Kedrick! He's a former Army officer . . . that's what you're thinking all the time . . . an officer and a gentleman. But he's something more, do you hear? He's more. He's a gentleman . . . that's true enough, but the man's a fighter, he loves to fight! Under all the calmness and restraint there's a drive and power that Dornie Shaw could never equal. Dornie may be faster, and I think he is, but don't you forget for one instant that Kedrick won't be through until he's down, down and dead."

Loren Keith was shocked. In his year's association with Burwick he had never seen the man in a passion, and had never heard him speak with such obvious respect, and even—yes, even fear, of any man. What had Alton Burwick seen that he himself had not seen?

He stared at Burwick, puzzled and annoyed, but some of the man's feeling began to transmit itself to him, and he became distinctly uneasy. He bit his lips and watched Burwick pacing angrily.

"It's not only him, but it's Shad. That cool, thin-faced Texan. As for Laine . . ."—Burwick's eyes darkened—"he may be the worst of the lot. He thinks he has a personal stake in this."

"Personal?" Keith looked inquiringly at the older man. "What do you mean?"

Burwick dismissed the question with a gesture. "No matter. They must go, all of them, and right now." He turned and his eyes were cold. "Keith, you fronted us in Washington. If this thing goes wrong, you're the one who will pay. Now go out there and get busy. You've a little time, and you've the men. Get busy!"

When he had gone, Burwick dropped into his chair and stared blindly before him. It had gone too far to draw back even if he was so inclined, and he was not. The pity of it was that there had been no better men to be had than Keith and Gunter. Yet, everything could still go all right, for he would know how to meet any investigating committee, how to soft-pedal the trouble, turn it off into a mere cow-country quarrel of no moment and much exaggerated. The absence of any complaining witness would leave them helpless to proceed, and he could make it seem a mere teapot tempest. Keith was obviously afraid of Ransome. Well, he was not.

Burwick was still sitting there when the little cavalcade of horsemen streamed by, riding out of town on their blood trail. The number had been augmented, he noticed, by four new arrivals, all hard, desperate men. Even without Keith, they might do the job. He heaved himself to his feet and paced across the room, staring out the window. It went badly with him to see Connie Duane die, for he had plans for Connie—maybe. His eyes narrowed.

***

Out on the desert the wind stirred restlessly, and in the brassy sky above a lone buzzard circled as if aware of the creeping tension that was slowly gripping the country beneath it. Far to the north, toward Durango, a cattle buyer pulled his team to a halt and studied the sky. There was no hint of storm, yet he had felt uneasy ever since leaving town on his buying trip down to Yellow Butte and Mustang. There had been rumors of trouble down that way, but then there had been intermittent trouble there for some time, and he was not alarmed. Yet he was somehow uneasy, as though the very air carried a warning.

South of him, and below the rim, Laredo Shad and Kedrick turned aside from the Mustang trail and headed toward Yellow Butte. It was only a little way out of their line of travel, but both men wanted to see what had happened there. Yet, when they approached the town, aside from the blackened ruins of the destroyed buildings, everything seemed peaceful and still. Eight or ten families had moved back into the town and a few had never left. They looked up warily as the two riders drew near, then nodded a greeting.

They knew now that these two were siding with them against the company, but hardship and struggle had wearied them, and they watched the two enter the settlement without excitement. The saloon had opened its doors in the large roomy office of the livery stable, and they went there now. A couple of men leaned on the bar, and both turned as they entered, greeted them, and returned to their conversation.

It was growing cool outside and the warmth of the room felt good. Both men stepped to the bar, and Kedrick ordered and paid. Shad toyed with his drink. He seemed uneasy, and finally he turned to Tom. "I don't like it," he said, low-voiced, "somehow or other Burwick is goin' to know about Ransome, an' he'll be in a sweat to get Connie out of the way, an' you an' me with her."

Kedrick agreed, for his own mind had been reading sign along the same trail. The only way out for the company now was to face the committee, if Ransome managed one, with a plausible tale and an accomplished fact, and then let them make the most of it.

"Burwick's a snake," Shad commented. "He'll never quit wigglin' until the sun goes down for the last time. Not that one. He's in this deep, an' he ain't the man to lose without a fight."

Horses' hoofs sounded on the road outside, and,

when they turned, Pit Laine and Dai Reid were dismounting before the door. They walked in, and Laine looked at Kedrick, then moved on to the bar. Dai looked worried, but said nothing. After a minute, Laine turned suddenly and went outside. "What's the matter?" Kedrick asked.

"It be worry, bye, and some of it shame, an' all for that sister o' his. Who would think it o' her? To go over to the other side? He's that shy about it, you would scarce believe. When a man looks at him, he thinks it's his sister they are thinkin' on, and how she sold out to that traitor to mankind, that rascal, Keith."

Kedrick shrugged. "Ambition and money do strange things. She has the makings of a woman, too."

Laine opened the door. "Better come out," he said, "we've got trouble."

They crowded outside. Men were hurrying toward the houses, their faces grave. "What is it?" Kedrick asked quickly.

"Burt Williams signaled from the top of the butte. There's riders coming from Mustang, a bunch of them."

As they looked, the small dark figure of a man appeared on the edge of the mesa once more. This time they saw his arm wave, once—two—three times, and continue until he had waved it six times. When he had completed, he gestured to the southeast. Then he signaled four more times from the southwest.

"Ten riders," Laine spat. "Well, we've got more than that here, but they aren't as salty as that crowd."

Burt Williams, favoring his broken arm, knelt behind a clump of brush on top of Yellow Butte and studied the approaching horsemen through the glass. He knew all in this group by sight but not by favor. One by one he named them off to himself: "Keith, Dornie Shaw, Fessenden, an' Goff . . . Poinsett. No, that's not Poinsett. That's one of the Mixus boys. Yep, an' there's the other."

He swung his glass. The four riders, spaced well apart, were approaching at a steady pace. None of their faces was familiar. He stared at them a while, but finally placed only one of them, a badman from Durango who ran with Port Stockton and the Ketchum outfit. His name was Brokow.

Stirred, he searched the country all around the town for other movement, then turned back to the larger cavalcade of riders. Had he held on a certain high flat a minute longer he would have seen two unmounted men cross it at a stooping run and drop into the wide arroyo northeast of town. As it was, he had been studying the approaching group for several minutes before he realized the Poinsett was not among them. He was with neither group.

Worried, Williams squinted his eyes against the sun, wondering how he could apprise them of the danger down below, for the absence of Poinsett disturbed him. The man was without doubt one of the most vicious of the company killers, a bitter man, made malignant by some dark happening in his past, but filled now with a special sort of venom all his own. Williams would have worried even more had he seen Poinsett at that moment.

The attack had been planned carefully and with all of Keith's skill. He surmised who they would be looking for, and hoped their watcher would over-look the absence of Poinsett, for it was he who Keith wanted in the right position for Poinsett was un-questionably the best of the lot with a rifle. At that moment, not two hundred yards from town, Poin-sett and his companion, Alf Starrett, were hun-kered down in a cluster of brush and boulders at one side of the arroyo. Poinsett had his Spencer .56 and was settling into position for his first shot. Starrett, with a fifteen-shot Henry .44, was a half dozen yards away.

Poinsett pulled out a huge silver watch and con-sulted it. "At half after two, he says. All right, that's when he'll get it." With utmost composure he be-gan to roll a smoke, and Alf Starrett, a hard-faced and wizened little man, noticed that his fingers were steady as he sifted tobacco into the paper.

Bob McLennon had planned the defense of Yel-low Butte, if such a defense became necessary, and, while Bob had been something of a hand with a gun, he definitely had not been a soldier or even an Indian fighter. Moreover, they had not expected an all-out battle for the town. Whatever the reason, he had committed a fatal error, for that pile of boulders and brush offered almost perfect concealment while affording complete coverage of the town, its one street, and the back as well as front of most of the buildings.

Keith had been quick to see this on his earlier visits to the town, and had planned to have Poin-sett and Starrett approach the place some time be-fore the main force moved in. In this, owing to their own experience, they had been successful.

Poinsett finished his cigarette and took up his rifle,

then settled down to careful watching and checking of the time. He had his orders and they were explicit. He was to fire on the first target offered after half past two—and his first shot must kill.

Shad and Kedrick had returned to the saloon and Pit Laine was loitering in front. Dai had gone across the street. Laine was in a position out of sight of Poinsett, but the latter had glimpsed Dai. The Welshman, however, offered only a fleeting target and Poinsett did not consider firing. His chance came at once, however.

The door of one of the nearest shacks opened and a man came out. He wore a broad-brimmed gray hat, torn at the crown, and a large, checked shirt tucked into jeans supported by suspenders. He turned at the door and kissed his wife. Poinsett took careful aim with his .56, choosing as his target point the man's left suspender buckle. Taking a good, deep breath, he held it and squeezed off his shot.

The big bullet struck with a heavy thump. The man took a lurch sidewise, tried to straighten, then went down. His wife ran from the door, screaming. Up the street a door banged and two men ran into the street, staring. Starrett's first shot knocked the rifle from the hand of one, splintering the stock. Poinsett dropped his man, but the fellow began to drag himself, favoring one leg that even at this distance they could see covered with a dark blotch at the knee.

Poinsett was a man without mercy. Coolly and carefully he squeezed off his second shot. The man stiffened, jerked spasmodically, and lay still.

"Missed my man," Alf said, apologetically, "but I ruin his shootin' iron."

Poinsett spat, his eyes cold. "Could happen to anybody," he said philosophically, "but I figured you burnt him anyways."

Within the saloon Kedrick had a glass half to his mouth when the shot boomed, followed almost at once by two more, their reports sounding almost as one.

"Blazes!" Shad whirled. "They ain't here yet?"

"They've been here," Kedrick said with quick realization. He swung to the door, glancing up the street. He saw the body of the last man to fall and, leaning out a bit, glimpsed the other. His lips tightened, for neither man was moving.

"Somebody is up the draw," he explained quickly. "He's got the street covered. Is there a back door?"

Kedrick dove for the door followed by the others as the bartender indicated the way, then caught up his shotgun. His pockets were already stuffed with shells. At the door Kedrick halted, then, flattened against the wall, stared up the draw. From here he could see the edge of the bunch of boulders and guessed the fire came from there. "Pinned down," he said. "They are up the draw."

Nobody moved. His memory for terrain served him to good purpose now. Recalling the draw, he remembered that it was below the level of the town beyond that point, but right there the boulders offered a perfect firing point.

Scattered shots came from down the draw, and nobody spoke. All knew that the three men down there could not long withstand the attack and would fall back on the town to be taken in the rear.

XII

Kedrick made up his mind quickly. Defense of the town was now impossible and they would be wiped out or burned alive if they attempted to remain here. "Shad," he said quickly, "get across the street to Dai and Pit. Yell out to the others and get them to fall back, regardless of risk, to the cañon at the foot of Yellow Butte."

He took a step back and glanced at the trap door to the roof. The bartender saw the intent and shook his head. "You can't do it, boy. They'd git you from down the crick."

"I'm going to chance it. I think they are still too far off. If I can give you folks covering fire, you may make it."

"What about you?" Shad demanded.

"I'll make it. Get moving!"

Laredo wheeled and darted to the door, paused an instant, and lunged across the street. The bartender hesitated, swore softly, then followed. Kedrick picked up a bottle of the liquor and shoved it into his shirt, then jumped for the edge of the trap door, caught it, and pulled himself through into the small attic. Carefully he studied the situation.

Hot firing came from downstream, and evidently the killers were momentarily stopped there. He hoisted himself through, swung to the ridge of the roof, and carefully studied the boulders. Suddenly he caught a movement, and knew that what he had first believed to be a gray rock was actually a shirt. He took careful aim with his Winchester, then fired.

The gray shirt jumped, and a hand flew up, then fell loose. Instantly a Spencer boomed and a bullet tore a chunk from the ridgepole near his face and splattered him with splinters. Kedrick moved downroof a bit, then, catching the signal from the window across the street, he deliberately shoved his rifle and head up and fired four fast shots, then two more.

Ducking his head, he reloaded the Winchester. Another bullet smashed the ridgepole and then a searching fire began, the heavy slugs tearing through the roof about three to four inches below the top.

Kedrick slid down the roof, hesitated at the edge of the trap door, and, seeing a distant figure circling to get behind the men in the wash, he took careful aim and squeezed off his shot. It was all of five hundred yards, and he had only a small bit of darkness at which to aim.

The shot kicked up sand short of the mark by a foot or more as nearly as he could judge, and he knew he had missed, but the would-be sniper lost his taste for his circling movement and slid out of sight. Kedrick went down the trap door and dropped again into the livery stable office.

Regretfully he glanced at the stock of whiskey, then picked up two more bottles and stuffed them into his pockets.

Hesitating only a second, he lunged across the way for the shelter of the livery stable. The Spencer boomed and he knew that the hidden marksmen had been awaiting this effort. He felt the shock of the bullet, staggered but kept going.

Reaching the livery stable, he felt the coldness of something on his stomach and glanced down. The bottle in his shirt had been broken by the bullet and he smelled to high heaven of good whiskey. Picking the glass out of his shirt, he located his horse's stall, led the Appaloosa out into the runway, and swung into the saddle.

The Spencer boomed again and again as he hit the road, riding hard, but he made it. The others cheered as he rode pell-mell through the cañon mouth and swung to the ground.

"This is no good," Laine said. "They can get behind us on the ridge."

Two men limped in from the draw, having withdrawn from boulder to boulder. Kedrick glanced around. There were fourteen men and women here who were on their feet. One man, he who had had the rifle knocked from his hand, had a shattered arm. The others were slightly wounded. Of them all, he had only seven men able to fight.

Quickly he gave directions for their retreat, then with Dai and Shad to hold the cañon mouth and cover them, they started back up the cañon.

Tom Kedrick measured his group thoughtfully. Of Laredo, Dai, and Laine, he had no doubts at all.

Of these others, he could not be sure. Good men, some of them, and one or two were obviously frightened. Nobody complained, however, and one of the men whose face was pale took a wounded man's rifle and gave him a shoulder on which to lean. He led them to the crevasse, and down into it.

Amazed, they stared around. "What d'you know?" the bartender spat. "Been here nigh seven year an' never knowed o' this place!"

There were four horses with the group, and they brought them all into the cave. One of the men complained, but Kedrick turned on him. "There's water, but we may be glad to eat horse meat." The man swallowed and stared.

Laine pointed at Kedrick's shirt. "Man, you're bleedin'!"

Kedrick grinned. "That isn't blood, it's whiskey! They busted one of the bottles I brought away!"

Pit chuckled. "I'd 'most as soon it was blood," he said, "seems a waste of good likker."

The seven able men gathered near the escape end of the crevasse, and one of them grinned at Kedrick. "I wondered how you got away so slick. Is there another way out down here?"

He shook his head. "If there is, I don't know it. I waited and got out through the cañon when it wasn't watched."

Laine's face was serious. "They could hold us here," he said anxiously. "We'd be stuck for sure."

Kedrick nodded. "I'm taking an extra canteen and some grub, then I'm going atop the butte to join Burt Williams. I'd like one man with me. From up there we can hold them off, I think."

"I'm your man," Laredo said quietly. "Wait'll I get my gear."

A rifle boomed, and then Dai Reid joined them. "They are comin' up," he said. He glanced at Kedrick. "One man dead in the boulders. I got the look of him by my glass. It was Alf Starrett. Poinsett was the other."

"Starrett was a skunk," Burnett, one of the settlers, said, "a low-down skunk. He kilt a man up Kansas way, an' a man disappeared from his outfit oncet that occasioned considerable doubt if he didn't git hisself another."

Kedrick turned to Pit Laine. "Looks like your show down here," he said. "Don't open fire until you have to, and don't fire even one shot unless it's needed. We'll be on top."

He led the way out of the crevasse and into the boulders and brush behind it. There was no sign of the attackers, and he surmised they were holed up, awaiting the arrival of some supporting fire from the rim back of the cañon.

Tom glanced up at the towering butte. It reared itself all of a hundred and fifty feet above him and most of it totally without cover. As they waited, a rifle boomed high above them and there was a puff of dust in the cañon mouth. Burt Williams had opened up.

Yet their first move toward the butte drew fire, and Laredo drew back. "No chance. We'll have to wait until dark. You reckon they'll hit us before then?"

"If they do, they won't get far." Tom Kedrick hunkered well down among the slabs of rock at the foot of the Butte. "We've got us a good firing point right here." He rolled a smoke and lit up. "What are you planning when this is over, Shad? Do you plan to stay here?"

The tall Texan shrugged. "Ain't pondered it much. Reckon that will take care of itself. What you aimin' to do?"

"You know the Mogollons southwest of here? I figured I'd go down there and lay out a ranch for myself." He smoked thoughtfully. "Down in east Texas, before I came west, a fellow arrived there named Ikard. Had some white-faced cattle with him, and you should see 'em! Why, they have more beef on one sorry critter than three longhorns. I figured a man could get himself a few Hereford bulls and start a herd. Might even buy fifty or sixty head for a beginning, and let 'em mix with the longhorns if they like."

"I might go for somethin' like that," Laredo said quietly. "I always wanted to own a ranch. Fact is, I started one once, but had to git shut of it." He studied the end of his cigarette. "That was in the Texas Panhandle, a ways south of Tascosa. Quite a ways. It was rough country. I mean rough to live in, not rough like this is. Why, you could stand on your front step down thataway an' see straight ahead for three days! Coyotes? Why, you should see 'em! They'd whup a grizzly, or near it, an' make these coyotes around here look like jack rabbits." He stared down the cañon toward the mouth, his rifle across his knees. He did not look at Kedrick, but he commented casually: "We need luck, Cap'n, plenty of luck."

"Uhn-huh"—Kedrick's face was sober—"right now we're bottled up, and, believe me, Burwick will stop at nothing. I wonder who was on watch up the cañon? Or supposed to be?"

"Somebody said his name was Hirst. Sallow-faced hombre."

"We'll have to talk to him. Was he down below?"

"Come to think of it, he wasn't. He must have hid out back there."

"Or sold out. Remember Singer? He wouldn't have been the only one."

Laredo rubbed out the last of his cigarette. "They'll be makin' their play soon. You know, Kedrick, I'd as soon make a break for it, get a couple of horses, an' head for Mustang. When we go, we might as well take Keith an' that dirty Burwick with us."

Kedrick nodded in agreement, but he wasn't thinking of the men below. There were at least four good men aside from Shad, Laine, and Dai Reid. That left the numbers not too unevenly balanced. The fighting skill and numbers were slightly on the enemy's side, as they had at least twelve men when the battle opened, and they had lost Starrett. That made the odds eleven to eight unless they had moved up extra men, which was highly probable. Still, they were expecting defense, not an attack.

He studied the situation. Suddenly a dark figure loomed on the rim of the cañon some hundred and fifty yards off, and much higher. He lifted his rifle and fired even as both Shad and Kedrick threw down on him with rifles, firing instantly. The man vanished, but whether hit or not they could not tell.

Desultory firing began, and from time to time they caught glimpses of men advancing from the cañon mouth, but never in sight long enough to offer a target, and usually rising from the ground some distance from where they dropped. The afternoon was drawing on, however, and the sun was setting almost in the faces of the attackers, which made their aim uncertain and their movements hesitant. Several times Shad or Kedrick dusted the oncoming party, but got in no good shots. Twice a rifle boomed from the top of the butte, and once they heard a man cry out as though hit.

"You know, Laredo," Kedrick said suddenly, "it goes against the grain to back up for those coyotes. I'm taking this grub up to Burt, an', when I come back, we're going to move down that cañon and see how much stomach they've got for a good scrap."

Shad grinned, his eyes flickering with humor. "That's ace high with me, podner," he said dryly. "I never was no hand for a hole, and the women are safe."

"All but one," Kedrick said, "that Missus Taggart who lives in that first house. Her husband got killed and she wouldn't leave."

"Yeah, heard one o' the womenfolks speak on it. That Taggart never had a chance. Good folks, those two."

***

Colonel Loren Keith stared gloomily at the towering mass of Yellow Butte. That man atop the butte had them pinned down. Now if they could just get up there. He thought of the men he had commanded in years past, and compared them with these outlaws. A pack of murderers. How had he got into this, anyway? Why couldn't a man know when he took a turning where it would lead him? It seemed so simple in the beginning to run off a bunch of one-gallused farmers and squatters.

Wealth—he had always wanted wealth, the money to pay his way in the circles where he wanted to travel, but somehow it had always eluded him, and this had seemed a wonderful chance. Bitterly he stared at the butte, and remembered the greasy edge of Burwick's shirt collar, and the malice in his eyes, Burwick who used men as he saw fit, and disposed of them when he was through.

In the beginning it hadn't seemed that way. His own commanding presence, his soldier's stride, his cold clarity of thought, all these left him despising Gunter as a mere businessman and Burwick as a conniving weakling. But then suddenly Burwick began to show his true self, and all ideas of controlling the whole show left Keith while he stared in shocked horror as the man unmasked. Alton Burwick was no dirty weakling, no mere ugly fat man, but a monster of evil, a man with a brain like a steel trap, stopping at nothing, and by his very depth of wickedness startling Keith into obedience.

Gunter had wanted to pull out. Only now would Keith admit even to himself the cause of Gunter's death, and he knew he would die as quickly. How many times had he not seen the malevolence in the eyes of Dornie Shaw, and well he knew how close Shaw stood to Burwick. In a sense, they were two of a kind.

His feeling of helplessness shocked and horrified Keith. He had always imagined himself a strong man, and had gone his way, domineering and supercilious. Now he saw himself as only a tool in the hands of a man he despised, yet unable to escape. Deep within him there was the hope that they still would pull their chestnuts out from the fire and take the enormous profit the deal promised.

One man stood large in his mind, one man drew all his anger, his hate and bitterness. That man was Tom Kedrick. From that first day Kedrick had made him seem a fool. Keith had endeavored to put Kedrick firmly in his place, speaking of his rank and his twelve years of service, and then Kedrick had calmly paraded such an array of military experience that few men could equal, and right before them all. He had not doubted Kedrick, for vaguely now he remembered some of the stories he had heard of the man. That the stories were true, and that Kedrick was a friend of Ransome's, infuriated him still more.

He stepped into the makeshift saloon and poured a drink, staring at it gloomily. Fessenden came in, Goff with him.

"We goin' to roust them out o' there, Colonel?" Goff asked. "It will be dark soon."

Keith tossed off his drink. "Yes, right away. Are the rest of them out there?"

"All but Poinsett. He'll be along."

Keith poured another stiff shot and tossed it off as quickly, then followed them into the street of Yellow Butte.

They were all gathered there but the Mixus boys who had followed along toward the cañon, and a couple of the newcomers who had circled to get on the cliff above and beyond the boulders and brush where the squatters had taken refuge. Poinsett was walking down the road in long strides. He was abreast of the first house when a woman stepped from the door. She was a square-built woman in a faded, blue cotton dress and man's shoes, run down at the heel. She held a double-barreled shotgun in her hands, and, as Poinsett drew abreast of her, she turned on him and fired both barrels, at point-blank range, and Poinsett took them right through the middle. Almost torn in two, he hit the ground, gasping once, his blood staining the gray gravel before their shocked eyes.

The woman turned on them, and they saw that she was no longer young. Her square face was red and a few strands of graying hair blew about her face. As she looked at them, her work-roughened hands still clutching the empty shotgun, she motioned at the fallen man in the faded, check shirt.

In that moment the fact that she was fat, growing old, and that her thick legs ended in the grotesque shoes seemed to vanish, and in the blue eyes were no tears, only her chin trembling a little as she said: "He was my man. Taggart never give me much, an' he never had it to give, but in his own way he loved me. You killed him . . . all of you. I wish I had more shells."

She turned her back on them and, without another glance, went into the house and closed the door behind her.

They stood in a grim half circle then, each man faced suddenly with the enormity of what they were doing and had done.

Lee Goff was the first to speak. He stood spraddle-legged, his thick, hard body bulging all his clothes, his blond hair bristling. "Anybody bothers that woman," he said, "I'll kill him."

XIII

Keith led his attack just before dusk and lost two men before they withdrew, but not before they learned of the hole. Dornie Shaw squatted behind the abutment formed by the end wall of the cañon where it opened on the plain near the arroyo. "That makes it easy," he said, "we still got dynamite."

Keith's head came up, and he saw Shaw staring at him, his eyes queerly alight.

"Or does that go against the grain, Colonel? About ten sticks of dynamite dropped into that crevasse an' Burwick will get what he wants . . . no bodies."

"If there's a cave back there," Keith objected, "they'd be buried alive!"

Nobody replied. Keith's eyes wandered around to the other men, but their eyes were on the ground; they were shunning responsibility for this, and only Shaw enjoyed it. Keith shuddered. What a fool he had been to get mixed up in this!

A horse's hoof struck stone, and as one man they looked up. Saddle leather creaked, although they could not see the horse. A spur jingled, and Alton Burwick stood among them.

Loren Keith straightened to his feet and briefly explained the situation. Burwick nodded from time to time, then added: "Use the dynamite. First thing in the morning. That should end it, once and for all." He drew a cigar from his pocket and bit off the end. "Had a wire. That committee is comin' out, all right. Take them a couple of weeks to get here, an' by that time folks should be over this an' talkin' about somethin' else. I'm figurin' a bonus for you all."

He turned back toward his horse, then stopped and, catching Dornie Shaw's eye, jerked his head.

Shaw got up from the fire and followed him, and Keith stared after them, his eyes bitter. Now what? Was he being left out of something else?

Beyond the edge of the firelight and beyond the reach of their ears, Burwick paused and let Shaw come up to him. "Nice work, Dornie," he said, "we make a pair, you an' me."

"Yeah." Dornie nodded. "An' sometimes I think a pair's enough."

"Well"—Burwick puffed on his cigar—"I need a good man to side me, an' Gunter's gone . . . at least."

"That company o' yours"—Dornie was almost whispering—"had too many partners, anyway."

"Uhn-huh," Burwick said quietly, "it still has."

"All right, then." Dornie hitched his guns into a firmer seating on his thighs. "I'll be in to see you in a couple of days at most."

Burwick turned and walked away, and Dornie saw him swing easily to the saddle, but it was all very indistinct in the darkness. He stayed where he was, watching the darkness and listening to the slow steps of the horse. They had a funny sound— a very funny sound. When he walked back to the campfire, he was whistling "Green Grow the Lilacs".

***

The attack came at daybreak and the company had mustered twenty men, of whom two carried packages of dynamite. This was to be the final blow, to wipe out the squatters, once and for all.

Shortly before the arrival of Burwick, Keith and Dornie Shaw with Fessenden accompanying them had made a careful reconnaissance of the cañon from the rim. What they found pleased them enormously. It was obvious, once the crevasse had been located, that not more than two men could fire from it at once, and there was plenty of cover from the scattered boulders. In fact, they could get within throwing distance without emerging in the open for more than a few seconds at a time. Much of the squatters' field of fire would be ruined by their proximity to the ground and the rising of the boulders before them.

The attack started well with all the men moving out, and they made twenty yards into the cañon, moving fast. Here, the great slabs fallen from the slope of Yellow Butte crowded them together. And there the attack stopped. It stopped abruptly, meeting a withering wall of rifle fire, at point-blank range!

Tom Kedrick knew a thing or two about fighting,

and he knew full well that his hideout would in the long run become a deathtrap. He put himself in Keith's place, and decided what that man would do. Then he had his eight men, carrying fourteen rifles, slip like Indians through the darkness to carefully selected firing positions far down the cañon from where Keith would be expecting them.

Five of the attackers died in that first burst of fire, and, as the gun hands broke for cover, two more went down, and one dragged himself to the camp of the previous night with a shattered kneecap. He found himself alone. The wife of Taggart had begun it—the mighty blast of rifle fire completed it. The company fighters got out of the cañon's mouth, and as one man they moved for their horses, Keith among them and glad to be going. Dornie Shaw watched him mount up, and swung up alongside him. Behind them, moving carefully as if they were perfectly disciplined troops, the defenders of the cañon moved down, firing as they came. A horse dropped, and a man crawled into the rocks, then jumped up and ran. Dai Reid swung wide of the group and started after him.

Another went down before they got away, and Kedrick turned to his group. "Get your horses, men. The women will be all right. This is a job that needs finishing now."

A quarter of a mile away, Brokow spotted a horse, standing alone, and started for it. As he arose from the rocks, a voice called out from behind: "A minute!"

Brokaw turned. It was only one man approaching him, the Welshman, Dai Reid. He stared at the man's Spencer, remembering his own gun was empty. He backed up slowly, his eyes haunted. "My rifle's empty," he said, "an' I've lost my Colt."

"Drop the rifle, then," Dai said quietly. "This I've been wanting, for guns be not my way."

Brokow did not understand, but he dropped his rifle. He was a big man, hulking and considered powerful. He watched in amazement as Reid placed his Spencer carefully on the ground, and then his gun belt. With bowlegged strides, the shorter man started for Brokow.

The outlaw stared, then started forward to meet Dai. As they drew near, he swung. His rock-like fist smashed Dai Reid flush on the chin, and Reid blinked only, then lunged. Twice more Brokow swung, blows filled with smashing panic born of the lack of effect of that first punch. Dai seemed unable to avoid them, and both connected solidly, and then his huge, big-knuckled hand grasped Brokow's arm and jerked him near. The hand slipped to the back of his head and jerked Brokow's face down to meet the rising of the Welshman's head. Stars burst before Brokow's eyes, and he felt the bone go in his nose. He swung wildly, and then those big hands gripped his throat and squeezed till Brokow was dead. Then Dai Reid dropped the outlaw to the sand, and, turning, he walked away. He did not notice the horse that stood waiting. It was a grulla.

In the headlong flight that followed the débâcle in the cañon's mouth, only Lee Goff had purpose. The hard-bitten Montana gunman had stared reality in the face when Taggart's wife turned on him. It was only coincidence that she so resembled his own mother, long since dead of overwork in rearing seven boys and five girls on a bleak Montana ranch. He headed directly for Yellow Butte and the Taggart home. He did not dismount, only he stopped by the door and knocked gently. It opened, and he faced Mrs. Taggart, her eyes red now, from weeping. "Ma'am,' he said, "I guess I ain't much account, but this here's been too much. I'm driftin'. Will you take this here . . . as a favor to me?"

He shoved a thick roll of bills at her, his face flushing deep red. For an instant, she hesitated, and then she accepted the money with dignity. "Thanks, son. You're a good boy."

There's an old Mormon Trail across northern New Mexico into Colorado and Utah. Lee Goff's bald-faced sorrel stirred the dust on that road all the way across two states before its rider began to look the country over.

Behind him, had he known, Tom Kedrick was riding to Mustang. With him were Laredo Shad, Pit Laine, Dai Reid, Burt Williams, and the others. They made a tight, grim-faced little cavalcade, and they rode with their rifles across their saddle forks.

Due west of them, had they only known, another little drama was taking place, for the riders they followed were not all the riders who had abandoned the fight in the cañon. Two of them, Dornie Shaw and Colonel Loren Keith, had headed due west on their own. Both men had their own thoughts and their own ideas of what to do, and among other things Keith had decided that he had had enough. Whether the others knew it or not, they were through, and he was getting out of the country.

There was some money back there in Mustang, and, once he had that, he was going to mount up and head for California. Then let Ransome investigate. After a few years he would return to the East, and, if the subject ever came up, he would swear he had nothing to do with it, that he only represented them legally in the first steps of the venture.

What Dornie Shaw was thinking nobody ever guessed, and at this moment he had no thought at all in his mind. For his mind was not overly given to thought. He liked a few things, although he rarely drank, and seemed never to eat much. He liked a good horse and a woman with about the same degree of affection, and he had liked Sue Laine a good bit, but the woman who really fascinated him was Connie Duane, who never seemed aware that he was even alive. Most of all he liked a gun. When cornered or braced into a fight, he killed as naturally and simply as most men eat. He was a creature of destruction, pure and simple. Never in his life had he been faced with a man who made him doubt his skill, and never fought with anything but guns—and he vowed he never would.

The two rode rapidly and both were mounted well, so by the time Kedrick was leaving Yellow Butte and lining out for town, they reached the bank to Salt Creek Wash. Here Keith swung down to tighten his saddle cinch while his horse was drinking. After a moment, Dornie got down, too.

Absently Keith asked: "Well, Dornie, this breaks it, so where do you think you'll go now?"

"Why, Colonel," Shaw said softly, in his gentle boy's voice, "I don't know exactly where I'm goin', but this here's as far as you go."

It took a minute for the remark to sink in, and then Keith turned, his puzzled expression stiffening into blank horror, then fear. Dornie Shaw stood negligently watching him, his lips smiling a little, his eyes opaque and empty. The realization left Loren Keith icy cold. Dornie Shaw was going to kill him. He had been an utter fool ever to allow this to happen. Why had he left the others and come off with Shaw? Why hadn't he killed him long since, from behind if need be, for the man was like a mad dog. He was insane, completely insane.

"What's on your mind, Shaw?" Without realizing it, he spoke as he might to a subordinate. Shaw was not conscious of the tone. He was looking at Keith's belt line. The colonel, he reflected, had been taking on a little weight here lately. "Why, just what I say. You've come as far as your trail takes you, Colonel. I can't say I'm sorry."

"Burwick won't like this. We're two of the men on whom he relies."

"Uhn-huh, that's the way it was. It ain't now. Back yonder"—he jerked his head toward the butte—"he sort of implied he'd got hisself one too many partners." He shoved his hat back a little. "You want to try for your gun? It won't help you none, but you can try."

Keith was frightened. Every muscle within him seemed to have tightened until he could not move, yet he knew he was going to. But at the last, he had something to say, and it came from some deep inner conviction: "Kedrick will kill you, Dornie. He's going to win. He'll kill Burwick, too."

Suddenly he remembered something; it had been only a fleeting expression on Dornie Shaw's face, but, something. "Dornie?" he shot the word out with the force of desperation. "There behind you! The grulla!"

Shaw whirled, his face white, an almost animal-like fury on it. As he turned, Keith gasped hoarsely and triumphantly, and his gun swung up, but he had never coped with a fighter like Shaw. In the flashing instant that he whirled and found nothing behind him, Dornie hurled himself backward. The shot split wide the air where he had stood an instant before, and then Dornie himself fired from the ground. Fired once, then a second time.

Keith caught the bullet through the midsection, right where that extra weight had been gathering, and took the second one in the same place. He fell, half in the trickle of water that comprised Salt Creek. Feeding shells into his gun, Dornie Shaw stared down at the glazing eyes. "How did you know?" he asked sullenly. "How did you know?"

XIV

Fessenden rode well forward in the saddle, his
great bulk carried easily with the movement of
the horse. His wide face was somber with
thought and distaste. Like the others, the wife of
Taggart had affected him as nothing else could
have. He was a hard man who had done more than
his share of killing, but he had killed men ruth-
lessly, thoughtlessly, men in mortal combat where
he himself might die as easily. Several times before
he had hired his gun, but each time in cattle or
sheep wars or struggles with equals, men as gun-
wise as he himself. Never before had he actually
joined in a move to rob men of their homes. Without conscience in the usual sense, he had it in this
case, for the men who moved West, regardless of
their brand, were largely men in search of homes.
Before, he had thought little of their fight. Several
times he had helped to drive nesters from cattle
range, and to him that was just and logical, for cows
needed grass and people lived on beef, and most of
the range country wasn't suited to farming, anyway. But in this case there was a difference, he now

realized, thinking of it for the first time. In this case men were not being driven off for cattle, but only for profit. To many, the line was a fine one to draw; to Fessenden and his like, once the matter was seen in its true light, that line became a gap, an enormous one.

Actually he rode in a state of shock. The victory Keith had wanted seemed so near. The taking of the few left in the cañon had seemed simple. His qualms against the use of dynamite he had shrugged off, if uncomfortably. Yet he had gone into the cañon with the others to get the thing over with, to get his money, and get out. And then, long before they expected it, came that smashing, thunderous volley, made more crashing by the close cañon walls, more destructive by the way the attackers were channeled by the boulders.

Shock started the panic, and distaste for the whole affair kept some of them, at least, on the move. Yet it was hard to believe that Clauson and Poinsett were dead, that Brokow had vanished, that Lee Goff was gone. For alone of the group, Goff had told Fessenden he was leaving. He had not needed to tell him why.

Behind him rode the Mixus boys, somber with disappointment at the failure of the attack. They had no qualms about killing, and no lines to draw even at the killing of women. They were in no true sense fighting men; they were butchers. Yet even they realized the change that had come over the group. What had become of Brokow or Goff they did not know, only that disintegration had set in, and these men had turned into a snarling pack of wolves, venting their fury and their hatred on each other.

Mustang was quiet when they rode into town. It was the quiet before the storm, and the town, like that cattle buyer who had turned back to Durango, sensed the coming fury of battle. No women were on the street, and only a few hardy souls loitered at the bars or card tables. The chairs before the St. James were deserted, and Clay Allison had ridden back to his home ranch, drunk and ugly.

An almost Sunday peace lay over the town when Fessenden drew up before the Mustang Saloon and swung down from his weary horse. Slapping his hat against his leg to beat off the dust, Fessenden stood like a great, shaggy bull and surveyed the quiet of the street. He was too knowing a Western man not to recognize the symptoms of disaster. Clapping his hat all awry upon his shaggy head, he shoved his bulk through the doors and moved to the bar.

"Rye," he said, his voice booming in the cavernous interior. His eyes glinted around the room, then back to the bartender.

That worthy could no longer restrain his curiosity. "What's happened?" he asked, swallowing.

A glint of irony came into the hard eyes of the gunman. "Them squatters squatted there for keeps," he said wryly, "an' they showed us they aim to stay put." He tossed off his drink. "All hell busted loose." Briefly he explained. "You'd 'a' figured there was a thousand men in that neck of the rocks when they opened up. The thing that did it was the unexpectedness of it, like steppin' on a step in the dark when it ain't there." He poured another drink. "It was that Kedrick," he said grimly. "When I seen him shift to the other side, I should've lit a shuck."

"What about Keith?"

"He won't be back."

They turned at the new voice, and saw Dornie Shaw standing in the doorway, smiling. Still smiling, he walked in and leaned against the bar. "Keith won't be back," he said. "He went for his gun out on Salt Creek."

The news fell into a silent room. A man at a table shifted his feet and a chair creaked. Fessenden wet his lips and downed his second drink. He was getting out of town, but fast.

"Seen that girl come in, short time back," the bartender said suddenly, "that Duane girl. Thought she'd gone over to the other side."

Dornie's head lifted and his eyes brightened, then shadowed. He downed his own drink and walked jauntily to the door. "Stick around, Fess. I'll be back." He grinned. "I'll collect for both of us from the old man."

The bartender looked at Fessenden. "Reckon he'll bring it if he does?"

The big gunman nodded absently. "Sure! He's no thief! Why, that kid never stole a thing in his life. He doesn't believe in it. An' he won't lie or swear . . . but he'll shoot the heart out of you an' smile right in your face while he's doing it."

The show had folded. The roundup was over. There was nothing to do now but light out. Fessenden knew he should go, but a queer apathy had settled over him, and he ordered another drink, letting the bartender pour it. The liquor he drank seemed now to fall into a cavern without bottom, having no effect.

***

On the outskirts of town, Tom Kedrick reined in. "We'll keep together," he said quietly. "We want Keith, Shaw, Burwick, the Mixus boys, and Fessenden. There are about four others that you will know that I don't know by name. Let's work fast and make no mistakes. Pit, you take Dai and two men and go up the left side of the street, take no chances. Arrest them if you can, we'll try them, and"—his face was grim—"if we find them guilty, they'll have just two sentences . . . leave the country or hang. The Mixus boys and Shaw," he said, "will hang. They've done murder."

He turned in his saddle and glanced at the tall Texan. "Come on, Shad," he said, "we'll take two men and the right side of the street, which means the livery stable, the Saint James, and the Mustang." Kedrick glanced over at Laine. "Pit," he said, "if you run into Allison or Ketchum, better leave 'em alone. We don't want 'em"

Laine's face was grave. "I ain't huntin' 'em," he said grimly, "but if they want it, they can have it."

The parties rode into town and swung down on their respective sides of the street. Laredo grinned at Kedrick, but his eyes were sober. "Nobody wants to cross Laine today," he said quietly. "The man's in a killin' mood. It's his sister."

"Wonder what will happen when they meet?"

"I hope they don't," Shad said. "She's a right pretty sort of gal, only money crazy."

The two men with them stood hesitantly, waiting for orders. Both were farmers. One carried a

Spencer .56, the other a shotgun. Shad glanced at them. "Let these hombres cover the street, Tom," he suggested. "You take the Saint James, an' I'll take the stable."

Kedrick hesitated. "All right," he agreed finally. "But take no chances, boy."

Laredo grinned and waved a negligent hand and walked through the wide door of the stable. Inside, he paused, cold and seemingly careless, actually as poised and deadly as a coiled rattler. He had already seen Abe Mixus's sorrel pony and guessed the two dry-gulchers were in town. He walked on a step and saw the barrel of a rifle push through the hay.

He lunged right and dove into a stall, drawing his gun as he went, and ran full tilt into the other Mixus! Their bodies smashed together, and Mixus, caught off balance, went down and rolled over. He came up, clawing for a gun. Laredo kicked the gun from under his hand and sent it spinning into the wide-open space between the rows of stalls.

With a kind of whining cry, Bean Mixus sprang after it, slid to his knees, and got up, turning. Laredo Shad stood, tall and dark, just within the stall, and, as Mixus turned like a rat cornered and swung his gun around, Laredo fired, his two shots slamming loudly in the stillness of the huge barn. Bean Mixus fell dead.

The rifle bellowed and a shot ripped the stall stanchion near Laredo's head. He lunged into the open, firing twice more at the stack of straw. The rifle jerked, then thundered again, but the shot went wild. Laredo dove under the loft where Abe Mixus was concealed, and fired two more shots through the roof over his head where he guessed the killer would be lying.

Switching his guns, he holstered the empty one and waited. The roof creaked some distance away, and he began to stalk the escaping Mixus, slipping from stall to stall. Suddenly a back door creaked and a broad path of light shot into the darkness of the stable. Laredo lunged to follow—too late.

The farmer outside with the shotgun was the man Sloan. As Abe Mixus lunged through the door to escape, they came face to face, at no more than twenty feet of distance. Abe had his rifle at his hip, and he fired. The shot ripped through the water trough beside Sloan, and the farmer squeezed off the left-hand barrel of his shotgun. The solid core of shot hit Mixus in the shoulder and neck, knocking him back against the side of the door, his neck and shoulder a mass of blood that seemed to well from a huge wound. He thought to get his gun up, but Sloan stepped around, remembering Bob McLennon's death and the deaths of Steelman and Slagle. The other barrel thundered and a sharp blast of flame stabbed at Abe Mixus. Smashed and dead, the killer sagged against the doorjamb, his old hat falling free, his face pillowed in the gray, blood-mixed dust.

Silence hung heavily in the wake of the shots. Into that silence Laredo Shad spoke. "Hold it, Sloan!" He stepped through the door, taking no glance at the fallen man. "The other one won't hang, either," he said. "They were both inside."

The two men drew aside, Sloan's face gray and sick. He had never killed a man before, and wanted never to again. He tried to roll a smoke, but his fingers trembled. Shad took the paper and tobacco from him and rolled it. The farmer looked up shamefacedly. "Guess I'm yaller," he said. "That sort of got me."

The Texan looked at him gloomily. "Let's hope it always does," he said. He handed him the cigarette. "Try this," he told him. "It will make you feel better. Wonder how Kedrick's comin'?"

"Ain't heard nothin'!"

Pit Laine stood in a door across the street. "Everythin' all right?" he called.

"Yeah," the other farmer called back, "on'y you don't hafta look for the Mixus boys no more! They ain't gonna be around."

***

Captain Tom Kedrick had walked up the street and turned into the door of the St. James Hotel. The wide lobby was still, a hollow shell smelling faintly of old tobacco fumes and leather. The wrinkled clerk looked up and shook his head. "Quiet today," he said. "Nobody around. Ain't been no shootin' in days."

Guns thundered from down the street, then again and again, then silence, and the two solid blasts of the shotgun. Both men listened, and no further sound came. A moment later Pit Laine called out and the farmer answered. The clerk nodded. "Same town," he said. "Last couple of days I been wonderin' if I wasn't back in Ohio. Awful quiet lately," he said, "awful quiet."

Tom Kedrick walked down the hall and out the back door. He went down the weathered steps and stopped on the grass behind the building. There was an old, rusty pump there, and the sun was hot on the backs of the buildings. He walked over to the pump and worked the handle. It protested, whining and groaning at the unaccustomed work, and finally, despairing of rest, threw up a thick core of water that splashed in the wooden tub. When he had pumped for several minutes, Kedrick held the gourd dipper under the pump and let it fill. The water was clear and very cold. He drank greedily, rested, then drank again.

Far up the backs of the buildings at the opposite end of town, a man was swinging an axe. Kedrick could see the flash of light on the blade, and see the axe strike home, and a moment later the sound would come to him. He watched, then wiped the back of his hand across his mouth, and started along in back of the buildings toward the Mustang.

He moved with extreme care, going steadily, yet with every sense alert. He wore his .44 Russians and liked the feel of them, ready in his hands. The back door of the Mustang was long unpainted and blistered by many hot suns. He glanced at the hinges and saw they were rusty. The door would squeak. Then he saw the outside stair leading to the second floor, and, turning, he mounted the stairs on tiptoe, easing through that door, and walking down the hall.

In the saloon below, Fessenden had eliminated half a bottle of whiskey without destroying the deadening sense of futility that had come over him. He picked up a stack of cards and riffled them skillfully through his fingers, and there was no lack of deftness there. Whatever effect the whiskey had had, it was not on his hands. Irritated, he slammed the cards down and stared at the bartender. "Wish Dornie'd get back," he said for the tenth time. "I want to leave this town. She don't feel right today."

He had heard the shots down the street, but had not moved from the bar. "Some drunk cowhand," he said irritably.

"You better look" the bartender suggested, hoping for no fights in the saloon. "It might be some of your outfit."

"I got no outfit," Fess replied shortly. "I'm fed up. That stunt out there to Yeller Butte drove me off that range. I'll have no more of it."

He heard the footsteps coming down the hall from upstairs and listened to their even cadence. He glanced up, grinning. "Sounds like an Army man. Listen!"

Realization of what he had said came over him, and the grin left his face. He straightened, resting his palms on the bar. For a long moment, he stared into the bartender's eyes. "I knew it! I knew that hombre would . . . ." He tossed off his drink. "Aw, I didn't want to leave town, anyway!"

He turned, moving back from the bar. He stood, spraddle-legged, like a huge grizzly, his big hands swinging at his hips, his eyes glinting upward at the balcony and the hall that gave onto it. The steps ceased, and Tom Kedrick stood there, staring down at him.

Neither man spoke for a full minute, while suspense gripped the watchers, and then it was Fessenden who broke the silence. "You lookin' for me, Kedrick?"

"For any of your crowd. Where's Shaw? And Keith?"

"Keith's dead. Shaw killed him back up on the Salt after you whipped us in the cañon. I dunno where he is now."

Silence fell once more and the two men studied each other. "You were among them at Chimney Rock, Fessenden," Kedrick said. "That was an ambush . . . dry-gulcher's stunt, Fess." Kedrick took another step forward, then side-stepped down the first step of the stairs which ran along the back wall until about six steps from the bottom, then, after crossing the landing, came down facing the room.

Fessenden stood there, swaying slightly on his thick, muscular legs, his brutal jaw and head thrust forward. "Aw, hell!" he said, and grabbed iron.

His guns fairly leaped from their holsters, spouting flame. A bullet smashed the top of the newel post at the head of the stairs, then ricocheted into the wall; another punctured a hole just behind Kedrick's shoulder. Tom Kedrick stepped down another step, then fired. His bullet turned Fessenden, and Kedrick ran lightly down four steps while Fessenden smashed two shots at him.

Kedrick dove headlong for the landing, brought up hard against the wall, and smashed another shot at the big man. It knocked a leg from under him, and he rolled over on his feet, colliding with the bar.

He had been hit twice, but he was cold sober and deadly. He braced himself and, with his left hand clinging to the bar, lifted his right and thumbed back the hammer. Kedrick fired two quick shots with his left gun. One ripped a furrow down the bar and hit Fessenden below the breast bone, a jagged, tearing piece of metal when it struck.

Fessenden fired again, but the bullet went wild, and his sixth shot was fired in desperation as he swung up his left hand gun, dropping the right into his holster. Taking his time, feeling his life's blood running out of him, he braced himself there and took the gun over into his right hand. He was deliberate and calm. "Pour me a drink," he said.

The bartender, lying flat on his face behind the bar, made no move. Tom Kedrick stood on the edge of the landing now, staring at Fessenden. The big gunman had been hit three times, through the shoulder, the leg, and the chest, and he still stood there, gun in hand, ponderous and invulnerable.

The gun came up and Fessenden seemed to lean forward with it. "I wish you was Dornie," he said.

Kedrick triggered. The shot nailed Fessenden through the chest again. The big man took a fast step back, then another. His gun slipped from his hand, and he grabbed a glass standing on the bar. "Gimme a drink!" he demanded. Blood bubbled at his lips.

Tom Kedrick came down the steps, his gun ready in his hand, and walked toward Fessenden. Holding his gun level and low down with his right hand, Kedrick picked up the bottle with his left and filled the empty glass. Then he pulled over another empty glass and poured one for himself.

Fessenden stared at him. "You're a good man,

Kedrick," he said, shaping the words patiently. "I'm a good man, too . . . on the wrong side."

"I'll drink to that." Kedrick lifted his glass, they clicked them, and Fessenden grinned crookedly over his.

"You watch that Dornie," he advised, "he's a rattler . . . mean." The words stumbled from his mouth and he frowned, lifting the glass. He downed his drink, choked on it, and started to hold out a big hand to Kedrick, then fell flat on his face. Holstering his gun, Tom Kedrick leaned over and gripped the big right hand. Fessenden grinned and died.

XV

Connie Duane headed for Mustang only a short time after the survivors of the fight at Yellow Butte began to arrive. Restless, after leaving the men who were returning to the squatters' town, she had begun to think of what lay ahead, of Fred Ransome and the impending investigation, and of her uncle's part in it. All his papers as well as many of her own remained under lock in the gray stone house in Mustang, but if she was to get her own money back from Burwick, or was to clear any part of the blame from her uncle, she knew it must be done with those papers. She struck the old Mormon Trail and headed south. She was on that trail when the sun lifted, and she heard the distant sound of shots.

Turning from the trail, she reined her horse into the bed of Salt Creek and rode south, passing the point where only a short time later Loren Keith was to meet his death at the hands of Dornie Shaw. Once in Mustang she believed she would be safe, and she doubted if anyone would be in the stone house unless it was Burwick, and she knew that he rarely left his chair.

Arriving in Mustang, she rode quickly up the street, then cut over behind the stone house and dismounted. She went into the house through the back door and went very quietly. Actually she need not have bothered, for Alton Burwick was not there. Making her way up the old stairs, she unlocked the door to the apartment she had shared with her uncle, and closed the door behind her.

Nothing seemed to have been disturbed. The blinds were drawn as she had left them and the room was still. A little dust had collected, and the light filtering in around the blinds showed it to her. Going to her trunk, she opened it and got out the ironbound box in which she carried her own papers. It was intact, and showed no evidence of having been tampered with. From the bottom of the trunk she took an old purse in which there were two dozen gold eagles, and these she changed to the purse she was now carrying.

Among other things there was an old pistol there, a huge, cumbersome thing. This she got out and laid on the table beside her. Then she found a Derringer seven-shot .22 caliber pistol her father had given her several years before he died, and she put it in the pocket of her dress.

Hurrying across the room, she went into the next room and began to go through her uncle's desk, working swiftly and surely. Most of his papers were readily available, and apparently nobody had made any effort to go through them, probably believing they contained nothing of consequence or that there would be plenty of time later. She was busy at this when she heard a horse walk by the house and stop near the back steps.

Instantly she stopped what she was doing and stood erect. The window here was partly open and she could hear the saddle creak very gently as whoever it was swung down. Then a spur jingled, and there was a step below, then silence.

"So? It's you."

Startled by the voice, Connie turned. Sue Laine stood behind her, staring with wide eyes. "Yes," Connie replied, "I came for some things of mine. You're Sue, aren't you?"

Without replying to the question, the girl nodded her head toward the window. "Who was that? Did you see?"

"No. It was a man."

"Maybe Loren has come back." Sue studied her, unsmiling. "How are they out there? Are they all right? I mean . . . did you see Pit?"

"Yes. He's unhappy about you."

Sue Laine flushed, but her chin lifted proudly. "I suppose he is, but what did he expect? That I was going to live all my life out there in that awful desert? I'm sick of it! Sick of it, I tell you!"

Connie smiled. "That's strange. I love it. I love it, and every minute I'm there, I love it more. I'd like to spend my life here, and I believe I will."

"With Tom Kedrick?"

Sue's jealousy flashed in her eyes, yet there was curiosity, too. Connie noticed how the other girl studied her clothes, her face.

"Why . . . I . . . where did you ever get that idea?"

"From looking at him. What girl wouldn't want him? Anyway, he's the best of the lot."

"I thought you liked Colonel Keith?"

Sue's face flushed again. "I . . . I . . . thought I did, too. Only part of it was because Tom Kedrick wouldn't notice me . . . and because I wanted to get away from here, from the desert. But since then . . . I guess Pit hates me."

"No brother really hates his sister, I think. He'd be glad to see you back with him."

"You don't know him. If it had been anybody but someone associated with Alton Burwick, why . . ."

"You mean, you knew Burwick before?"

"Knew him?" Sue stared at her. "Didn't you know? Didn't he tell you? He was our stepfather."

"Alton Burwick?" Connie stared in amazement.

"Yes, and we always suspected that he had killed our father. We never knew, but my mother suspected later, too, for she took us and ran away from him. He came after us. We never knew what happened to mother. She went off one night for something and never came back, and we were reared by a family who just took us in."

A board creaked in the hall, and both girls were suddenly still, listening.

Guns thundered from the street of the town, and both girls stared at each other, holding their breath. There was a brief silence, then a further spattering of shots. Then the door opened very gently and Dornie Shaw stood there, facing the two girls.

He seemed startled at finding the girls together, and looked from one to the other, his brown eyes bright, but now confused. Then he centered his eyes on Sue Laine. "You better get out," he said. "Keith's dead."

"Dead?" Sue gasped. "They . . . they killed him?"

"No, I did. Up on the Salt. He drew on me."

"Keith . . . dead." Sue was shocked.

"What about the others? Where are they?" Connie asked quickly.

Dornie turned his head sharply around and looked hard at her, a curious, prying gaze as if he did not quite know what to make of her. "Some of 'em are dead," he said matter-of-factly. "They whupped us. It was that Kedrick"—he spoke without emotion or shadow of prejudice as though completely indifferent—"he had 'em set for us an' they mowed us down." He jerked his head toward the street. "I guess they are finishin' up now. The Mixus boys an' Fessenden are down there."

"They'll be coming here," Connie said with conviction. "This is the next place."

"I reckon." He seemed indifferent to that, too. "Kedrick'll be the first one. Maybe"—he smiled—"the last one." He dug out the makings, glancing around the room, then back at Sue. "You git out. I want to talk to Connie."

Sue did not move. "You can talk to us both. I like it here."

As he touched his tongue to the paper, his eyes lifted and met hers. They were flat, expressionless. "You heard me," he said. "I'd hate to treat you rough."

"You haven't the nerve!" Sue flashed back. "You know what would happen to you if you laid hands on a woman in this country! You can get away with killing me, but this country won't stand for having their women bothered, even by a ratty little killer like you!"

Connie Duane was remembering the Derringer in her pocket and lowered her hand to her hip within easy grasp of the gun.

A sudden cannonade sounded, then a scattering of more shots. At that moment Kedrick was finally shooting it out with Fessenden. Dornie Shaw cocked an inquisitive ear toward the sound. "Gettin' closer," he said. "I ain't really in no hurry until Kedrick gets here."

"You'd better be gone before he does come." Connie was surprised at the confidence in her voice. "He's too much for you, and he's not half frightened like these others are. He'll kill you, Dornie."

He stared at her, then chuckled without humor. "Him? Bah! The man doesn't live who can outdraw Dornie Shaw! I've tried 'em all! Fess? He's supposed to be good, but he don't fool with Dornie! I'd shoot his ears off."

Calmly Connie dropped her right hand into her pocket and clutched the Derringer. The feel of it gave her confidence. "You had better go," she said quietly. "You were not invited here and we don't want you."

He did not move. "Still playin' it high an' mighty, are you? You've got to get over that. Come on, you're coming with me."

"Are you leaving?" Connie's eyes flashed. "I'll not ask you again!"

Shaw started to speak, but whatever it was he

planned to say never formed into words, for Connie had her hand on the Derringer, and she fired from her pocket. Ordinarily she was a good shot, but had never fired the gun from that position. The first bullet burned a furrow along Dornie Shaw's ear, notching it at the top, the second shot stung him along the ribs, and the third plowed into the table beside him.

With a growl of surprise, he dove through the door into the hall. Sue was staring at Connie. "Well, I never!" Her eyes dropped to the tiny gun that Connie had now drawn from her pocket. "Dornie Shaw! And with that! Oh, just wait until this gets around!" Her laughter rang out merrily, and despite herself Connie was laughing, too.

Downstairs, near the door, Dornie Shaw clutched his bloody ear and panted as though he had been running, his face twisting as he stared at his blood. Amazed, he scarcely noticed when Kedrick came up the steps, but, as the door pushed open, he saw him. For a fatal instant, he froze, then he grabbed for his gun, but he had lost his chance. In that split second of hesitation, Kedrick jumped. His right hand grasped Dornie's gun wrist, and Kedrick swung the gunman bodily around, hurling him into the wall. Shaw's body hit with a crash and he rebounded into a wicked right to the wind.

Shaw was no fighter with his hands, and the power of that blow would have wrecked many a bigger man. As it was, it knocked every bit of wind from the gunman's body, and then Kedrick shoved him back against the wall. "You asked me what I'd do, once, with a faster man. Watch this, Dornie!"

Kedrick lifted his right hand, and slapped the

gunman across the mouth. Crying with fury, Shaw fought against the bigger man's grip while Kedrick held him flat against the wall, gripping him by the shirt collar, and slapped him, over and back. "Just a cheap killer," Kedrick said calmly. "Somebody has already bled you a little. I'll do it for good."

He dropped a hand to Dornie's shirt and ripped it wide. "I'm going to ruin you in this country, Dornie. I'm going to show them what you are . . . a cheap, yellow-bellied killer who terrorizes men better than himself." He slapped Dornie again, then shoved him into the wall once more, and stepped back.

"All right, Shaw! You got your guns! Reach!"

Almost crying with fury, Dornie Shaw grabbed for his guns, but as he whipped them free, all his timing wrecked by the events of the past few minutes, Kedrick's gun crashed and Shaw's right-hand gun was smashed from his hand. Shaw fired the left-hand gun, but the shot went wild, and Kedrick lunged, chopping down with his pistol barrel. The blow smashed Dornie Shaw's wrist and he dropped the gun with a yelp.

He fell back against the wall, trembling, and staring at his hands. His left wrist was broken, his right thumb gone, and, where it had been, blood was welling.

Roughly Kedrick grabbed him and shoved him out the door. Shaw stumbled and fell, but Kedrick jerked him to his feet, unmindful of the gasps of the onlookers, attracted by the sounds of fighting. In the forefront of the crowd were Pit Laine, Dai Reid, and Laredo Shad, blinking with astonishment at the sight of the most feared gunman in the country treated like a whipped child.

Shaw's horse stood nearby, and Kedrick motioned to him. "Get on him . . . backward!"

Shaw started to turn and Kedrick lifted his hand and the gunman ducked instinctively. "Get up there! Dai, when he's up, tie his ankles together."

Dornie Shaw, befuddled by the whipping he had taken, scarcely aware of what was happening, lifted his eyes. He saw the grulla tied near the stone house. It was the last straw; his demoralization was complete.

Feared because of his deadly skill with guns and his love of killing for the sake of killing, he had walked a path alone, avoided by all, or catered to by them. Never in his life had he been manhandled as he had been by Tom Kedrick. His ego was shattered.

"Take him through the town." Kedrick's voice was harsh. "Show them what a killer looks like. Then fix up that thumb and wrist and turn him loose."

"Turn him loose?" Shad demanded. "Are you crazy?"

"No, turn him loose. He'll leave this country so far behind nobody will ever see him again. This is worse than death for him, believe me." He shrugged. "I've seen them before. All they need, that kind, is somebody to face them once who isn't afraid. He was fast and accurate with his guns, so he developed the idea he was tough. Other folks thought the same thing. He wasn't tough. A tough man has to win and lose, he has to come up after being knocked down, he has to have taken a few beatings, and know what it means to win the hard way. Anybody can knock a man down. When you've been knocked down at least three times yourself, and then get up and floor the other man, then you can figure you're a tough hombre. Those smoke poles of Shaw's greased his path for him. Now he knows what he's worth."

The crowd drifted away and Connie Duane was standing in the doorway. Tom Kedrick looked up at her, and suddenly he smiled. To see her now, standing like this in the doorway, was like life-giving rain upon the desert, coming in the wake of many heat-filled days.

She came down the steps to him, then looked past him at Pit. "Your sister's upstairs, Pit. You'd better talk to her."

Laine hesitated, then he said stiffly: "I don't reckon I want to."

Laredo Shad drew deeply on his cigarette and squinted through the smoke at Laine. "Mind if I do?" he asked. "I like her."

Pit Laine was astonished. "After this?"

Shad looked at the fire end of his cigarette. "Well," he said, speaking seriously, "the best cuttin' horse I ever rode was the hardest to break. Them with lot of git up an' go to 'em often make the best stock."

"Then go ahead." Pit stared after him. Then he said: "Tell her I'll be along later."

XVI

For three weeks there was no sign of Alton Burwick. He seemed to have vanished into the earth, and riders around the country reported no sign of him. At the end of that time three men got down from the afternoon stage and were shown to rooms in the St. James. An hour later, while they were at dinner, Captain Tom Kedrick pushed open the door and walked into the dining door. Instantly one of the men, a tall, immaculate man whose hair was turning gray at the temples, arose to meet him, hand outstretched. "Tom! Say, this is wonderful! Gentlemen, this is Tom Kedrick, the man I was telling you about. We served together in the War Between the States! Tom . . . Mister Edgerton and Mister Cummings."

The two men, one pudgy with a round, cheerful face, the other as tall as Frederic Ransome with gray mutton-chop whiskers acknowledged the introduction. When Kedrick had seated himself, they began demanding details. Quietly, and as concisely as possible, he told them his own story from his joining the company in New Orleans.

"And Burwick's gone?" Edgerton asked. He was the older man with the mutton-chop whiskers. "Was he killed?"

"I doubt it, sir," Kedrick replied. "He simply vanished. The man had a faculty for being out of the way when trouble came. Since he left, with the aid of Miss Duane and her uncle's papers, we managed to put together most of the facts. However, Burwick's papers have disappeared, or most of them."

"Disappeared?" Edgerton asked. "How did that happen?"

"Miss Duane tells me that when she entered the house before the final trouble with Shaw, she passed the office door and the place was undisturbed and the desk all in order. After the crowd had gone and when we returned, somebody had been rifling the desk and the safe."

"You imply that Burwick returned. That he was there then?"

"He must have been. Connie . . . Miss Duane . . . tells me that only he had the combination and that he kept all the loose ends of the business in his hands."

Cummings stared hard at Kedrick. "You say this Shaw fellow killed Keith? How do we know that you didn't? You admit to killing Fessenden."

"I did kill Fessenden. In a fair fight, before witnesses. I never even saw Keith's body after he was killed."

"Who do you think killed John Gunter?" Cummings demanded.

"My guess would be Burwick."

"I'm glad you're not accusing Keith of that," Cummings replied dryly.

"Keith wouldn't have used a knife," Kedrick replied quietly, "nor would he have attacked him from behind as was obviously the case."

"This land deal, Kedrick," Ransome asked, "where do you stand in it?"

"I? I don't stand at all. I'm simply not in it."

Cummings looked up sharply. "You don't stand to profit from it at all? Not in any way?"

"How could I? I own nothing. I have no holdings or claim to any."

"You said Burwick promised you fifteen percent?"

"That's right. But I know now that it was merely to appease me long enough to get me on the spot at Chimney Butte where I was to be killed along with the others. Burwick got me there, then rode off on the pretext that he wanted to look at a mineral ledge."

"How about this girl? The Duane girl?" Cummings asked sharply. "Does she stand to profit?"

"She will be fortunate to get back the money that her uncle invested."

"See, Cummings?" Ransome asked. "I told you Kedrick was honest. I know the man."

"I'll give my opinion on that later, after this investigation is completed. Not now. I want to go over the ground and look into this matter thoroughly. I want to investigate this matter of the disappearance of Alton Burwick, too. I'm not at all satisfied with this situation." He glanced down at the notes in his hand, then looked up. "As to that, Kedrick, wasn't Fessenden a duly elected officer of the law when you shot him? Wasn't he the sheriff?"

"Elected by a kangaroo election," Kedrick

replied, "where the votes were counted by two officials who won. If that is a legal election, then he was sheriff."

"I see. But you do not deny that he had authority?"

"I do deny it."

Connie Duane was awaiting him when he walked back to his table. She smiled as he sat down, and listened to his explanation. She frowned thoughtfully. "Cummings? I think there is something in Uncle John's papers about him. I believe he was acting for them in Washington."

"That explains a lot." Kedrick picked up his coffee cup, then put it down abruptly, for Laredo Shad had come into the room, his face sharp and serious. He glanced around and, sighting Kedrick, hurried toward him, spurs jingling. Kedrick got to his feet. "What's wrong? What's happened?"

"Plenty! Sloan was wounded last night and Yellow Butte burned!"

"What?" Kedrick stared.

Shad nodded grimly. "You shouldn't have turned that rat loose. That Dornie Shaw."

Kedrick shook his head irritably. "I don't believe it. He was thoroughly whipped when he left here. I think he ran like a scared rabbit when he left, and, if he did want revenge, it would be after a few months, not so soon. No, this is somebody else."

"Who could it be?"

Tom's eyes met Connie's and she nodded, her eyes frightened. "You know who it could be. It could be Burwick."

Burwick had bothered him, getting away scot-free, dropping off the end of the world into oblivion as he had. Remembering the malignant look in the man's eyes, Kedrick became even more positive. Burwick had counted on this land deal, he had worked on it longer than any one of them, and it meant more to him.

"Shad," he said suddenly, "where does that grulla tie in? It keeps turning up, again and again. There's something more about all this than we've ever known, something that goes a lot deeper. Who rides the grulla? Why is it he has never been seen? Why was Dornie so afraid of it?"

"Was he afraid of the grulla?" Shad asked, frowning. "That doesn't figure."

"Why doesn't it? That's the question now. You know, that last day when I had Shaw thoroughly whipped, he looked up and saw something that scared him, yet something that I think he more than half expected. After he was gone down the street, I looked around, and there was nothing there. Later, I stumbled across the tracks of the grulla mustang. That horse was in front of the house during all the excitement!"

Frederic Ransome walked over to their table. "Cummings is going to stir up trouble," he said, dropping into a chair. "He's out to get you, Kedrick, and, if he can, to pin the killing of Keith on you, or that of Burwick. He claims your story is an elaborate buildup to cover the murder of all three of the company partners. He can make so much trouble that none of the squatters will get anything out of the land, and nothing for all their work. We've got to find Burwick."

Laredo lit a cigarette. "That's a tough one," he said, "but maybe I've got a hunch."

"What?" Kedrick looked up.

"Ever hear Burwick talk about the grulla?"

"No, I can't say that I did. It was mentioned before him once that I recall, and he didn't seem interested."

"Maybe he wasn't interested because he knowed all about it," Shad suggested. "That Burwick has me puzzled."

Connie looked up at him. "You may be right, Laredo, but Pit and Sue Laine were Burwick's stepchildren and they knew nothing about the horse. The only one who seemed to know anything was Dornie Shaw."

Tom Kedrick got up. "Well, there's one thing we can do," he said. "Laredo, we can scout out the tracks of that horse and trail it down. Pick up an old trail, anything. Then just see where it takes us."

***

On the third day it began to rain. All week the wind had been chill and cold and the clouds had hung low and flat across the sky from horizon to horizon. Hunched in his slicker, Laredo slapped his gloved hands together and swore. "This finishes it!" he said with disgust. "It will wipe out all the trails for us."

"All the old ones anyway," Kedrick agreed. "We've followed a dozen here lately, and none of them took us anywhere. All disappeared on rock, or were swept away by wind."

"Escavada's cabin isn't far up this cañon," Shad suggested. "Let's hit him up for chow. It will be a chance to get warm, anyway."

"Know him?"

"Stopped in there once. He's half Spanish, half Ute. Tough old blister, an' been in this country since before the grass came. He might be able to tell us something."

The trail into the cañon was slippery and the dull red of the rocks had been turned black under the rain. It slanted across the sky in a drenching downpour, and, when they reached the stone cabin in the corner of the hills, both men and horses were cold, wet, and hungry.

Escavada opened the door for them and waved them in. He grinned at them. "Glad to have company," he said. "Ain't seen a man for three weeks."

When they had stripped off their slickers and peeled down to shirts, pants, and boots, he put coffee before them and laced it with a strong shot of whiskey. "Warm you up," he said. "Trust you ain't goin' out again soon. Whiskey's mighty fine when a body comes in from the cold, but not if he's goin' out again. It flushes the skin up, fetches all the heat to the surface, then gives it off into the air. Man freezes mighty quick, drinkin' whiskey."

"You ever see a grulla mustang around, Escavada?" Laredo asked suddenly, looking up at the old man.

He turned on them, his eyes bright with malicious humor. "You ain't some of them superstitious kind, be you? Skeered o' the dark like? An' ghosts?"

"No," Kedrick said, "but what's the tie-up?"

"That grulla. Old story in this here county. Dates back thirty, forty years. Maybe further'n that. Sign of death or misfortune, folks say."

Laredo looked inquiringly at Kedrick, and

Kedrick asked: "You know anything about it? That horse is real enough. We've both seen the grulla."

"So've I," the old man said. He dropped into a chair and grinned at them. His gray hair was sparse, but his eyes were alive and young. "I seen it many times, an' no misfortune come my way. Not unless you call losin' my shovel a misfortune."

He hitched his chair nearer the woodpile and tossed a couple of sticks on the fire. "First I heerd of it was long ago. Old folks used to tell of a Spanish man in armor, ridin' a mouse-colored horse. He used to come an' go about the hills, but the story back of it seems to be that a long time back some such feller was mighty cruel to the Injuns. That story sort of hung around an' a body heered it ever' now and again until about fifteen, sixteen years back. Since then she's been mighty lively."

"You mean, you heard the story more since then?" Kedrick asked.

"Uhn-huh. Started with a wagon train wiped out by Injuns up on the Salt. Ever' man jack o' them kilt dead . . . womenfolks, too, the story was. There was a youngster come off scot-free, boy about five or six years old. He crawled off into the brush, an', after, he swore them Injuns was led by a white man on a grulla horse, a white man in armor!"

"Wild yarn," Shad said, "but you can't blame the kid, imaginin' things after what he must've seen."

"He said that hombre in the armor went around with a long knife, an' he skewered ever' one of the bodies to make sure they was real dead. He said once that hombre looked right square at him, layin' in the brush, an' he was skeered like all git out, but must've been he wasn't seen, 'cause he wasn't bothered."

"An' this grulla has been seen since?" Shad asked. "Reg'lar?"

"Uhn-huh, but never no rider clost enough to say who or what. Sometimes off at a distance, sometimes just the horse, standin'. Most folks git clear off when they see that horse."

He got up and brought back the coffee pot. "Right odd you should ast me about him now," he commented. "Right odd."

Both men looked at him, and, sensing their acute interest, he continued. "Been huntin' here lately. Ketched me a few bees off the cactus an' mesquite, figurin' to start a beeline. Well, I got her started, all right, an' I trailed them bees to a place far south o' here. South an' west, actually. Most o' this country hereabouts is worked out of bees. I been at it so long I was workin' a good ways off. Well, my beeline took me over toward the Hogback. You know that place? She's a high-curvin' ridge maybe five or six hundred feet at the crest, but she rises mighty close to straight up for four hundred feet. Crawlin' up there to locate the cave them bees was workin' out of, I come on a cave like a cliff dwellin', on'y it wasn't. She was man-made, an' most likely in the past twenty years or so. What started me really lookin' was my shovel . . . the one I lost. She was right there on that ledge, so I knowed it hadn't been lost, but stole off me, so I began huntin' around. I found back inside this place it was all fixed up for livin'. Some grub there, blankets, a couple of guns, an' under some duffel in the corner an old-time breastplate an' helmet."

"You're serious?" Kedrick demanded incredulously.

"Sure as I'm alive! But"—Escavada chuckled—"that ain't the best of it. Lyin' there on the floor, deader'n last year's hopes, was a young fellow. He had a knife, an old-time Spanish knife that a feller in armor might have carried, an' it was skewered right th'ough him!"

"A young man ... dead?" Kedrick suddenly leaned forward. "Anything odd about him? I mean ... was he missing a thumb?"

Escavada stared. "Well, now, if that don't beat all! He was missin' a thumb, an' he was crippled up mighty bad in the other arm. Carried her in a sling."

"Dornie Shaw!" Laredo leaped to his feet. "Dornie Shaw, by all that's holy!"

"Shaw?" Escavada puckered his brows, his old eyes gleaming. "Now that's most odd, most odd! Shaw was the name o' that boy, the one who didn't git killed with the wagon train!"

Kedrick's face was a study. Dornie Shaw—dead! But if Dornie had been the boy from the wagon train, that would account for his superstitious fear of the grulla mustang. But to suppose that after all these years Dornie had been killed by the same man, or ghost if you believed in ghosts, that killed the rest of them so many years before was too ridiculous. It was, he thought suddenly, unless you looked at it just one way.

"Man can't escape his fate," Escavada said gloomily. "That boy hid out from that knife, but in the end it got him."

Kedrick got up. "Could you take us to that place, Escavada? Down there on the Hogback."

"I reckon." He glanced outside. "But not in this rain. Rheumatiz gits me."

"Then tell me where it is," Kedrick said, "because I'm going now!"

***

They were crossing the head of Coal Mine Creek when Laredo saw the tracks. He drew up suddenly, pointing. The tracks of a horse, well shod. "The grulla," Kedrick said grimly. "I'd know those tracks anywhere."

They pushed on. It was late and the pelting rain still poured down upon their heads and shoulders. The trails were slippery, and dusk was near. "We'd better find us a hole to crawl into," Shad suggested. "We'll never find that horse in this weather."

"By morning the tracks will be gone, and I've a hunch we'll find our man right on that cliff dwelling where Escavada saw Dornie's body."

"Wonder how Dornie found the place?"

"If what I think is right," Kedrick replied, wiping the rain from his face, "he must have run into an old friend and been taken there to hide out. That old friend was the same rider of the grulla that killed his family and friends with the wagon train, and, when he saw that armor, he knew it."

"But what's it all about?" Shad grumbled. "It don't make sense! An' no horse lives that long."

"Sure not. There may have been half a dozen grullas in that length of time. This man probably tried to capitalize on the fears of the Indians and Mexicans who live up that way to keep them off his trail. We'll probably find the answer when we reach the end of our ride."

The Hogback loomed, black and ominous, before them. The trail, partly switchback and partly sheer climb, led over the sharp, knife-like ridge. They mounted, their horses laboring heavily at the steep and slippery climb. Twice Tom Kedrick saw the tracks of the grulla on the trail, and in neither case could those tracks have been more than an hour old.

Kedrick glanced down when they saw the opposite side, then dismounted. "This one is tricky," he said grimly. "We'd better walk it."

Halfway down, lightning flashed, and in the momentary brightness Laredo called out: "Watch it, Tom! High, right!"

Kedrick's head jerked around just as the rifle boomed. The bullet smacked viciously against the rock beside him, spattering his face with splinters. He grabbed for his gun, but it was under his slicker. The gun boomed again, five fast shots, as fast as the marksman could work the lever of his rifle.

Behind Tom Kedrick the anguished scream of a wounded horse cut the night and Shad's warning yell was drowned in the boom of the gun again, and then he flattened against the rock barely in time to avoid the plunging, screaming horse! His own Appaloosa, frightened, darted down the trail with the agility of a mountain goat. The rifle boomed again, and he dropped flat.

"Shad? You all right?"

There was a moment before the reply, then it was hoarse, but calm. "Winged me, but not bad."

"I'm going after him. You all right?"

"Yeah. You might help me wrap this leg up."

Sheltered by the glistening rain-wet rock, with gray mist swirling past them on the high ridge of the Hogback, Kedrick knelt in the rain, and, shielding the bandage from the rain with a slicker, he bound the leg. The bullet had torn through the flesh, but the bone was not broken.

XVII

When the wound was bandaged, Kedrick drew back into the shelter of the slight overhang and stared about. Ahead and below them was a sea of inky blackness. Somewhere down that mountain would be their horses, one probably dead or dying, the other possibly crippled. Around them all was night and the high, windy, rain-wet rocks. And out there in the darkness a killer stalked them, a killer who could at all of three hundred yards spot his shots so well as to score two hits on a target seen only by a brief flash of lightning. Next time those shots could kill. And there was no doubt about it. Now the situation was clear. It was kill or be killed.

"Sure," Laredo said dryly, "you got to get him, man. But you watch it. He's no slouch with that Spencer!"

"You've got to get off this ridge," Kedrick insisted. "The cold and rain up here will kill you."

"You leave that to me," Shad replied shortly. "I'll drag myself down the trail an' find a hole to crawl into down on the flat below this Hogback. Might even find your palouse down there. You got grub an' coffee in those saddlebags?"

"Yeah, but you'd better not try a fire until I come back."

Shad chuckled. "Make sure you come back. I never did like to eat alone."

Slipping his hands under his slicker through the pockets, Tom gripped his guns. His rifle, of course, was in his saddle scabbard. He was going to have to stalk a skilled killer, a fine marksman, on his own ground in absolute darkness with a handgun. The killer had a Spencer .56.

Lightning flashed, but there was no more shooting. Somewhere out there the killer was stalking them. He would not give up now, or retreat. This, for him, was a last stand unless he killed them both. His hideout now was known, and, if they escaped, he would no longer be safe. That he did not intend to be driven from the country was already obvious by the fact that he had stayed this long.

Kedrick crawled out, using a bush to cover his movement, and then worked along the windy top of the ridge toward a nest of boulders he had seen ahead of him by the lightning flash. The wind whipped at his hat, and flapped the skirt of his slicker. His right-hand gun was drawn, but under the slicker.

He crawled on. Lightning flashed and he flattened out on the rocks, but the Spencer bellowed, the bullet smashing his eyes and mouth full of gravel. Rolling over, he held his fire, spitting and pawing desperately at his blinded eyes.

There was no sound but the wind and rain. Then in the distance, thunder roared and rumbled off among the peaks, and, when the lightning flashed again, he looked out along the high ridge of the Hogback. Lashed by the driving rain, its rocks glistened like steel under clouds that seemed a scarce arm's length above Kedrick's head. Mist drifted by him, touching his wet face with a ghostly hand, and the little white skeletons of long-dead pines pointed their sharp and bony fingers toward the sky.

Rain pelted against his face, and he cowered, fearing the strike of a bullet at each flash of lightning, smelling the brimstone as the lightning scarred the high ridge with darting flame. He touched his lips with his tongue and stared until his eyes ached with strain. His mouth was dry and his stomach empty, and something mounted within him. Fear? Panic? He could stay still no longer. With infinite patience, he edged forward, working his way a little over the edge of the ridge toward the hulking black clumps of some juniper, ragged trees, whipped to agonized shapes by generations of wind.

There was no sound but the storm, no sight of anything. He moved on, trying to estimate how far away the cliff house would be, to guess if he could reach it first or get between it and the killer out there. Flame stabbed the night and something burned sharply along his shoulders. He let go everything and rolled, went crashing down a dozen feet before he brought up in a tangle of dead limbs.

But the killer was not waiting. He loomed suddenly dark on the crest, and, crouching like a hunted animal, every instinct alert, Kedrick fired! The dark figure jerked hard, and then the Spencer bellowed. The bullet plastered a branch near him, and Kedrick knew that only his own shot had saved his life. He fired again, and then deliberately hurled himself backward into the night, falling, landing, crawling. He got to his feet and plunged into the absolute darkness, risking a broken limb or a bad fall, anything to get the distance he needed. Then lightning flashed, and, as if by magic, the Spencer boomed. How the man had followed his plunging career he could not know, but he felt the stab and slam of the bullets as they smashed about him. This man was shooting too close. He couldn't miss long.

His shoulders burned, but whether that shot had been a real wound or a mere graze he did not know. Something fluid trickled down his spine, but whether it was rain water through the slit coat or his own blood, he could not guess.

He moved back, circling. Another shot, but this slightly to his left. Quickly he moved left and a shot smacked right near where he had been standing. The killer was using searching fire now, and he was getting closer.

Kedrick moved back, tripped and fell, and bullets laced the air over him. Evidently the man had a belt full of ammunition, or his pockets stuffed. Kedrick started to rise, but his fingers had found a hard smoothness, not of rock, but of earth and gravel! Carefully he felt about in the darkness. The path! He was on a path, and no doubt the path to the cliff house.

He began to move along it, feeling his way carefully. Once, off to his left, he heard a rock roll. He took a chance and fired blind, then rolled over three times and felt the air split apart as the shots slammed the ground where he had been. He fired again, then again, always moving.

Lightning flashed, and he saw a hulking thing back on the trail the way he had come, a huge, glistening thing, black and shining. Flame sprang from it, and he felt the shock of the bullet, then steadied himself and fired again.

Deliberately then, he turned and worked his way down the path. Suddenly he felt space before him, and found the path here took a sharp turn. Another step and he might have plunged off! How near was his escape he knew in another instant when lightning flashed and he saw far below him the gray white figure of the Appaloosa standing in the rain.

He worked his way down the cliff, then found a ledge, and in a moment his hands found the crude stone bricks of the cliff house. Feeling his way along it, he felt for the door, and then, pushing it open, he crawled into the inner darkness and pushed the door shut behind him.

After the lashing of wind and rain the peace seemed a miracle. Jerking off his soaking hat, he tossed it aside, and threw off the slicker. There was a chance the killer would not guess that he knew of this place, and undoubtedly, had he not known, he would have passed it in the darkness and storm. Working his way along the floor, he found a curtain dividing this from an inner room. He stepped through it and sat down hard on the bunk. Feeling for his left-hand gun, he found the holster empty, and he had fired five shots with his right gun. Suddenly the curtain stirred and there was a breath of wind, then it vanished. The killer was in the other room! He had come in!

Kedrick dared not rise for fear the bed would creak, but he heard a match strike, and then a candle was lighted. Feet shuffled in the other room. Then a voice. "I know you're in there, Kedrick. There's water on the floor in here. I'm behind a piece of old stone wall that I use for a sort of table. I'm safe from your fire. I know there's no protection where you are. Throw your guns out and come with your hands up! If you don't, I'm going to open fire an' search every inch of that room!"

Over the top of the blanket curtain, which was suspended from a pole across the door, Tom Kedrick could see the roof in the other room. The cave house was actually much higher than need be; evidently the killer had walled up an overhang or cave. Kedrick could see several heavy cedar beams that had served to support a ceiling, now mostly gone. If that was true in the other room, it might be true in his, also.

He straightened to his feet, heard a sudden move, then fired! From the other room came a chuckle. "Figured that would draw fire! Well, one gun's empty. Now toss out the other an' come out. You haven't a chance!"

Kedrick did not reply. He was reaching up into the darkness over his head, feeling for the beams. He touched one, barely touched it, then reached up with both hands, judging the distance he had to jump by the width of the beams in the other room. What if it were old and would not support his weight? He had to chance that.

He jumped, his fingers hooked well over the edge, and soundlessly he drew himself up. Now Kedrick could see into the lighted room, but he could not locate the killer. The voice spoke again. "I'm giving you no more time, Kedrick. Come out or I start to shoot! Toss that other gun first!"

Silence lay in the room, a silence broken by the sudden bellow of a gun! The killer fired, emptied a six-gun, then emptied another. Tom Kedrick waited, having no idea how many guns the man had, or what he might have planned for. Then six more carefully spaced shots were fired, one of them ricocheting dangerously close to Kedrick's head.

A long pause, and then a sound of movement. "All right, if you're alive in there now, you got a shot comin', but if you want to give up, you can. I sort of want you alive." Suddenly the blanket was jerked from its moorings, and Alton Burwick stood in the opening, a gun gripped in his fist, ready to fire. Kedrick made no sound, and the man stared, then rushed into the room. Almost whining with fury, he jerked Kedrick's hat from the bed, then the slicker, and, as the latter fell to the floor, with it fell Kedrick's other pistol, which falling from the holster had hooked into some tear in the slicker. He stared at it furiously, and then jerked the bed aside. Almost insane with fury, he searched, unbelieving and whining like an angry hound on a trail.

He stopped, his pent-up fury worn away, and stood there, his chest heaving with his exertions, his fist still gripping the pistol. "Gone! Gone!" he cried, as if bereft. "When I had him right here!"

Kedrick's fingers had found a tiny sliver of wood, and deliberately he snapped it against Burwick's cheek. The fat man jerked as if stung, then looked up. Their eyes met, and slowly he backed away, but now he was smiling. "Oh, you're a smart one,

Kedrick! Very smart! Too bad it couldn't have been you with me instead of that weakling Keith! All front and show, but no bottom to him, no staying quality! But"—he sighed—"I've got you anyway, and you'll suffer for what you've done." He scooped Kedrick's other pistol from the floor and backed away. "All right, get down!"

Kedrick dropped to the floor, and the fat man waved irritably at the gun he clutched. "No use to bluff. That's empty. Throw it down!"

"What's it all about, Burwick?" Tom asked suddenly. "Why this place? The armor? What about Dornie Shaw?"

"Ah? How did you know about that? But no matter, no matter." He backed to the wall, watching Kedrick and holding the gun. "Why, it was gold, boy! Gold, and lots of it! It was I stirred those Indians up to attacking that caravan. I wanted the gold they carried, and most of it belonging to Dornie's pa. I knew about it. Followed them from Dodge. Knew when they drew it from the bank there, and how much. They fooled me, though. When the Indians hit, they'd buried it somewhere. It could have been a lot of places, that was the trouble.

"They might have buried it sooner, somewhere else along the trail. I've dug and I've hunted, but I've never found it. Maybe I will someday, but nobody else is going to! Wondered why I wanted the land? Profit, sure. But I wanted this place, a couple of sections in here, all for myself. Figured on that, working it out somehow. The gold's somewhere between here and Thieving Rock. Has to be."

Kedrick nodded. "That clears up a lot of things.

Now you drop that gun, Burwick, and come as my prisoner."

Burwick chuckled fatly. "Try to bluff me? I'd've expected that from you. Nervy one, huh? Bet you got that Connie Duane, too. By the Lord Harry, there's a woman! No scare to her. Not one bit. Drop your gun, boy, or I'll put my first bullet through your kneecap."

He was going to shoot, and Tom Kedrick knew it. Coolly he squeezed off his own shot, an instant faster. He shot for the gun hand, but the bullet only skinned the thumb knuckle and hit Burwick in the side. The fat man jerked and his face twisted, and he stared at the gun, lifting his own. Coolly Kedrick fired again, then again. The bullets struck with an ugly smack, and Burwick wilted, the gun going from his limp fingers to the floor. Kedrick stepped in and caught him, easing him down. The flabby cheeks were suddenly sagging and old.

Bitterly the man stared upward at him. "What happened? That . . . that . . . ?"

"The gun was a Walch twelve-shot pistol," Tom explained. "I started carrying them a few days ago, replacing the Forty-Four Russians."

Burwick stared at him, no hatred in his eyes. "Smart," he said. "Smart! Always one trick better than me, or anybody. You'll . . . do, boy."

XVIII

On the streets of Mustang the sun was warm after the rain. Tom Kedrick, wounded again but walking, stood beside Connie Duane. Shad was grinning at them. "Look mighty fine in that tailored suit, Tom. You goin' to be gone long?"

"Not us. We'll be married in Santa Fé, and then we're headin' for the Mogollons and that ranch."

"Seems a shame not to hunt for that gold," Laredo complained. "But, anyway, the real treasure was that box full of Burwick's papers. Sure made Cummings hunt his hole. But I do regret that gold."

"I don't," Connie replied. "It's caused too much trouble. Alton Burwick spent his life and a good many other lives after it. Let it stay where it is. Maybe a better man will find it, who needs it more than we do!"

"Gosh," Laredo said suddenly, "I got to light a shuck. I'm late to meet Sue. So long, then!" They watched him go, waiting for the stage.

Everything was quiet in Mustang—three whole days without a killing.

About the Editor

Jon Tuska is the author of numerous books about the American West as well as editor of several short story collections, *Billy the Kid: His Life and Legend* (Greenwood Press, 1994) and *The Western Story: A Chronological Treasury* (University of Nebraska Press, 1995) among them. Together with his wife Vicki Piekarski, Tuska cofounded Golden West Literary Agency that primarily represents authors of Western fiction and Western Americana. They edit and copublish forty titles a year in two prestigious series of new hardcover Western novels and story collections, the Five Star Westerns and the Circle Ⓥ Westerns. They also coedited the *Encyclopedia Of Frontier and Western Fiction* (McGraw-Hill, 1983), *The Max Brand Companion* (Greenwood Press, 1996), *The Morrow Anthology of Great Western Short Stories* (Morrow, 1997), and *The First Five Star Western Corral* (Five Star Westerns, 2000). Tuska has also been editing an annual series of short novel collections, Stories of the Golden West, of which there are seven volumes.

The Classic Film Collection

The Searchers by Alan LeMay

Hailed as one of the greatest American films, *The Searchers,* directed by John Ford and starring John Wayne, has had a direct influence on the works of Martin Scorsese, Steven Spielberg, and many others. Its gorgeous cinematic scope and deeply nuanced characters have proven timeless. And now available for the first time in decades is the powerful novel that inspired this iconic movie. (Coming February 2009!)

Destry Rides Again by Max Brand

Made in 1939, the Golden Year of Hollywood, *Destry Rides Again* helped launch Jimmy Stewart's career and made Marlene Dietrich an American icon. Now available for the first time in decades is the novel that inspired this much-loved movie. (Coming March 2009!)

The Man from Laramie by T. T. Flynn

In its original publication, *The Man from Laramie* had more than half a million copies in print. Shortly thereafter, it became one of the most recognized of the Anthony Mann/ Jimmy Stewart collaborations, known for darker films with morally complex characters. Now the novel upon which this classic movie was based is once again available—for the first time in more than fifty years. (Coming April 2009!)

The Unforgiven by Alan LeMay

In this epic American novel, which served as the basis for the classic film directed by John Huston and starring Burt Lancaster and Audrey Hepburn, a family is torn apart when an old enemy starts a vicious rumor that sets the range aflame. Don't miss the powerful novel that inspired the film the *Motion Picture Herald* calls "an absorbing and compelling drama of epic proportions." (Coming May 2009!)
